The Philosophical Detective Returns

Also by Bruce Hartman:

Perfectly Healthy Man Drops Dead

The Rules of Dreaming

The Muse of Violence

The Philosophical Detective

A Butterfly in Philadelphia

Big Data Is Watching You!
(also published as *I Am Not a Robot)*

Potlatch: A Comedy

The Devil's Chaplain

Parole

The Philosophical Detective Returns

Bruce Hartman

Swallow Tail Press

The Philosophical Detective Returns

Published by Swallow Tail Press
Philadelphia, PA, USA
www.swallowtailpress.com
Not for sale or distribution outside the
United States of America

Cover illustration: "The Ancient of Days" by William Blake

Also available in ebook format.

ISBN: 978-0-9997564-4-7

Author's Note

This is a work of fiction. Any resemblance to actual events or persons, living or dead, is entirely coincidental or used for fictional purposes only. I need hardly add that "Jorge Luis Borges" is a purely fictional product of my own imagination, not to be confused with the famous Argentine writer of the same name.

1. Impostors

When I arrived in New York in the spring of 1971, I'd been out of the Army a little over two months. My military career had been brief and uneventful, if your idea of uneventful includes running twenty miles with a fifty-pound pack, collapsing from heat prostration, and being left to die in a malarial swamp. And all that took place in Fort Polk, Louisiana, which is as close as I ever got to Vietnam. Let's just say I had issues. The Army decided, after getting to know me better, that they wished I'd stayed home, and that's where they sent me, along with my panic attacks, memory lapses and nightmares. When I returned to Boston, my girlfriend Katie tried to pick up the pieces of my shattered self, with mixed results—the more she loved me, the more I doubted myself. "I'm not sure I know who you are anymore," she said one night as we sat in a coffee shop on Commonwealth Avenue. "I'm sure I don't," I told her. She gently suggested that what I needed was to get back in touch with reality. She was right: reality and I had developed a strained, often distant, relationship. And so, setting off on a quest to confront that issue once and for all, I caught the Trailways bus to New York City, where, I told myself, there's so much reality you can't avoid being in touch with it.

What I needed was a guide, a mentor, a teacher who could help me find my way back to reality. In an ironic twist of fate, the mentor I found—inching his way across Washington Square Park with his cane, smiling and impeccably dressed, as always, in a dark gray suit and tie—was the last person I would have consulted about anything relating to reality: Jorge Luis Borges.

Borges, the blind Argentinian fabulist and poet, was visiting New York University to conduct a seminar on the detective stories of Edgar Allan Poe. Three years earlier, before I was thrown out of graduate school, I'd served a term as his driver, seeing eye dog, Sancho Panza and Dr. Watson in and around Cambridge, Massachusetts, where he spent most of a year avoiding his duties at Harvard while he solved a series of baffling crimes. Now in his seventies, he was an improbable blend of bookishness and fatalistic machismo, obsessed with labyrinths, infinity, knife fights, and the Kabbalah. His paradoxical short stories had earned him an international reputation, even (like Dante and Kafka) his own adjective—"Borgesian"—to describe the uniquely fantastical world he inhabited. This was the man who stepped into my path when I needed to get back in touch with reality.

"Nick Martin!" he called out, having recognized my voice when I asked a passer-by for directions to the subway. Pivoting on his cane, he wrenched himself free from the graduate teaching assistant who'd been assigned as his escort, lurched toward me and clamped his tourniquet-like grip above my elbow. "Thank God you're here."

You could call it coincidence—chance, luck, whatever—but Borges (he told me later) saw our meeting in Washington Square Park that Friday afternoon as destiny. When the world began, he said, that meeting had been penciled into the book of time, pending the occurrence of an infinite number of intervening events, until it was finally entered in ink, so to speak, by actually happening. My confusion about the location of the subway station made the meeting with Borges inevitable. Five minutes later, he would have been heading toward his apartment and I would have been in the station waiting for an uptown train. We would never have met again.

And a lot of other things would never have happened. The crimes celebrated in the newspapers as the "Morgue Murders" would have gone unsolved. Public institutions such as the NYPD, the FBI and the Office of Chief Medical Examiner would have been discredited. Charles Dickens's pet raven, Grip—best known as a character in *Barnaby Rudge*—would not have ended up in the Free Library of Philadelphia. And the Seal of Solomon, a priceless signet ring said to have been given to King Solomon by the Archangel Michael, would never have found its way to the Hebrew University Museum in Jerusalem.

With his arm clutched around my elbow, I followed Borges and the graduate student—her name was Mary Ann Chalmers—across the park to Fifth Avenue, proceeding, as in one of Zeno's paradoxes, in increments of half a step, then a quarter of a step, an eighth of a step, and so on, until I despaired of ever reaching our destination. Then, defying all logic, we arrived at a stately high-rise two blocks north of Washington Square and took the elevator to the tenth floor. Borges's apartment, which belonged to an elderly NYU classics professor on sabbatical in Paris, looked like it hadn't been redecorated since the 1940s. It boasted venetian blinds, a well-stocked library, and an old TV set that took up half of the living room. Its best feature was a cheerful live-in house-keeper who introduced herself as Señora Sanchez. She invited us in and immediately offered us drinks from a portable bar she wheeled into the living room. It was three in the afternoon.

Mary Ann Chalmers, a raven-haired New Englander who had the haunted, half-mad look of a character in one of Poe's more fantastic tales, asked for Dubonnet on the rocks, and Borges ordered "whisky—by which of course I mean scotch." We guided him into a plush wing chair, where he sat with his walking stick (he never called it a cane) planted in the carpet like a royal sceptre. Mary Ann Chalmers and I—unsure of our status and wary of each other as potential rivals—took seats at the opposite ends of a wide sofa across from Borges's wing chair. I enjoyed a cold Rheingold beer as I broke the news to Borges that I wouldn't be able to shepherd him around in New York as I had done in Cambridge.

"Of course you will," he beamed, sipping his scotch.

"I have a job," I objected.

"Nonsense."

Before I could respond, we were joined by his neighbor from across the hall, a big friendly man named Murray Kellerman, who apparently had a standing invitation to drop in when cocktails were being served. Murray, in his early thirties, sat on a cane chair he pulled up near the end of the couch, asked for a bourbon and ginger, and quickly became the life of the party. He had curly brown hair, a pair of lively brown eyes and a knack for telling stories that made everyone laugh. He was one of those instantly likeable people that you trust implicitly—a merry prankster eager to include everyone in the fun (though as we would soon learn, he also had his serious side).

Under Murray's influence, even Mary Ann cheered up enough to crack a furtive smile and ask the Señora for another Dubonnet. "And ask Señor Borges if he'd like another whisky," she told the housekeeper instead of asking him herself.

Borges winced when he heard that and wagged his index finger in a Latin American gesture that means no. With all eyes on him, he took the opportunity to expound on one of his favorite themes: the nothingness of personality. "You call me Borges," he said, still wagging his finger, "but I should warn you that I am an impostor."

I shouldn't have been surprised, but I was. By the time we parted company in Cambridge, aided by my girlfriend Katie's researches, I had come to precisely that conclusion—that the man I knew as Borges was an impostor. It unnerved me, though, to hear him admit it as if it were a well-known fact.

His sightless gaze made a wide sweep around the room. "Everyone who thinks that he, or she"—he tipped his head gallantly toward the suspicious Ms. Chalmers—"has a continuing identity, a 'self' (and this means everyone who's ever lived, except possibly the Buddha), is mistaken in that belief, and is thus an impostor when he insists on his personal identity."

"This is some kind of joke, right?" Señora Sanchez laughed.

"Only to the extent that everything is a joke," Borges said.

Mary Ann Chalmers knew enough to take the joke seriously. "But if that's true," she said darkly, "then you're not really Borges."

He smiled and shook his head. "Of course not. The real Borges, if there is one, is an impostor who at this moment is probably posing as me."

"Like Chuang Tzu and the butterfly," Murray ventured.

"Something like that." Borges beamed in delight that Murray had caught the allusion.

"I know who you are," Murray explained. "I'm a big fan of yours. I've read all your books."

Borges nodded modestly. His modesty was false, but so, in all likelihood, was Murray's claim to have read all his books.

"And you're not just a writer," Murray added. "You're the Director of the National Library of Argentina, *and*"—he paused for special emphasis—"you're a famous detective." Murray must have read the book on how to flatter Borges.

It worked: Borges looked like a boy who'd been sent to the head of the class. "You're too kind," he mumbled. "I have no official standing as a detective."

"I hope you'll be able to tackle some cases while you're here in New York," Murray said.

"Only if there are some murders," Borges smiled, holding up his palms. "Let's not hope for that."

"There are three murders a day in New York," Señora Sanchez said. "You can read about them in the *Daily News.*"

The Señora had a point. New York in the 1970s wasn't the high-flying, latté-sipping, Uber-hopping paradise it is today. It had murders and muggings galore, rampant air pollution and graffiti, addicts shooting up in the streets. The *Daily News* said New Yorkers lived in a climate of fear.

Still Borges didn't hesitate to correct her. "Outside of movies and detective stories," he said, "murders (except the most obvious ones, such as gangsters stabbing each other in knife fights) aren't really very common. And mysterious ones—the kind that require a detective to solve them—are quite rare."

Murray's bright expression darkened into a deep frown. "There were six million of them in the Holocaust," he said grimly. "Just counting Jews."

"But those are hardly a mystery. We know who the perpetrators were."

"The main ones," Murray said, shaking his head, not in disagreement but in sorrow. "But tracking down all their accomplices could keep a detective busy for a lifetime." A note of bitterness colored his voice. "Not to mention finding everything they stole from their victims."

This turn in the conversation put a damper on our merriment. Chatting about murder was one thing—but people actually getting murdered, by the millions, that was something else again. We all stared down into our drinks, except Borges, who gazed forward in his usual affable, absent way, thin wisps of white hair curling around his bald head like a halo.

"I'm sorry I brought up such a depressing topic," Murray said. "It's just that I've been doing some amateur detective work in that field myself. I've got a personal interest in it."

That piqued Borges's interest. "Tell us about it. Your personal interest."

"No, I've said enough. No reason for everybody to get depressed."

"I want to hear it," Borges pressed him.

"This is serious," Murray hesitated. "I wouldn't want to see it turn up in one of your stories."

"My stories are serious."

There was no way to escape from that. Murray asked the Señora for another drink and told his tale. He was the grandson and sole living heir of Klaus Mannheimer, a wealthy Jewish industrialist and art collector from Vienna who died in the Holocaust. Mannheimer was a Zionist and an expert on mysticism, golems and the Kabballah; it was rumored in the family that he dabbled in magic. At an auction in Vienna in 1934, four years before Nazi Germany annexed Austria, Mannheimer had acquired an art treasure known as the Seal of Solomon, a signet ring made of solid gold inlaid with diamonds, sapphires and other precious gems—which was said to have belonged to the Biblical King of Israel—with the stated purpose of returning it to its rightful place in Jerusalem. At that time the ring was valued at over eight million Austrian marks. Shortly before the Nazi takeover, Mannheimer entrusted it to Matthias Netzer, an attorney in Zurich, Switzerland, for safekeeping until he could escape from the Reich. But his exit was blocked, and in 1941 he was deported to Auschwitz along with his wife and every other member of his family. The Seal of Solomon was never seen or heard of again.

"My mother was Klaus Mannheimer's only child," Murray told us. "She became estranged from her parents when she married my dad and came to the United States in 1935. I was born in 1939 and grew up in Yorkville on the upper East Side. I hardly remember my mother—she was killed in an auto accident when I was three. When my dad died a couple of years ago, I started investigating the family history and found out about the ring."

"You learned about it *after* your father died?" Borges asked.

"I found a letter from Klaus Mannheimer to my mother, dated 1940. Of course it was in German and I couldn't read it. But when I had it translated I got the whole story. I hired an investigator in Zurich to make some inquiries and learned that Matthias Netzer died in 1965. There was no mention of the ring in his will or the records of his estate."

Borges asked the obvious question. "Did he have any survivors?"

"He had a wife, who recently died, and two sons, Peter and Bernhard, who are now in their forties. Peter Netzer is a doctor, a prominent pathologist who's been at Zurich General Hospital for many years. The younger brother, Bernhard, hasn't been so successful—in and out of teaching jobs, two broken marriages, a reputation for bizarre, self-destructive behavior; undoubtedly an alcoholic."

"So what did you do when you learned all this?"

"I wrote to an organization in London—it's called Restitution—that tracks Holocaust victims and provides information and help to survivors and their families. They told me that Klaus Mannheimer and his entire family died in Auschwitz, and that I was the sole living heir. I didn't believe them at first, but they provided genealogical charts that convinced me it was true."

"So you are the rightful heir of a priceless treasure," Borges smiled. "What did you do next?"

"I wanted to see if the ring had surfaced since the war, so I contacted some art and antiquities dealers here in New York and posed as the agent of a wealthy collector who might want to buy the ring if it ever came on the market. Most of the dealers knew its history, which in Europe goes back to Renaissance Italy. One of them researched the auction records and confirmed that it was sold at auction in Vienna in 1934, consistent with my grandfather's letter."

"But none of them have heard of it since?"

"No, or so they claim. I don't know if I believe them or not. Frankly I think art dealers are mostly a pack of thieves."

"Did you speak with the Netzer family?"

"Not directly." Murray stood up and started pacing from one end of the room to the other. "But here's what happened. The FBI has links to the organization I mentioned, Restitution, with the goal of gathering information about potential claims for valuables stolen by the Nazis or stashed in Swiss banks. An FBI agent called Wallace Harkins got my name from Restitution and offered to help me pursue a claim."

"The FBI?"

"I didn't want to get the FBI involved, but they sort of insisted. Agent Harkins has actually been very helpful. I showed him the letter from my grandfather and told him what I'd learned about the Netzers. He contacted the Swiss equivalent of the FBI—the Swiss Federal Police—and had them interview the Netzers. They denied any knowledge of the matter."

"Naturally."

"They wouldn't speak to me or to Agent Harkins."

"Of course not. That would make it too easy." Borges held his hands out in front of him, fingertips touching, as if waiting for Murray to continue. A full minute passed before he realized that this wasn't going to happen. "So is that where the story ends?" he asked incredulously. "With the detective in a cul-de-sac? Mysteries don't end like that."

Murray smiled as he realized that Borges was judging his story by its literary merits. "No, of course not," he said, slipping back into his seat. "A couple of weeks ago I read in the *Times* that Dr. Peter Netzer, of Zurich, had accepted an appointment as the new Chief Medical Examiner of New York."

"Ah!" Borges exclaimed. "An unexpected twist. Very good! Perhaps your story will have a surprise ending after all."

"I certainly hope so," Murray nodded. "Dr. Netzer will be assuming his duties at the city morgue on Monday."

2. The Librarians of Babel

I had arrived in the city three weeks earlier with a hundred dollars in my pocket and a determination to leave my issues behind and seek my fortune in the Big Apple. My immediate ambition was to find a job in publishing. With a degree in comparative literature and a year of graduate study—okay, 'study' is an exaggeration; let's just say I was enrolled in graduate school for a year—I could make a convincing case for having the right qualifications. My first day in New York I walked all over Manhattan and sat on park benches wondering where I was going to sleep. Someone had suggested the Sloan House YMCA on 34th Street near Penn Station, so I hiked over there and waited in line for a room, which cost $5.00 a night. At that rate I could only afford to sleep every other night. My problem was solved by three Peruvian brothers I met in the line who'd come to New York to study Business English. They'd worked out a method of reducing the cost by renting a double room for $8.00, sneaking in an extra man, and sleeping four across on two beds pushed together. By rounding out the quartet I was able to sleep for $2.00 a night—not a bad price for midtown Manhattan, even if only two of us could get out of bed at the same time. The Peruvians snored like bucksaws and stayed up half the night playing cards and telling dirty jokes, but they never objected to my sleepwalking and occasional raving nightmares. And I was on the same street as the Empire State Building, in case I wanted to jump off.

After three weeks of polite but unanimous rejection, the only job I could find (and it was part time, just thirty hours a week) was at the *Anglo-American Cyclopedia,* an obscure 24-volume reference work that relied on door-to-door salesmen to convince anxious parents that their sons and daughters faced a lifetime of penury if they grew up without it. Anglo-American's biggest selling point—which according to the salesmen made it far superior to its arch-rival, the *Encyclopaedia Britannica*—was its world-renowned Subscriber Reference Service. Purchasers received a book of coupons which entitled them to submit questions to the experts at the Reference Service. Being one of those experts, I can attest, did not require any expertise beyond the ability to live on $90 a week. Our office filled the 33rd floor of a high-rise on Third Avenue, a warren of cubicles stretching as far as the eye could see, each housing a formica-topped desk, a molded plastic chair and a college graduate with no particular skills— we were called "reference assistants"—all under the oversight of Miss B. Kunkel, a gray-haired librarian who wore a chain attached to the side-pieces of her glasses (which, however, had never been known to dangle during working hours).

Miss Kunkel explained my duties at a brief meeting in her office the day I was hired. She sat at her desk in front of a heavy wooden cabinet that seemed to hoard all the world's secrets. "The universe may be infinite," she said, "but our encyclopedia, though under constant revision, is not. For this reason the set comes with a hundred numbered coupons, which, in numerical order, the purchaser may send in with questions on any topic not covered in the encyclopedia."

"I see," I nodded, anxious to make a good impression.

"Provided, of course, that the question is not beyond the scope of our service."

"Of course." I nodded again, though I'd begun to have misgivings. A hundred coupons, while generous, hardly seemed sufficient to bridge the gap between an infinite universe and a 24-volume encyclopedia published in 1953. "But what do we do when they've used up their hundred coupons?"

Miss Kunkel seemed bemused by my question, as if it foreshadowed excessive sympathy for over-inquisitive subscribers. She picked up her phone to summon my supervisor. "Quite frankly," she said, "we've never received a coupon numbered higher than three."

My supervisor was a stunningly beautiful Greek-American woman named Lucinda Samos, fresh out of library school. She was tall and statuesque, with almond eyes, a sensuous mouth, and a figure that any hourglass would have been proud of. Not in my wildest dreams (if my wildest dreams had been about librarians) would I have imagined that a librarian could be so attractive. When she tapped on the door, Miss Kunkel handed her a thick loose-leaf binder and sent us on our way.

"I'm Lucinda," she said, her voice as soft and silky as the scarf she wore around her neck. "I'll be your mentor."

As she guided me to my desk, my fellow reference assistants—there seemed to be hundreds of them, men and women of all ages, colors and creeds—popped their heads over the tops of their cubicles and just as quickly disappeared back inside.

I told Lucinda a little about myself, emphasizing that as a reference assistant I was a rank beginner in need of constant mentoring and supervision. That made her smile, but she was inured to admiration. After a few preliminaries she gave me all the training I would ever receive.

"You see this?" She handed me the loose-leaf binder Miss Kunkel had given her. "This is your Bible. Your prayer book. Your catechism."

"My catechism?"

"Actually it's the form book for the responses you're allowed to give to the idiots who send in their coupons."

I was taken aback by her irreverent attitude. "But... aren't we obligated to provide a serious answer to every question?"

"You have to handle fifty questions a day," she smiled. "Six to ten photocopied pages per question. That means you can spend about ten minutes on each one. If you can't find something in the library or the morgue, you have to pick out the best response from the form book. Good luck!"

The morgue?

She ducked out of sight and left me alone in my cubicle before I could ask her what she was talking about.

3. The Tell-Tale Art

Before I left Borges's apartment that first night, he corralled me into agreeing to stop by the next morning—it was a Saturday—to help him with his research. He was preparing his seminar on Poe's detective stories, he said, and Miss Chalmers would be unavailable. It was a dangerous temptation, roughly in the same category as Odysseus sailing past the Sirens after cleaning the wax out of his ears. But I'd enjoyed seeing the old sage again and meeting his neighbor Murray, with his quest for a fabulous inheritance. I had asked Lucinda out for coffee on Sunday (it wasn't a date, we'd agreed, just a chance to get acquainted), but other than that— unless I wanted to spend it coaching the Peruvians on their Business English—my weekend was wide open.

I arrived at the apartment around eleven o'clock. Borges sat in the big wing chair, dressed for work in his gray suit and tie. Work was something he did in his head; there were no books or writing materials within reach. Señora Sanchez hovered over him like an overprotective mother, bringing him a carafe of maté (a kind of Argentinian tea that is sipped through a silver straw), warm biscuits, cold cuts, cucumbers, slices of deviled egg—none of which she offered to me—and whisking the dirty dishes away as soon as he stopped eating.

"As I'm sure you know," he said, sipping his maté, "Edgar Allan Poe invented the detective story. He wrote just three of them, all very well known: 'The Murders in the Rue

Morgue,' 'The Mystery of Marie Rogêt,' and 'The Purloined Letter.' I assume that you've read them?"

"Sure," I said. "Is there anyone who hasn't?"

Borges took another sip of his maté. "There's a professor in Baltimore who thinks that three of my best-known stories were conceived as conscious imitations of Poe's three detective stories, and that I wrote them, in each case, exactly a hundred years after Poe's original. He's working on a scholarly book expounding that theory in elaborate detail."

"Sounds like a mad idea," I said.

"There's madness in his method," Borges conceded, "though I understand that he musters his evidence quite convincingly. As for the project he imagines for me—the project of duplicating Poe's detective stories in that way..." His voice trailed off and he rolled his sightless eyes toward the ceiling.

"Is that what you did?" I asked.

"That would have been mad, too," he smiled. "Not to say I wouldn't have done it, if it had occurred to me. But as you know, I detest mirrors, reflections and duplications of all kinds. Imitating Poe was the last thing my rather prosaic mind would have attempted. It was Poe who had the genius to anticipate my stories and improve upon them—a hundred years before I wrote them."

"Poe anticipated *you?*"

"Quite so. I created Poe as my precursor, just as Kafka created his own precursors."

"But—"

"Countless other writers, more talented than I—Conan Doyle, Chesterton, Ellery Queen—have rendered this service to Poe. Had we not done so, his tales would strike us as contrived, inconsequential curiosities from an earlier era. I doubt if the professor in Baltimore would ever have read them."

Señora Sanchez must have noticed me eyeing Borges's food. In fact I was famished, not having had a bite since the night before. "Have you had breakfast?" she asked me.

I shook my head.

"I'm so sorry!" she said, and ran off to the kitchen to find me something to eat.

Borges sat staring into space, or into the absence of space (to him the two would have been the same). "The question is why," he said. "Not why did I write my stories, supposedly in imitation of Poe, but why did Poe write his three detective stories in the first place? Surely not just to anticipate mine."

"Surely not," I agreed.

"It's a mystery I intend to solve before I give my seminar," he said, nodding with resolution. "With your help, of course."

Alarm bells rang in my head. I hemmed and hawed as best I could—mentioning my job, my shortage of funds, my lack of a place to live—but nothing would stop him.

"Thinking over Poe's three stories," he went on, "it has occurred to me that a certain French writer is mentioned in two of them. Crébillon."

"Crébillon?"

"He wrote poetic tragedies in the early to mid-1700s."

"Never heard of him," I said, hoping that would disqualify me from any duties involving Crébillon.

"Nobody has. I would wager that my graduate assistant, Miss Chalmers, who styles herself a Poe scholar, has never heard of him. Yet he's hiding in plain view in two of Poe's most famous stories."

"Probably just a coincidence," I said.

"I need you to help me find out why."

"Why what?"

"Why Poe and his alter ego C. Auguste Dupin were so familiar with Crébillon, and Poe made a point to mention him twice in three stories. Didn't you say you were working for an encyclopedia? Which one?"

"It's called the *Anglo-American Cyclopedia.*"

"Ahh!" He smiled and shook his head. "Not exactly an authoritative source."

"Not at all. In fact—"

"Only one encyclopedia can make that claim. The 11th edition of the *Encyclopaedia Britannica,* first published in 1909."

"It must be a little out of date by now."

"Nonsense. Are you aware that the *Anglo-American Cyclopedia* originated as an unauthorized reprint of the *tenth* edition of the *Britannica,* published in 1903, which itself was mostly a reprint of the ninth edition of 1889? Now *that* is out of date."

"It's under constant revision," I said, echoing Miss Kunkel.

For some reason that made him laugh. "I'm sure it is. A hundred years from now..." His voice trailed off.

"Would you like me to try to find something about Crébillon in our encyclopedia?" I asked. If that was the only help he needed, I could handle it.

"Oh, no," he said.

"How can I help you, then?"

"I believe there's a row of second-hand book dealers not far from here, on Fourth Avenue south of Union Square. Book Row, they call it." He shoved a wad of cash into my hand. "Take this and get me a set of the 11th edition of the *Britannica*. Preferably the 29-volume compact edition on India paper, published in 1911."

"All twenty-nine volumes?"

"Of course."

I asked the obvious question. "How are you going to read it?"

"Don't worry. You can read it to me."

In truth I was relieved that Borges didn't own a set of the *Anglo-American Cyclopedia*. If he'd sent in one of his coupons I probably wouldn't have been able to help him.

As I learned from Lucinda, there were only two places we were allowed to look for the answer to a question sent in by a subscriber. One was the Reference Service library—a single room about the size of a large bedroom, stocked with random discards from the editorial departments. On an altar-like table at one end stood the latest edition of the *Anglo-American Cyclopedia,* which the staff treated like a holy book, not to be consulted except on certain ceremonial occasions. Obviously you couldn't look in the *Cyclopedia* for a topic that was not covered in it; on the other hand, until you did look, you didn't know if the topic was covered there or not. If no answer could be found in the library (which was almost always the case), the next place to look was the "morgue"—a vast, dimly-lighted file room in the center of the floor where a bull-faced woman named Peg hoarded newspaper clippings on every conceivable subject, though never on the one you were looking for. She guarded the door with scissors in hand and you entered at your peril. If you could escape from Peg and find your way back to your cubicle with six to ten xeroxed pages that vaguely addressed the question sent in with the coupon, you sent them over to Cornelia Herrington, the typist, with a cover letter claiming to have answered the question, and prayed that the subscriber would be satisfied. One thing I noticed: Miss Kunkel was right—all the coupons I'd been given to answer were numbered 1, 2, or 3.

The reason for this soon became apparent. The loose-leaf response manual—our Bible, prayer book, and catechism— consisted of hundreds of form letters explaining why any given question could not be answered. In each case certain fine print in the purchase agreement was cited: *We reserve the right to reject any question that is beyond the scope of our service.* Looking for health information? Scientific or technical data? Historical or literary interpretation? Philosophical or theological doctrine? Child rearing advice? Geographical information beyond a listing of state capitals? In each case the oracle of the response manual would deliver the same daunting message: *We're sorry, but your question is beyond the scope of our service.*

There was one ray of hope in this cloud of unknowing. In rare instances—I could never figure out what the criteria were—we were allowed to use the last form letter in the binder, Form Letter 323, which featured a large blank space (to be filled in by the reference assistant) and a statement that the answer was from an "Authoritative Source." Consulting an Authoritative Source was an occult process which involved a complicated series of steps, like questioning the oracle of

Delphi. I had to talk to Lucinda, who would arrange a consultation with Miss Kunkel, who would then lock herself in her office with the shades drawn, to emerge several hours later, dazed and haggard, with the answer scrawled on a notepad.

"Then is Miss Kunkel the Authoritative Source?" I asked Lucinda.

She answered with an enigmatic smile. Later I learned that the Authoritative Source was kept under lock and key in the cabinet behind Miss Kunkel's desk.

4. *Das Fluch*

As Borges and I talked about Poe and Crébillon and the various encyclopedias and the research he wanted me to do, I had noticed a light tap as Murray Kellerman appeared at the door. He pushed it open and waited politely for us to finish before he walked into the living room, carrying a small yellowed envelope in his hand. He whispered to Señora Sanchez and she offered him a cup of tea as he sat down, replenishing Borges's maté as she did so.

Borges paid no attention to all this until he'd finished giving me my assignment. Then he said, "Ah! Here's Kellerman. Did you bring what I asked you to bring?"

"I sure did," Murray said, waving the envelope.

Borges smiled at me. "I am intrigued by Kellerman's story about his grandfather and the stolen ring, the FBI investigation, and the prominent pathologist in Zurich who's moving to New York to run the morgue, and his unstable, alcoholic brother—Peter and Bernhard Netzer, I believe are their names. So when he told me about this letter I asked him to bring it over so you can read it to us."

Murray handed me the old envelope, which was covered with cancelled stamps that said "Deutsches Reich" and featured an idealized portrait of Hitler. I carefully removed the letter, which was yellow and faded, though still legible. It was written in German.

"I don't read German," Murray said. "I had to ask a book dealer over on Fourth Avenue to translate it for me, and now I can't find the translation."

"You know German, don't you?" Borges asked me.

"A little," I admitted.

"Well, at least you can sound it out so I can understand it."

I read the letter aloud, struggling to translate as I went, and relying on Borges to supply the words I didn't know. It was largely as Murray had described, with all the claims about Solomon's signet ring and its origins and all the details about how Mannheimer had entrusted it to the attorney in Zurich, Matthias Netzer, until he could get his family out of Germany. When I came to the end, I turned it over and found a postscript that appeared to have been written in the same hand, but in a more pronounced state of agitation.

"There's a postscript here," I said, showing it to Murray. "Do you want me to translate that too?"

"I don't remember seeing that before," Murray said.

"Go ahead and translate it," Borges said.

"All right, here it is: 'If, as now appears, Counselor Netzer takes advantage of my...'" I stumbled over the next word. "*Unfähigkeit?*"

"Inability," Borges said.

"'...my inability to escape from the Reich and appropriates to himself the ring of Solomon and its prodigious value— thus preventing its return to Jerusalem and depriving me and my family of our only remaining...' *Vermögensverhältnisse?*"

"Resources."

"'...and dooming us to deportation and probable death at the hands of the Nazis—I want you to know that with my dying breath, so help me God, I hereby invoke on Matthias Netzer, and all his...' *Abkömmlingen?*"

"Descendants."

"'...and on *all those who come into possession of the Seal of Solomon*'—this part is underlined—'as a result of his faithless dealings, and their descendants after them, the ancient *Fluch*'—I don't know that word—'that will follow them down through the generations to the end of time.'"

Murray and I both stared at Borges as if he were an oracle. "What is a *Fluch?*" Murray asked him.

"A *Fluch* is a curse," Borges said. "Your grandfather has invoked on Matthias Netzer and his descendants—and on all those who come into possession of the ring—an ancient curse that will follow them to the end of time."

We sat in silence for a long moment, even Señora Sanchez, whose sense of melodrama, well-honed by afternoon TV, must have been piqued by the mention of a curse. I assumed that Murray, who hoped to come into possession of the ring, was weighing the pros and cons of risking a *Fluch*—the idea sounded even worse in German than it sounded in English—that would follow him to the end of time. "All this proves," he finally said, "is that my grandfather believed in curses. He also believed in golems, the Kabbalah, and a lot of other nonsense."

"The Kabbalah isn't nonsense," Borges said. "Golems, of course, are mythological, but that doesn't make them nonsensical. The same is true of the ring of Solomon."

I had the feeling that he knew more than he was willing to tell us. "What do you know about the ring of Solomon?" I asked him. "Is this the Solomon in the Bible we're talking about?"

Borges was uncharacteristically reticent, hesitating before he answered. "Yes, we're talking about the Biblical King Solomon," he said. "I can tell you what I know about him and his signet ring, but my knowledge is sketchy and probably out of date."

"I thought you knew everything," Murray said.

Borges chuckled as if he thought Murray had made a good joke. "My vast erudition—or vast ignorance, the two are the same—on this subject, as on many others, I owe to two sources: the *Thousand and One Nights* and the 11th edition of the *Encyclopaedia Britannica.*"

All the more reason, I thought, to purchase a set of the 11th edition as Borges had requested. For some reason he hadn't asked me to buy him a set of the *Thousand and One Nights*—probably because he had it memorized. I doubted if Murray believed him, but I knew it was true: those two works, and a handful of others equally obscure and out of date, in which fact and fiction are commingled indiscriminately, were the source of most of his learning.

"The *Thousand and One Nights,*" Borges said, "better known in the English-speaking world as the *Arabian Nights*, is a labyrinth so vast and circular, so layered with fantastic themes and tales within tales, that no one can read it in a single lifetime. Certainly not I, though in my younger days I pored over the ten volumes of Burton's translation and its six-volume supplement until I was seeing double. That, I am tempted to say—plus the 11th edition of *Britannica,* a work of similarly monstrous complexity which I tried to read from cover to cover—are probably what robbed me of my sight, if not of my sanity. I read far into the night, beyond the time when dream and reality lose their distinctness, and now I can never read them again. I can only tell you what I remember, or think I remember, from their pages."

He took a sip of his maté and went on: "King Solomon is revered by Muslims (under his Arabic name, Suleiman) as well as by Jews and Christians. The Jews, wary of occultism, extoll his wisdom, good deeds and worldly magnificence; Muslims and Christians have often seen him as a sorcerer and mystic. It is said that he had a magical signet ring given him by the Archangel Michael to aid in the construction of the Temple of Jerusalem. Upon that ring was engraved the seal and most holy name of God—in Christian sources with a five-pointed star, in Jewish and Muslim sources with a six-pointed star of David. By the power of that seal Solomon could understand the language of the birds (this is confirmed by Chaucer) and he could command spirits—called *jinn* or genies by the Muslims, angels or demons by the Christians and Jews—to do his bidding. That was how he built the Temple, in about 1000 B.C. He used the ring to capture one demon, and from that demon he extracted the names of many others, whom he then enslaved to build the Temple."

"What happened to the ring after that?" Murray asked.

"Long after the Temple had been completed, Solomon's ring or seal continues to appear in the literature of the Near East, whenever a demon or genie needs to be enslaved, a treasure uncovered, an enormous distance traveled in an instant. His power over the jinn is referenced in the Qur'an itself, which, Muslims believe, existed before the creation of the world. The ring figures prominently in the *Arabian Nights*. In one of the most famous stories, 'The Fisherman and the

Genie,' the jar in which the genie is imprisoned is said to have been closed with the seal of Solomon."

Murray glanced at me with an amused, skeptical smile. "But how did that signet ring get from the *Arabian Nights* to a Viennese auction house in 1934? That's where my grandfather bought it."

"The ring disappeared from history when the Second Temple was destroyed by the Romans in 70 A.D. It is said that the high priest, with his dying breath, uttered a curse that would follow the ring in the hands of its robbers and despoilers down through the generations until it was returned to its rightful place in a restored Temple."

"You read that in the *Arabian Nights?*"

"No, in the 11th edition of *Britannica,*" Borges said. "Your grandfather's ring could be the real thing. Perhaps it was discovered in Jerusalem and brought back from the Crusades, though I doubt it. Quite likely it's a medieval forgery—especially since it's encrusted with gems. None of the ancient accounts mention gold or precious stones. In fact they describe it as being made of brass and iron."

"To tell you the truth, I don't really care," Murray said. "The gold and gems are what make it valuable."

Thinking a few moves ahead (as he always did), Borges disagreed (as he always did). "The efficacy of the curse would depend on its being authentic."

"Don't tell me you believe in the curse!"

"Curses have a venerable pedigree," Borges said. "There's the Biblical curse on Cain for killing his brother, the curse on the house of Atreus in Greek mythology, the curse of Tutankhamen, and of course the curses pronounced on precious gems such as the Hope diamond. The classic instance, for our purposes, is found in *The Moonstone*, by Wilkie Collins, a friend of Charles Dickens—"

"Wait a minute," Murray said. "Isn't that a novel?"

"Possibly the best mystery novel ever written," Borges nodded, unfazed by Murray's skepticism. "It centers around a sacred gem stolen from a temple in India, which carried an ancient curse, much like the one your grandfather invoked for his ring, ensuring certain disaster to anyone who laid hands on it, and to all who received it after him, to the end of the generations of men."

"Not just a novel," Murray said. "A fairy tale."

"Yet the curse was no supernatural fancy. It was the mission of a hereditary secret society that searched for the gem and exacted vengeance on those who usurped it."

"But it's still just a story, isn't it?"

"Just a story?" Borges smiled. "Perhaps. But if I were the Netzers, I'd think twice about ignoring a story like that. You, on the other hand, being the legitimate heir—assuming the ring is authentic—might be able to use its powers to your advantage, as Solomon did."

Murray laughed. "Well, I'm not planning to conjure any demons."

"Don't be so sure," Borges warned him. "You never know when that might come in handy."

5. Clueless

Sunday I was off from work, which wasn't quite the blessing it might have been in a perfect world. At Sloan House we weren't allowed to stay in our room during the day, even if we all could have fit into it. This was a YMCA, after all, and on Sunday the residents were expected to attend religious services, which seemed to be of the Calvinist persuasion. Exercising my free will, I elected to slip out a side door along with the Peruvians. The weather was damp and cold as only springtime in New York can be, with a nasty wind whistling through the canyons of skyscrapers. My roommates traipsed off to a Peruvian bar on Tenth Avenue to drink pisco sours and watch soccer on TV, leaving me with two hours to kill before it was time to meet Lucinda. The city was quiet and surprisingly boring on a gray Sunday morning. I considered taking the subway down to Book Row to buy the encyclopedia for Borges, whose wad of cash was burning a hole in my pocket, but I doubted if the secondhand book stores would be open on Sunday, and I decided I needed a respite from Borges as much as from my job. It proved to be a wise decision. The following day—also supposedly a day off—I would visit his apartment and find myself caught up in a murder investigation that would eat up most of my time for the next two weeks.

I spent the next two hours doing what I usually did in my spare time: walking the streets of New York. I'm a compulsive walker who likes nothing better than to set myself on autopilot and wander aimlessly and almost unconsciously around whatever city I happen to be in. That morning my steps sketched a random pattern I couldn't remember an hour later. I think I walked up Ninth Avenue to 96th Street, then down Broadway to 59th. After that my memory goes blank. I must have crossed the park to Fifth Avenue and hiked up one of the avenues on the East Side. At noon I met Lucinda at a coffee shop near the Metropolitan Museum.

It wasn't a date, we both understood that. Just meeting for coffee—no drinks, no dinner, no exchanging the stories of our lives. Just the chance, for me, to spend an hour or two with a lovely, lively woman who happened to be my mentor and supervisor, and for her, to extend some welcoming hospitality to a coworker who'd recently arrived in New York without knowing anybody. When she asked why I'd left Boston, I couldn't tell her about Katie—I'm not sure why, if it wasn't a date—so I had to make a few things up, stretch the truth a little, describe my decision in terms that were a little too abstract. Coming home from the Army, I told her (yes, I'm ashamed to admit, I failed to mention that I'd never made it out of boot camp), I felt as if I'd lost my sense of who I was: fragmented, disconnected, unable to focus. Clueless, as Katie put it, though I didn't tell Lucinda that. "My friends didn't know who I was anymore, and neither did I."

"Have you figured that out yet?" Lucinda asked.

"Still clueless," I admitted. "Got any ideas?"

"I'm not a psychologist," she said. "I couldn't tell you what's going on from that point of view. But, as a librarian, I might be able to help you."

That struck me as very funny. "You could tell me where to look it up?"

"What does a good librarian do?" she smiled. "She takes all the disconnected fragments of knowledge that have accumulated over the centuries and shows you how to navigate through them to find what you need to know. Clues for the clueless," she laughed. "That's what we do."

"Even if it's your self you're looking for?"

"*Know thyself.* Isn't that the basis of all philosophy?"

Lucinda turned out to be an amazing woman. She'd been raised in Queens, where she still lived. Her father, a Greek immigrant, was a veteran of the anti-German resistance during World War II and now worked as a bank teller; her mother was a high school English teacher. She had an older brother who was a surgeon at Presbyterian Hospital. She had studied art history and philosophy at Columbia, graduating near the top of her class, and then enrolled in its library school. Her position as supervisor at the *Anglo-American Cyclopedia* reference service was her first professional job.

Although I laughed at her metaphor—I considered it a metaphor—of the librarian as a kind of magus of self-knowledge, I took it more seriously than I let on, because it seemed to relate to a recurrent dream, or nightmare, I'd been having. In my dream I wandered alone through a vast library, picking up books from the shelves and opening them eagerly, only to find in every case that they were written in languages I couldn't understand. The only person I could see was Miss Kunkel, sitting behind an enormous desk in the center of the library. I pushed my way through the stacks and called her name but could never reach her or make her listen to me. This went on until one of the Peruvians shook me and told me in choice Business English to find another nightmare.

I decided not to mention that dream to Lucinda just yet.

6. Inquisitions

I'm an old man now, older than Borges was then, addicted to pain killers, rehearsing my bows for the final curtain. I have two daughters, Ingrid and Gracie, grown women now who have loved me and looked after me, each in her own way, since their mother died. They aren't in this story, not having been born or even conceived when it took place. Yet they are part of it, at this point in my life the most important part. They're the future that happened only because of the way it turned out—it's the backstory to their own lives, a tale of deceptions and discoveries they will never know about. They will never read this. A daughter shouldn't know too much about her parents' early lives, especially their relationship with each other, which, but for certain random events or choices that are better left unmentioned, might have taken a different path, leading them to other lovers, who could have been, but wouldn't have been, her parents.

When I think back on my younger days, those years before the internet, before smart phones, before Google, Wikipedia and all the rest, what I see in my mind's eye is a world of unimaginable complexity and deliberation. To buy a book you had to go to a book store; to send mail you had to go to the post office; to meet someone, you actually had to be in the same room with them. To do research you went to a library, searched through card catalogs and bibliographies, took notes in longhand, submitted search requests, waited for the requested materials, sacrificed your eyesight to the microfilm reader and then groped your way through a maze of shelves and stacks—all to accomplish, over days or weeks or a lifetime, what can now be done on Google and Wikipedia in fifteen minutes.

No wonder the *Anglo-American Cyclopedia*, in its wisdom, reserved the right to reject questions that were beyond the scope of its service. Without that limitation, our library would have needed to be as vast as the universe itself. I only wished I'd had a similar agreement with Borges. No question was too arcane, no allusion too obscure, no book too scarce to arouse his curiosity. Yes, I could have greeted his demand for a 29-volume set of the *Encyclopaedia Britannica* (11th edition, India paper, 1911) with haughty disregard: *I'm sorry, sir, but that request is beyond the scope of my service.* But when he shoved that wad of cash into my hand—three hundred dollars, I realized when I counted it—I felt like a down-at-the-heels encyclopedia salesman thirsting for a commission. I asked Murray Kellerman if he knew any secondhand book dealers, and he recommended August Schneider, the old Austrian who'd translated the Mannheimer letter for him. And so on Monday morning, I ventured down Fourth Avenue to see if I could find what Borges was looking for.

In those days Fourth Avenue below Union Square was still known as Book Row, though most of the old-time dealers had long since folded their tents. Only a few shabby bookstores remained, and the shabbiest belonged to August Schneider, well into his eighth decade, who stood in the doorway, wreathed in cigar smoke, following my movements with a lynx eye in case I tried to pilfer a twenty-five-cent paperback from the cart on the sidewalk. When I brushed past him he followed me inside and sat behind a cluttered desk just inside the door, sizing me up as I peered between the bulging shelves of old books.

"A hundred dollars that will cost you," he said, pointing to a leather-bound set that stood lined up on his desk. His sagging face, like everything else in the store, had been yellowed by cigar smoke beginning before I was born. "And let me tell you, for twenty-nine volumes that's a bargain."

"I guess you talked to Murray."

"Murray?" he laughed. "Yah, I talked to Murray."

"Is that the *Britannica?*"

"Eleventh edition, India paper, 1911." He picked up the first volume and flicked through it like a deck of cards. "Very nice set."

"A hundred dollars is pretty steep," I said, "for something that's so out of date."

"The whole world's in this encyclopedia," he smiled. "How could it be out of date?"

"Still..."

"So the money's coming out of your pocket?"

Murray must have told him that it wasn't. In fact Borges had given me an extravagant sum which, I hoped, would pay for the encyclopedia, a taxi to deliver it to him, and some of the other expenses I'd racked up on his account.

"I should be so rich as that blind man," Schneider said with a crooked smile. "Your friend Murray told me all about him. He's been writing books since the twenties."

He pulled out a flimsy, yellowed paperback, entitled *Inquisiciones,* and held it out just beyond my reach. "Borges's first book. It's about the Spanish Inquisition."

"The title is in Spanish," I said, "and it means 'inquisitions,' in the sense of investigations, but I don't think it's about the Spanish Inquisition."

"So you're an expert? All I know is, it's a rare book, a valuable book. But don't get any ideas. It's not for sale."

Was he trying to entice me to spend the rest of my money on that book? I changed the subject. "You translated a letter for Murray," I said.

"Yah, I translated a letter for your friend Murray." His eyes twinkled mischievously.

"You left out the part about the curse. *Das Fluch.*"

"*Das Fluch?* Was there a curse in that letter? That part I must have missed."

It was a short, uncomfortable taxi ride to Borges's apartment with three boxes containing the 11th edition of the *Encyclopaedia Britannica* bouncing on the seat beside me. I passed the time imagining what I would do with the money I'd have left over, which, after paying the taxi fare, would be almost two hundred dollars. I needed that money badly, and I knew Borges would never ask for his change. I could keep it all without considering myself a thief. But I realized with a sinking sensation that this was Borges's way of drafting me into his service. Now I owed him, and he owned me. Whatever he asked me to do from now on, I couldn't say no.

I landed with my three boxes on the sidewalk in front of Borges's building. The doorman, Henri, who considered himself a member of a higher social class, acted like the *maître d'* of an exclusive French restaurant, which he claimed to have been. At first he blocked my way, but was persuaded by a five-dollar bill to let me take the boxes through the lobby, though not as far as the elevator. There was a storage area for deliveries, he told me—"Mr. Borges receives many packages"—but I salvaged what was left of my pride by insisting that I wasn't a deliveryman, but a friend bearing gifts. The lie stuck in my throat. I knew in my heart that I should have used the servants' entrance.

Señora Sanchez knew a fellow servant when she saw one. She didn't take her eyes off the TV screen as I struggled with my boxes into the apartment and added them to a pile of unopened packages on the floor. "He's across the hall with Murray," she said, munching potato chips from a bowl on her lap. "Just knock and walk in."

Murray was also subletting his apartment from a professor who was on sabbatical. It had the kind of makeshift, faux-Scandinavian decor that was popular in those days—a low couch, a couple of sling chairs, a glossy white coffee table piled with art books from the overstock tables at Marboro Books. There was one comfortable armchair in the living room, a portable stereo, a black and white TV. Murray sat at a card table contemplating a chess board while Borges slouched in the armchair, twirling his walking stick, apparently lost in thought. What was it like for such a mind to be trapped in blindness? I wondered. What he saw wasn't darkness, he'd told me, but a bluish luminescence that enveloped him as he wandered in the maze of memory and imagination.

Suddenly he rapped his walking stick on the parquet floor and turned toward Murray. "Queen to Queen's four."

Apparently the two of them were playing chess. How could Borges keep track of all the pieces on a board he couldn't see?

Cursing under his breath, Murray moved the queen as Borges had directed.

"Checkmate," Borges murmured.

"I give up," Murray laughed. The plastic pieces clattered as he swept them off the board.

"It's not in the spirit of chess to react that way when you lose," Borges admonished him with a smile. "Chess is a duel of honor between gentlemen. The winner doesn't make the last move—he doesn't actually capture the king—and in recognition of that, the loser must gracefully concede."

"I'll try to remember that."

"The game of life must be played the same way."

To my astonishment, Borges rose to his feet and strode across the room as if he could see where he was going. He stopped a few inches from the window and pretended to look outside at a pair of pigeons which had roosted on the ledge. By that time I was standing beside him, gently touching his elbow. "There are pigeons on the window ledge," he said.

"Yes," I said. "They're all over New York."

"Sometimes I forget there's a city out there," he said, and let me guide him back to his chair.

"I'm amazed that you can play chess," I told him, glancing at Murray who was on his hands and knees picking up the chess pieces he had knocked on the floor.

"It would be more amazing if I couldn't," Borges said. "The labyrinth I'm accustomed to living in has many more than sixty-four black and white squares."

"Maybe I'd do better wearing a blindfold," Murray said, setting the pieces back on the board. "Less distraction. Is that your secret?"

"Poe, or at least his fictional detective Dupin, would have thought so," Borges said. "You'll recall that in 'The Murders in the Rue Morgue,' he compares chess unfavorably with draughts (which is now usually called checkers). In chess, he says, what is only complex is mistaken for what is profound. Winning is mostly a matter of *attention,* not analysis."

"What does he mean by analysis?" Murray asked.

"Analysis, as Poe sees it—and remember, he's elaborating a theory of how a detective solves a crime—is the exertion of the intellect: the detective's ability to identify with his opponent and retrace the steps by which he committed the crime—and in the investigation, to seduce him into error or hurry him into miscalculation."

"In other words," Murray said, "he sees detective work as a battle of wits between the detective and the criminal. I don't think that's what it's like in the real world—I mean, for the police. They rely on witnesses, fingerprints, lab results—"

"What the police do in your so-called real world is a shabby exercise in solving crimes through brute force, rather than the intellect. I have no interest in such things."

The usually affable Murray shot a disapproving glance at Borges, to which Borges, lost in his blue mist, paid no attention. "There are real crimes committed out there," Murray said, turning his pleading eyes toward me. "Like what Matthias Netzer did to Klaus Mannheimer. Stealing that priceless ring and then ingeniously covering his tracks so that his family would still be denying any knowledge of it twenty-five years later. That's more a matter for the police, wouldn't you say, than for some amateur sleuth?"

"Frankly," Borges said, "I doubt if the police have ever solved a truly ingenious crime. That only happens in books."

As it happened, we soon had an opportunity to test that hypothesis. A sharp knock on the door brought our discussion down from the clouds, as Murray welcomed Agent Wallace Harkins of the FBI. Agent Harkins was the friendly agent who'd taken an interest in Murray's inheritance claim and enlisted the Swiss police to investigate the Netzers. I have to say that my image of the intrepid, indomitable G-man came down a few notches when I met Agent Harkins. He looked more like a waiter or a car salesman, with a smooth, boyish face, a florid complexion, and a protruding lower lip. He wore a cheap gray suit, a pale blue tie that matched his eyes, and an expression that said, unconvincingly, that he was the smartest person in the room.

He greeted Murray but paid no attention to Borges or me. "Bernhard Netzer arrived in New York yesterday," he told Murray. "This morning he was found hanging from a tree in Central Park."

7. The Hanged Man

Bernhard was the younger of the Netzer brothers, and by far the less impressive of the two, according to Agent Harkins, who had collected information on them over the past several months from his counterparts in Zurich. Peter (the pathologist) was universally admired for his achievements, if not for his colorless personality; he had received many professional honors and appointments. Bernhard was the perennial problem child. He studied literature in France and Germany but returned to Switzerland without a degree, tried his hand at writing, organic farming and politics, squandering a good deal of family money in the process. The only things he succeeded at were drinking and chasing women, to the extent that you can succeed in those fields: at the age of forty he was a twice-divorced alcoholic with a paranoid streak who devoted most of his energy to infuriating his mother (who had recently been run over by a tram). The two brothers made no secret of their loathing for each other, especially after Peter had an affair with Bernhard's wife, Helga, and married her. Apart from those oddities, the Netzers were a typical Swiss family, solidly middle class. There was nothing in their lifestyle or financial profile that suggested some hidden source of great wealth.

"What was Bernhard Netzer doing in New York?" Borges asked. "Isn't it the other brother who has the job here?"

Harkins squinted at Borges as if noticing him for the first time. "I don't believe we've met."

Borges dipped his head slightly. "Jorge Luis Borges."

"Dr. Borges is a noted detective," Murray said. "This is his assistant, Nick Martin."

"You've brought in private detectives?"

"The very best," Murray said. "You can tell them anything you'd tell me."

"All right," Harkins said, frowning. "To answer your question: Yes, it's the other brother, Peter, who just started as Chief Medical Examiner. He's been here a few days with his wife, staying at the Plaza Hotel. Apparently Bernhard followed them here—he checked into the Plaza yesterday afternoon. The three of them had dinner together, went back to their separate rooms about ten, and that's the last time Bernhard was seen alive."

"You'll be investigating his death, I assume," Borges said.

Harkins frowned again. "It's a matter for the local police." He turned back to Murray. "I talked to an NYPD detective about it and they're looking into the possibility of homicide."

"Did he mention why?" Murray asked.

"*She,*" Harkins smirked, as if his answer were a joke. "The detective is a woman, if you can believe that."

Borges threw up his hands. "Doesn't anyone in this country read Agatha Christie?"

The FBI agent seemed rattled by Borges's outburst, but he went on, fixing his eyes on Murray. "Detective Bernadette Foley," he said. "I just wanted to give you a heads-up. She considers you the prime suspect."

"Me?"

"When Bernhard Netzer's death hit the news wire, the NYPD received a call from that Restitution group in London, who told them all about the Netzers' Nazi connections and the fact that you've accused them of stealing that ring from your grandfather. That gives you a pretty good motive, doesn't it?"

"A motive to kill them?"

"Why search for a motive," Borges said, "when you've got a curse?"

Harkins blinked incredulously. "A curse?"

"Didn't you say the mother had been run over by a tram?"

Agent Harkins's florid complexion had risen a few shades, well into the purple zone. He still thought he was the smartest person in the room, but he might have begun to wonder what kind of room he was in. Borges made matters worse by launching into a lengthy discourse on the futility of beginning a crime investigation with *motive*. "If you start with a suspect's motive," Borges said, "you will look only for facts that confirm that bias—you can always find them—and ignore any that don't. This will lead to a solution that seems self-evident but which in fact is false. You might as well begin with a curse. Are you aware that there's a curse on that ring?"

"What the hell are you talking about?"

"If instead you look at *all* contemporaneous facts and circumstances," Borges went on, "there will be only one possible solution: the correct one. The motive will be obvious, and any external causes—the curse, destiny, divine intervention—can be disregarded." He raised his hand to silence any possible objection. "The solution, as Poe said, is a matter of logic, as in a mathematical problem. I offer that as an ironclad rule of detection."

"Are you talking about *Edgar Allan* Poe? Is that the Poe you're talking about?"

"Is there any other?"

I have to say I sympathized with Agent Harkins. First Agatha Christie, then a curse, and now Edgar Allan Poe, had been cited by Borges within the span of two minutes. Somehow I doubted if those topics were on the syllabus at FBI school. Luckily a confrontation was averted by the sudden arrival of Señora Sanchez, who tapped on the door and pushed her refreshment cart into Murray's apartment. She circulated like an airline stewardess, exchanging pleasantries as she offered coffee, tea, juices and tasty Latin American snacks. Borges sank into his armchair with a carafe of maté, Murray perched on the couch beside Harkins, balancing his coffee cup on his knees, and I contented myself with one of the sling chairs, an elastic contrivance which, every time I changed my position, threatened to catapult me onto the floor.

Harkins drained his coffee cup with unseemly haste. "I didn't know I was coming over here to hear lectures about curses and mystery writers," he said.

Murray gave him his most diplomatic smile. "I'm more than happy to cooperate with the FBI, but I still need to have my own team involved." He gestured toward Borges and me. "I have a lot at stake here."

Harkins considered that as he waited for Señora Sanchez to refill his cup. "All right, Murray, here's the thing," he said. "Whether or not you murdered Bernhard Netzer is a matter for the local police, not the FBI. Frankly I don't give a damn, as long as you stay out of jail until we can pull the trigger on our sting operation."

That expression startled Borges back into the conversation. "Sting operation?" he repeated. "What does that mean?"

"Maybe you could look it up in one of your Agatha Christie books," Harkins said.

"A sting operation," Murray told Borges, "is when the police play along with some illegal activity—like dealing in stolen goods—until they can catch the criminals in the act."

Borges's eyebrow edged upwards in a characteristic blend of puzzlement and suspicion. "Is that what's going on here?"

"I think I told you I contacted some art dealers to find out if Solomon's ring had ever come on the market," Murray said. "When I did that, I gave the name Michael Forbis and pretended that I represented a private collector who wanted to buy it."

"A harmless fiction," Borges said approvingly.

"You could call it that." Murray didn't look so sure he agreed that it was harmless. "After I reached out to the art dealers, Agent Harkins—who's been very generous with his help on my restitution claim—asked me to work with the FBI to help catch them—"

"Don't use that word," Harkins barked. "*Catch* is something you do in a trap. This isn't entrapment."

"Right. So then what word—"

"Identify." Harkins spat out the correct formulation as if he were applying for a search warrant: "To identify any art and/or antiquities dealers who may be involved in importing, selling or otherwise disposing of stolen art works or antiquities in violation of international law and/or the laws of the United States."

"Did you identify any such dealers?" Borges asked.

"There's one dealer who's been very interested in locating the ring and selling it to my supposed client," Murray said. "A dealer named Bridget O'Hara, who runs an upscale auction gallery on Madison Avenue."

"We've been watching her for some time," Harkins said. "She's done this type of thing before, and we know she'll do it again. Murray's been working with us on that."

"Working with you?" Borges asked. "Doesn't that mean you're using him as bait for your—"

"Again I caution you against using any metaphors arising from hunting, fishing or trapping activities. The Agency specifically prohibits the use of such metaphors."

Borges erupted with fury at this infringement of poetical freedom. "Prohibits such metaphors?" he cried, pounding his walking stick on the floor. "Must I consult your agency before I compose my next poem? Do you also regulate periphrasis, metonymy and synecdoche?"

Harkins didn't take the bait, so to speak. By this time he'd concluded that Borges was more than slightly insane. And all he cared about was getting the art dealer into his clutches. "When was the last time you talked to Bridget O'Hara?" he asked Murray.

"I met her at her gallery a couple of weeks ago, right after I read that Peter Netzer was coming to New York," Murray said. "She said she expected to have the ring soon. Of course she didn't know I knew who the seller was."

"Is that the last time you talked to her?"

"She called me the middle of last week," Murray said. "Said there'd been some kind of glitch. I asked her, Does the owner still want to sell? and she hesitated a little. Maybe they're having second thoughts, I don't know. But finally she said not to worry, the ring would be available soon."

8. Detective Foley

In that benighted era, everybody smoked (which may be why most of them are dead). Cigarette commercials portrayed smoking as the key to relaxation, wisdom and popularity. So as Señora Sanchez collected our used cups and plates we all leaned back in our seats and lit up. We smoked quietly, inhaling, exhaling, and (in Borges's case) blowing smoke rings, as we considered the situation from our individual perspectives. Harkins, high on the hope that Bridget O'Hara would soon put the sale together, puffed with the self-satisfied smirk of a gambler watching his opponent double down on a bad hand. Murray smoked anxiously, I smoked obliviously, and Borges—encircled by swirling orbits of smoke he couldn't see—maintained a sphinxlike silence, as if he'd propounded an impossible riddle and was waiting for someone to solve it. His poetic outrage had vanished like the morning mist.

This spell of contemplation was broken by a sharp rap on the door.

"Come in!" Murray blurted without knowing who was there.

The door flew open, framing a long-limbed Irish beauty in a Burberry raincoat, a crimson scarf around her elegant neck. She had blazing blue eyes, apple-red lips and a crown of copper-gold hair held back with a silver clasp. I assumed it was Bridget O'Hara, but that was a mistake. This was Bernadette Foley—*Detective* Bernadette Foley, as she insisted on being called whenever possible. No wonder I'd been mistaken. She was way too young and beautiful to be a detective, but as we were to learn, her youth and beauty were a kind of disguise. She was a woman not to be trifled with.

"Mr. Kellerman?" She held up her badge and stepped inside. "Detective Bernadette Foley, NYPD. May I come in?"

We all laughed because she was already inside. "Sure," Murray said. By this time we were all on our feet, even Borges, trying to be gentlemanly. "Make yourself at home."

She settled into the other sling chair and the rest of us sat back down. "I'd like to ask you some questions." Her bravado faltered when she noticed Agent Harkins. "What are you doing here?"

"Mr. Kellerman and I have some matters to discuss," Harkins said smoothly. "About the international art smuggling investigation I described to you earlier."

"What does Mr. Kellerman have to do with that?"

"He's cooperating with us, helping us get close to a dealer who's suspected of being involved in that type of activity."

The detective fixed her searing blue eyes on Harkins. "Here in the city?"

"The dealer's in New York, but—"

"If there's some fencing of stolen art going on in New York, that's for the NYPD to investigate. You know that."

Harkins rolled his eyes, which was a mistake. I later learned, as a handy rule of thumb, that you do not roll your eyes at Detective Bernadette Foley unless you want to have them torn from their sockets. "This is a sting operation we've been working on for a long time," he said. "We're not going to let the NYPD screw it up."

I thought she might pull off her scarf and strangle him. Instead—and more chillingly—she stared him down and lowered her voice. "I'll pass that comment on to my superiors. The Police Commissioner will love it."

Harkins groped for his cigarettes and stuck one in his mouth.

"Can I offer you something?" Señora Sanchez asked, approaching with her cart. "Coffee? Tea? Juice?"

Foley glared at Harkins. "Please refrain from smoking," she said. "It's like a gas chamber in here. Anyway"—she aimed a predatory smile at Murray—"the fencing of stolen art isn't what I'm here to talk to you about."

"You're here because of the death of Bernhard Netzer," Murray said.

"Exactly. Which has nothing to do with the FBI's sting operation."

"We'll see about that," Harkins said.

"I'm sorry to hear about Mr. Netzer," Murray said, "but I don't know anything about how he died."

"You hated him, though, didn't you?" Foley said. "That's what the Restitution group told us. You called him a thief and a lot of worse things and said you were going to bring him down."

"Not him specifically," Murray said. He sounded defensive and I didn't blame him. She seemed to be accusing him of murder. "The whole family. They are thieves and a lot of worse things. And as to bringing them down, I meant legally."

"Have you ever met Bernhard Netzer or spoken to him?"

"No."

"And yet you went to his hotel last night and asked to speak to him, didn't you?"

"I went there to try to speak with his brother, Peter Netzer, and the clerk told me they were both staying there. But neither of them was there when I got there."

"What time was that?"

"I think it was about eight o'clock." He glanced at Harkins, then at me, as if we could confirm what he'd said. "What time did he die?"

"You tell me."

"I'm not a murderer." His eyes pleaded with the detective. "I don't know what I can do to convince you of that. I'm actually a pretty decent guy."

She snorted out a little laugh and stared back at him until he couldn't stand it any longer and turned away. Then she leaned forward and handed him one of her cards. "I'm going to ask you to come down to the precinct and sign a statement."

Harkins was determined to keep Murray out of jail. "Is this definitely a homicide case?" he asked Foley. "Do you have a ruling on that? I thought there was a finding of suicide."

"We expect to have an independent ruling on the cause of death by tomorrow."

"An independent ruling? What do you mean?"

"Things have gotten a little weird," she said, less belligerent than before. "When the police recovered the body, they took it right to the morgue."

"The same morgue where Peter Netzer works?"

"That's right. Dr. Netzer started his new job there this morning, just two hours before they brought the body in. The officers had a pretty good idea who it was—his passport was in his pocket—but still, the first thing Dr. Netzer had to do was identify his brother's body."

"That is sort of weird," Murray said.

"It gets weirder."

Harkins pounced. "Don't tell us Peter Netzer actually performed the autopsy on his brother?"

She bit her lip. "He said it would be shirking his duty to pass that responsibility off on somebody else."

The autopsy conducted by Dr. Peter Netzer, we learned, had resulted in a finding of suicide as the cause of death. And a suicide note—the contents of which Foley refused to disclose—had been found in Bernhard Netzer's hotel room. Ordinarily the Chief Medical Examiner has the last word, but for some reason which Detective Foley wouldn't disclose, the District Attorney's office was insisting on a second autopsy conducted by an independent pathologist.

"There must be a pretty good reason for that," Agent Harkins said.

"There is," Detective Foley agreed, "but I can't go into it." She glared at Murray. "Bottom line, if the second autopsy doesn't confirm suicide as the cause of death, we're going to be focusing on you."

"And if it does?"

"In that event, no homicide case will be opened."

Detective Foley belted up her Burberry and prepared to leave. "I have a favor to ask you," she said to Agent Harkins. "We've been trying to get in touch with any relatives the victim may have had in Switzerland. You said you'd opened some contacts over there?"

Harkins frowned. "Can't you ask the brother?"

"Obviously we'd rather not depend on him for our information."

"Bernhard Netzer had a couple of ex-wives," Harkins said. "One of them, believe it or not, is Peter Netzer's current wife Helga. She's here in New York with him."

That was all Foley could get out of him. He wasn't doing her any favors.

"I might be able to help," Borges chimed in. "I was educated in Switzerland. That was decades ago, but I've maintained some ties in the country. In fact one of my friends from the German-speaking region is still active in the Swiss federal police. It would be a simple matter of calling him and asking for help."

Foley blinked at him suspiciously. "And you are...?"

He bowed modestly. "Dr. Jorge Luis Borges, Director of the National Library of Argentina."

She gawked at him for a long moment, trying to make sense of what he'd just said.

"He's also a noted detective," Murray said. "Working with me on recovering the ring."

"Do any of you speak German?" Borges asked. "Perhaps better than I? No, well then tomorrow morning I'll give it a try. It's too late to call them today."

"I don't like this," Harkins said. "We have our procedures for making inquiries in foreign countries. In fact we've already—"

"I'd appreciate your talking to your friend," Foley said to Borges, cutting Harkins off. Then she turned to Murray: "I'll call you tomorrow and let you know how the second autopsy turns out. If there's a finding of homicide, you'll need to get your butt down to the precinct station or I'll send somebody out to bring you in."

"No problem," Murray said. "I have nothing to hide."

"That's what they all say," she smiled. "Right before they ask for a lawyer."

"You can interview him in my office," Harkins said.

Foley replied with an icy stare. "Just to be clear, Agent Harkins," she said. "We're not running this case out of your office."

9. The Mystery of Peter Mark Roget

Tuesday morning was sunny and springlike, but my outlook was decidedly blue. At the office I opened a dozen questions before finding one that was within the scope of our service. A subscriber from Racine, Wisconsin, asked, with Coupon No. 1, "Who was the eighth avatar of Vishnu?" Merely understanding the question was a challenge, which gave me an excuse to consult my lovely mentor before heading to the library. As a supervisor Lucinda occupied a corner cubicle, large enough to contain an uncomfortable chair for me. We didn't talk much about the avatars of Vishnu, which, Lucinda explained, are incarnations of an Indian god. Over coffee on Sunday I had told her about Borges and Murray and the curse on the ring of Solomon. I doubted if she believed much of what I said; I probably would have been better off keeping my mouth shut. But she had a bright, open smile that invited all sorts of foolish disclosures, and that Sunday tête-a-tête, though it wasn't a date, had generated a little warmth on both sides. And now, sitting in her cubicle, I told her about the Bernhard Netzer murder and how I had unexpectedly become involved in its investigation. She seemed impressed, having read about it in the *Times* that morning. She asked me a lot of questions I couldn't answer and then quickly changed the subject. Was it skepticism? I wondered. Did she think I was making it all up?

"Follow me," she said. She rose to her full, impressive height, like a marble statue of a Greek goddess, and led me through the maze of cubicles to the morgue, where bull-faced Peg guarded her trove of newspaper and magazine clippings with fierce determination.

Peg eyed me warily as I stated my request, and then, to my immense surprise, waddled to the back of the room and pulled out a file marked, "Vishnu, Avatars of." Her expression left no doubt in my mind that she would impale me with her scissors if I didn't return it promptly, complete and with all pages in the right order.

"Now you can see why I love to work here," Lucinda said as she guided me back to my cubicle. "An encyclopedia is a microcosm. It's a map of knowledge, a reflection of everything people have thought and learned and done."

"Everything?" I wondered aloud.

"Of course, not *everything* can be in the encyclopedia."

"For some things," I suggested, "you need to consult an authoritative source."

"Yes," she laughed. "But for most things, you can just look in the morgue."

At lunchtime I had to hurry downtown, having agreed, for some unfathomable reason, to take Borges out to lunch. This called for a mad rush followed by the excruciating, sub-glacial pace of prizing him in and out of the taxi to go to a restaurant six blocks away. The overall experience bordered on the surreal. Droves of office workers, animated by a glimpse of spring weather, surged over the sidewalks in a primaveral frenzy. Yellow cabs swarmed over the streets like hornets in heat. The gentle maritime breeze only served to remind me that I was trapped on an island from which there was no escape without paying a toll. The light at the end of the tunnel was New Jersey.

At times like this, Borges made an excellent companion. He was so oblivious to the external world—if he even believed in its existence—that its imperfections had scant effect on him. For all the hardships he'd endured, at heart he was a friendly, sociable man who loved to talk. And he would talk about anything, so long as it was what he wanted to talk about.

I took him to a popular sidewalk cafe in the West Village called O. Henry's, where we sipped Italian white wine before ordering our food. The busy tables were small and crowded together with narrow paths for the waitresses and busboys, and it took some doing to get Borges properly wedged into his seat with his walking stick propped beside him. The neighboring tables were alive with clattering dishes and chattering academics from NYU. I wondered if any of them knew who Borges was.

He was still seething at what he insisted on calling the FBI's ban on metaphors. "Not Hitler," he said as we sipped our wine, "not Stalin, not even the man whose name I will not utter"—he meant Juan Perón, the fascist dictator of Argentina in the 1940s and '50s—"ever tried to extend tyranny this far. To silence poetry is to strangle humanity. If some ancient Ozymandias had been able to prevent Homer from singing about the wine-dark sea, do you think we'd be sitting here today? I think not. We'd still be living in the trees."

The waitress—a perky Midwesterner who introduced herself as Pat—had to humor him for a good five minutes before she could extract his food order. This was Greenwich

Village, after all, where in the 1970s mad poets and philosophers lurked behind every lamp post. By the time she brought
our next glass of wine, Borges had expanded his defense of
Homer far beyond the use of metaphors. "Homer was the
first blind poet known to history," he said, "although there
must have been many others before him. It was the only
occupation open to a blind man in the ancient world: if he
was not a poet he would have been stoned to death." He
took a long sip of his wine. "That may still be the case for all
I know."

"Fortunately you are a poet," I said.

"Indeed."

"As well as a philosopher and detective."

"I have never practiced philosophy," he said, "except fic-
tionally, and most of what I know about crime detection I
learned from reading Poe and Chesterton. My first love has
always been poetry. A poet, unlike a philosopher, does not
attempt to understand the entire universe, just a small part of
it: that part which can be perfectly described in a few words.
The exception, of course, is Homer, who understood more
than any philosopher. But Homer would have been a failure
as a detective. At the end of his life he went mad because he
couldn't solve a riddle."

The waitress, Pat, had returned with our plates. "It
sounds like you know a lot," she said to Borges, setting his
Waldorf salad carefully in front of him. "Are you a professor?"

He parried the question with a wave of his hand. "All my
apparent erudition can be found in the 11th edition of the
Encyclopaedia Britannica."

"We had a set of the *Anglo-American Cyclopedia* back home," she said. "I learned a lot from that."

"I hope not too much," Borges said.

"Did you send in any of the coupons?" I asked Pat as she ground fresh pepper on my fettucine alfredo.

"Oh, yes. I sent in the first one. I wanted to know why the precession of the perihelion of Mercury is forty-three arc seconds per century larger than the calculation based on Newtonian orbital mechanics. I was planning to become an astrophysicist. But I never got an answer."

"They said your question was beyond the scope of their service."

"How did you know?"

I grimaced bitterly. "They did the same thing to me."

"That's when I came to New York to become a waitress. It's not so bad."

She perked off toward another table while Borges and I dug into on our lunches. "By the way," Borges said, "I meant to thank you for getting the encyclopedia. It's a very nice set."

I dreaded what was coming next. "Have you been... reading it?"

"Miss Chalmers came over this morning and read certain articles aloud at my request."

I breathed a sigh of relief that Miss Chalmers knew how to read.

"She's helping me prepare for my Poe seminar. Of course, I have to tell her exactly where to look for the information I need. An encyclopedia—even the 11th edition of *Britannica*—is utterly useless unless you already know what you're looking for."

"I meant to tell you," I said. "The bookseller I bought it from—his name is August Schneider—has a copy of one of your early books: *Inquisiciones.*"

Borges's face tightened. "Paper wrappers, Buenos Aires, 1925?"

"Yes, that's it."

He set his fork down on the table and leaned toward me. "I must have that book. Go back and get it."

"Schneider says it's not for sale."

"Nonsense."

"I have to agree with the gentleman about that," Pat said, appearing beside us with dessert menus. "If they say it's not for sale, that means it is for sale, only at a much higher price than you want to pay."

"Precisely," Borges agreed. "Go back and get it," he told me. "Surely you had some money left over? I'm always looking for copies of my early books."

We ordered coffee—maté not being on the menu—and Pat hurried off to fetch it.

"What's the name of this place?" Borges wondered.

"O. Henry's," I said. "Named after a writer, I think."

"Yes, O. Henry was quite famous in his day for his short stories, which always had a surprising twist at the end. His method of composition was the same as Poe's: write the ending first, then start at the beginning and write whatever leads to the end. The oddest thing about him was his belief that if he read the dictionary straight through, he would gain the sum of human knowledge."

Pat had returned and now she stood filling our cups with coffee. "That's not really so odd, is it?" she asked Borges. "For somebody who started his stories at the end?"

"Why do you say that?" Borges asked.

"If you know the ending of a story, then you know the meaning of everything leading up to it, don't you? That's what it would be like knowing the definition of every word in the dictionary. You'd understand everything." She turned and walked away.

"There are no facts in the dictionary," Borges said, shaking his head. "No proofs or disproofs of the existence of God, no critiques of Horace's odes or Berkeley's idealism, no tips on where to get the best Russian salad in Buenos Aires—and yet..."

"She's gone," I whispered.

"—and yet this young lady thinks she would *understand everything* if she knew all its definitions. And O. Henry thought that by reading through it he could gain *the sum of human knowledge.*"

I glanced around to see if anyone was listening to our conversation. To our right a couple of well-dressed ladies nibbled salads and chatted about a Broadway musical they planned to attend. To our left some bearded academics who must have been mathematicians or physicists were engaged in a heated discussion of quantum mechanics. No one else—apart from our waitress—seemed concerned with the sum of human knowledge.

"O. Henry wasn't the first to entertain such a mad scheme," Borges went on. "Other thinkers have asked themselves: If every word can be correctly and precisely defined, then by combining those words in every possible way, couldn't every true fact, every meaningful theory, every correct doctrine (and the refutation of every fact, theory and doctrine) be deduced in a kind of mathematical process?

Leibniz took the next step and postulated what he called *blind thought*—thinking carried out like algebra with symbols whose meanings remain unknown. And then of course there are the Kabbalists—"

"Anyone need a refill?" The waitress hovered over us with a pot of scalding coffee, threatening to pour it into our cups from two feet above.

"No, thanks," I smiled back at her. "Just the check, please." She hurried off to get our check.

"An encyclopedia is better than a dictionary, isn't it?" I asked Borges hopefully. "At least it consists of facts. The 11th edition—"

"An encyclopedia, even the best one—even a perfect one, which would be a linguistic image of everything in the universe, including itself—is a kind of labyrinth," he cut me off, "which like any labyrinth is incomprehensible unless you see the whole thing. You must either wander at random or start somewhere specific—by looking up something you've at least heard of—and proceed along an endless series of bifurcating paths, each of which leads to an entirely different set of facts. How could the sum of human knowledge ever be attained through such a process?"

"The fallacy," Pat said as she laid our check on the table, "is in envisioning the sum of human knowledge as a *quantity of facts* without any overarching logic. Before all those facts, what you need is a *conceptual structure* to make sense of them."

"In that case," Borges said, "what you need isn't a dictionary or an encyclopedia. What you need is *Roget's Thesaurus.*"

"We had one of those back home too," Pat said. "I think it came with the encyclopedia."

I have to say that I thought our discussion, which had soared so high, had tumbled to a new low. *Roget's Thesaurus!* "Isn't that just a dictionary of synonyms and antonyms?" I objected.

"It may have become that in later editions," Borges said, "but as originally conceived by Peter Mark Roget in the nineteenth century, the *Thesaurus* was just what the young lady described: an arrangement of language in a structure that was not alphabetical, like a dictionary, but conceptual. The first two concepts (as in the book of Genesis) are existence and nonexistence, followed by substantiality and insubstantiality, and proceeding from the abstract to the concrete through a structure of exactly one thousand concepts which, in its subdivisions, encompasses *the sum of human knowledge.*"

"But is that knowledge of the world or only of the mind?" Pat asked.

Borges's face had taken on a reddish, almost luminescent glow. "Do you seriously believe that the two are different?" he demanded, rapping his walking stick on the sidewalk for emphasis. "Spinoza said, *the order and connection of ideas is the same as the order and connection of things.* It follows that perfect knowledge of the mind and its ideas is also perfect knowledge of the world. The human mind, when fully explored, is a map of the cosmos."

It was humbling to acknowledge (if only to myself) that the waitress had a far better grasp of what Borges was talking about than I did. This conversation had been far beyond the scope of my service. I reached in my wallet and pulled out some cash—it was part of the money I'd had left after buying the encyclopedia—and handed it to Pat, who shoved it in her apron pocket, smiled, and glided to the next table, where she happily joined the debate on quantum mechanics.

"That is the challenge we face in solving a crime," Borges said as he pushed himself into standing position with his walking stick. "We struggle with our meager thoughts and ideas. And yet small as they are, our ideas come to us in a logical structure—they can't exist otherwise—and that structure is identical to the structure of the world. What we must do is study the facts and circumstances of the crime in every detail (disregarding the false clues planted by the criminal) until we have a clear and complete picture of it in our minds. That, I believe, is what Poe meant by analysis."

I clutched his arm to guide him to the sidewalk. "Is it the practice in this country," he asked, "for the waitress to take such an active role in the conversation?"

"Sometimes it is, I guess."

"Well, I hope you left her a generous tip."

10. Nullibiety

That evening it was eerily quiet in Murray's apartment. No cops, no FBI agents, no murder accusations or metaphor suppression in progress. Borges and Murray were absorbed in a chess game, which, by all appearances, might have been a fight to the death. Murray hovered desperately over the chess board while Borges, ensconced in his armchair, studied it fixedly with his mind's eye. Their conversation consisted entirely of cryptic instructions such as "Pawn to King's four," "Knight to King's three," and the like, after which they receded into a monastic silence.

"Murray," I said, hoping to lighten the mood with a little small talk, "what kind of work do you do?" It was a remarkable fact that I still didn't know what Murray did for a living.

He glanced up from the chess board with a mischievous look in his eye. "I'm either an unemployed actor or an unemployed mathematician."

"Everybody in New York is an unemployed actor," I pointed out.

"True," he agreed. "But being unemployed, I might as well say I'm an unemployed mathematician, or an unemployed sculptor, or an unemployed concert pianist. You can be unemployed at an infinite number of occupations."

"Nullibiety—the condition of existing nowhere—is infinite," Borges agreed.

"And," Murray added, "you can impress women by picking the right occupations to be unemployed from. I've found they get a lot friendlier when I tell them I'm an unemployed brain surgeon."

We bantered on like this until Borges intoned the inevitable "Checkmate!" and Murray admitted defeat, more gracefully than I'd seen him do it before. "I'm going to beat you someday," he told Borges. "You just wait."

When they finished their game, Murray handed me that afternoon's *New York Post,* folded open to the following article:

TRAGEDY, UPROAR GREET
NEW MEDICAL EXAMINER
By Rachel Price

The city's new Chief Medical Examiner, Dr. Peter Netzer, took office Monday in the midst of personal tragedy and a public uproar about possible links to a Nazi past. The body of Dr. Netzer's brother, Bernhard Netzer, of Zurich, Switzerland, was found in Central Park and brought to the city morgue just as Dr. Netzer assumed his duties. The death has been ruled a suicide.

Dr. Netzer, through a spokesman, denied allegations that his family is in possession of art works stolen from Jews during the Nazi era. The Mayor's office issued a statement extending condolences to Dr. Netzer and his family, while calling for a full investigation of the alleged Nazi connections.

"Nothing in there we didn't know," Murray said, trying to sound optimistic. But we all knew that the suicide finding was open to question. A second autopsy, unless it confirmed the earlier finding of suicide, would spell trouble for Murray.

"It wasn't suicide," Borges declared.

"How can you be so sure?"

"Why would anyone endure the ordeal of traveling to New York in order to kill himself? Have you ever gone through customs at Kennedy Airport? Have you taken the cab ride into Manhattan? No one in his right mind would do that just to kill himself. He could do it at home."

"But what about the suicide note?"

Borges dismissed the note with a wave of his hand. "Nothing is easier to fake than a suicide note."

Murray wasn't quite ready to accept that. "We'll have to see what the second autopsy shows."

"It doesn't matter what the second autopsy shows," Borges said. "The truth is a matter of logic."

"Isn't it more a matter of facts?" Murray objected.

"The two are indistinguishable. As I told that young waitress this afternoon—quoting Spinoza—the order and connection of ideas is the same as the order and connection of things."

"You talked to a waitress about this?"

"It was at O. Henry's," I explained. "Your name wasn't mentioned."

"Look at the logic," Borges said. "Didn't the art dealer—what's her name? Bridget O'Hara?—tell you two weeks ago that she expected to have the ring in her possession in the near future?"

"It was about two weeks ago—"

"And at that time wasn't Peter Netzer expected to arrive for his new job in New York? Which he did, and brought his wife along, as expected. And then his brother, expectedly or not, also showed up. Those are the three people who knew about the ring, so isn't it fair to assume that when the art dealer spoke to you, she expected one of them to bring it to her in New York?"

"I see your point, but—"

"And since Bernhard died a violent death within a few hours of his arrival, one can only assume that he was the person bringing the ring and that he was killed by someone who wanted to steal it. And everything that makes his death look like suicide—including the note and the autopsy performed by his brother—has been manufactured to confuse the police."

"Then—I hate to ask—who do you think killed him? His brother?"

"I doubt it very much. How likely is it that his brother would wait until he came to New York to kill him? The same goes for the brother's wife."

"Maybe the art dealer, then?" Murray suggested.

"Highly unlikely. The art dealer still thinks she'll have the ring soon. Didn't she tell you that a couple of days ago?"

Murray had turned suddenly pale as he listed the potential suspects and Borges dismissed each of them in turn. "You're not saying *I* killed him, are you?"

"Of course not. He was killed by someone who wanted the ring. You have a legitimate inheritance claim that has every chance of succeeding. And yet"—I braced myself for what might come next—"the fact that you were seen at the hotel around the same time as the murder will count against you. It is, in fact, the kind of circumstantial evidence that has sometimes sent men to the gallows."

"We don't have a gallows in New York," Murray said.

"The electric chair, then, if that's any comfort. By the way, you still haven't told us why you went to the Netzers' hotel."

"All right," Murray said, a little sheepishly, "I'll tell you what happened. I'd been thinking about all this and realized that I've relied way too much on the FBI. They're the ones who supposedly investigated in Switzerland and told me the Netzers refused to cooperate. But how do I know they're telling me the truth? For all I know, they're using the Netzers the same way they're using me, as bait for their sting operation against Bridget O'Hara. It occurred to me, since Peter Netzer was in New York, that maybe I should reach out to him before getting involved any deeper with the FBI. Maybe I could persuade him and his family to give up their claim to the ring without going through setting up a phony sale and waiting years for my inheritance. So I called the morgue and asked when Dr. Netzer would be starting there. They said Monday, and I asked where he was staying. They didn't want to tell me but I kept at it until I finally wheedled it out of them."

"Murray's famous charm," I said.

"Right. They said he was staying at the Plaza. I agonized about it all day Sunday and finally went over there about eight o'clock that night. I walked up to the desk and asked to speak to Dr. Netzer. 'Which one?' the clerk asked. 'We have a Peter Netzer and a Bernhard Netzer.' That took me by surprise—I had no idea both of them were here. I'd gone there to see Peter, so I asked for him. The clerk asked my name, and I told him."

"What name did you give him?" Borges asked.

"Murray Kellerman. What do you think? He rang Peter Netzer's room and there was no answer. 'Bernhard, then,' I told the clerk, but there was no answer there either. 'They must have gone out,' he said. So I asked for Peter's extension number so I could try calling him myself."

"Did the clerk give it to you?" Borges asked.

"Yes, and I wrote it down on one of their cards. People were coming and going, I didn't know who any of them were. I tried to call Peter Netzer from a courtesy phone in the lobby. Still no answer, so I came home."

"Was that all, then?"

"Yes—well, no, there was one other thing. The clerk asked me, 'Are you with the lady?' and I said, 'What lady?' and he just looked at me like he thought I was lying. Finally he said, 'Pardon me, sir, I must have been mistaken.' What do you make of that?"

"I haven't the slightest idea. But I can only hope, for your sake, that the new autopsy confirms the ruling of suicide."

It was a hope that would soon be shattered. A few minutes later the telephone rang and Murray answered. Borges and I heard one side of a very one-sided conversation, the kind you might have with a police officer ordering you to come down to the station to answer questions in a murder investigation.

When Murray hung up the phone he gave us the details. The second autopsy report had come in with a finding of probable homicide. He had been instructed to report to Detective Foley's office at nine o'clock the next morning. He had the right to be represented by counsel; anything he said could and would be used against him in a court of law. It's never a good day when a police officer tells you that.

"When you see Detective Foley," Borges told Murray, "please tell her that I made the call she requested to the Swiss Federal Police. I wasn't able to find out anything about other relatives Bernhard Netzer may have had in Switzerland."

"I'll pass that on while she's beating a confession out of me."

"But just between us, I was able to open my own line of communication with the Swiss police. I talked to Inspector Fritz Egli—very pleasant fellow, though a bit confused. Something I said must have given him the impression that I am the Prefect of the New York City police."

"The New York City police doesn't have a Prefect," Murray said.

"I know that," Borges said, "but I don't think Inspector Egli does. At any rate he's promised to keep me informed about the investigation in Switzerland."

"What investigation?"

"The investigation of Bernhard Netzer. He's suspected of killing his mother."

It took a moment for that to sink in. "Did you tell him that Bernhard Netzer is dead?"

"Again I'm afraid I might have given Herr Egli the wrong impression," Borges smiled. "He seems to think Bernhard Netzer is still alive."

After we said goodnight to Murray, I helped Señora Sanchez escort Borges back to his apartment. He collapsed into his wing chair—I sat on the sofa—and the kind Señora brought us each a drink: whisky for Borges, beer for me.

"Murray's in big trouble," I said.

"He'll be fine as long as we find the real murderer."

"How are we going to do that?"

"The usual way."

"I do the legwork and you provide the ratiocination?"

"Exactly. You'll also be the narrator, of course, when it comes time to tell the story. The Watson, if you will."

Every great detective must have a Watson, he'd told me once. Some lesser being he can share his thoughts with, and who can tell his story, though he seldom understands it. I preferred to think of myself as Virgil escorting Dante through Hell, or Sancho Panza, bringing a glimmer of common sense to Don Quixote.

"What if I won't?" I said.

"Won't what?"

"Won't be your Watson."

"Then I suppose Murray will go to the electric chair."

That was a shocking way of putting it. Yet I had to admit that it contained a grain of truth. With the relentless Detective Foley leading the NYPD against him, and the FBI using him as a pawn to be sacrificed as soon as he'd served their purpose, Murray wouldn't have a fighting chance without Borges on his side.

"Nick," Borges said in a surprisingly intimate tone, like a kindly father counseling his son, "I'm offering you an opportunity to do something important. Marooned in my wing chair, dependent on others for every necessity of life, I am—despite the authoritative pose I sometimes strike—as helpless as a turtle washed up in the surf and left flailing on its back.

And you—I hope you don't mind my saying this—appear to me to be in approximately the same position. You don't seem to know who you are or what you're doing."

"Well," I said gently, not wanting to sound dismissive, "you've sort of taken control of my life, haven't you?"

"Only because I'm afraid of what would happen if I didn't. I know you, Nick, much better than you think I do, because I was young once and now I'm an old man. If I've taken control of your life, it's so I can turn it back over to you when you know what to do with it."

I couldn't resist a note of irony. "And in the meantime I'm to be your Watson."

"Don't underestimate the importance of Watson. At the end of the day it's his story. He's the narrator; he controls the story and how it gets told. Even his famous obtuseness may be a disingenuous ploy. Believe me, Nick, there's no more important character in a story than the narrator."

For Borges, as I had to learn over and over again, it was impossible to separate life from literature. Sooner or later everything he thought about took the form of a story. A murder involves three stories, he told me later—the victim's story, the murderer's story, and the detective's story—each of which has a beginning, a middle and an end. The victim's story and the murderer's each has its own cast of characters and its own plot, which overlap at one critical moment. The detective's story begins where the victim's ends. Its only purpose is to reconstruct the other two stories and find the point where they converge. And the narrator is the godlike intelligence who grasps these stories in their manifold divergences and weaves them together into a coherent representation of reality.

And all of this, Borges told me, was invented by Edgar
Allan Poe. The great mystery, he said, was why? Why did Poe
invent the detective story?

Thereby, or at least nearby, hung a tale. Which—
fortunately for me, who had to get up and go to work at 8:00
o'clock the next morning—Borges postponed to another day.

11. The Aleph

Wednesday. My day began at 5:30, when the first Peruvian bounded out of bed. By 6:00 they were all shaved and showered, dressed, and ready to start another day of Business English. Roberto was kind enough to roll me over and stand me up before they charged out to breakfast. In view of my penchant for sleepwalking, he even pinched me to make sure I was fully conscious.

My office didn't open until nine, so I took my time getting there. It was a forty-minute walk from Sloan House to 53rd Street and Third Avenue, which allowed for a leisurely survey of the human race in all its varieties, glories and imperfections. I observed some glorious women and quite a few men in suits who ranked among the imperfections. Most people fell somewhere in between, average working stiffs like me rushing somewhere to avoid doing anything useful for the next eight hours. I liked to think that by evading the questions people sent in with their coupons, I was, in my own small way, making the world a better place. Most of the information they wanted would have done them more harm than good.

As I sat in my cubicle sifting through the mail, I thought about Borges's description of an encyclopedia as a labyrinth, which is incomprehensible unless you can see the whole thing. The number of facts in the universe is infinite, and the fraction of them contained in an encyclopedia infinitesimal. If the world is the totality of facts—everything that is the case, as some joker once said—then how can we ever know enough to understand anything? And yet here was a letter from Darryl C., of Chillicothe, Ohio, who had sent in his first question (handwritten with a cartoonish picture of an atom, electrons spinning around a pea-like nucleus, at the top), along with Coupon No. 1, asking whether a nuclear reactor should be equipped with an automatic shut-down switch to prevent overheating. He explained that he was an engineer who had been hired to design a nuclear power plant near Harrisburg, Pennsylvania. I shook my head in bemused disbelief. The question was clearly beyond the scope of our service, and even if I could find an answer I wouldn't have sent it to him. A little knowledge (and that was all I could ever offer) is a dangerous thing. I wished him well on his nuclear plant and rejected the question.

As I did my work that morning—searching for obvious answers in the library, digging for clippings in the morgue, choosing rejection letters from the form book—something preyed on my mind: Borges's designation of me as his Watson. I didn't like being cast in the role of the dim-witted companion whose role is to see and hear all the same things as the detective but never solve the crime. Still, as Borges had emphasized so strongly, the role of Watson carried with it the status of narrator, to which he attached so much importance.

In the event that I ever wrote the story down—which is what I'm doing now—I would control the narrative, which to some extent was the narrative of my own life. I didn't have to come across as dim-witted. No matter how the case turned out, I'd be able to make myself look smarter, wittier, more prescient than I really was. I could manipulate events and appearances so that I, and not Borges, would get credit for the brilliant insights, the witty aphorisms, perhaps even the solution to the crime. Of course being the narrator has its disadvantages. People today are so accustomed to unreliable narrators that when you tell a story, nobody believes a word you say.

Lost in thought, I glanced up and saw Lucinda peering over the edge of my cubicle. It seemed to me that her beautiful eyes, like black mirrors, as deep and timeless as outer space, contained the entire universe, and I was on the outside looking in, the merest reflection, an insubstantial play of light across the surface.

"Are you all right?" she asked in a worried voice. "Wait just a minute. I'll be back."

She vanished and I returned to my work, quickly sinking back into distraction as I awaited her return. But I was in for a jolt when I opened my last letter of the day. It came from a Mr. G. Alfano, of Manhattan, N.Y., whose address was a midtown post office box, and was accompanied by Coupon No. 1. The envelope was postmarked the day before. The letter read in its entirety as follows:

> *Was Atreus fulfilling a curse on his family when he carved up his brother's children and served them to him in a stew? What was the origin of that curse?*

A curse? The question struck me as uncanny. Hadn't Borges mentioned the curse on the house of Atreus when I translated the Klaus Mannheimer letter?

Lucinda appeared in the doorway and I showed her the letter. "What's the problem?" she asked. "This is an easy one."

"Isn't it a little weird getting this question so soon after I translated that letter about the curse on the ring of Solomon?" I reminded her what I'd told her about the curse on Matthias Netzer and his progeny.

"Just a coincidence," she assured me.

She led me to the library and looked up the curse on the House of Atreus in a book on Greek mythology. It wasn't a pretty picture—Atreus stewing Thyestes's children, Agamemnon sacrificing Iphigenia for the sake of a favorable wind, Clytemnestra butchering her husband Agamemnon in his bath, their son Orestes avenging his father's death by slaughtering Clytemnestra and her lover Aegisthus.

"Not your typical Greek family," I said. "But then the Netzers aren't exactly the Swiss Family Robinson."

When I arrived at Borges's apartment, he was sending off Mary Ann Chalmers with a heavy research assignment that included bringing him various books from the university library: Poe's essays and reviews, his letters, and two or three standard biographies. He sat in the wing chair in his gray suit and conservative tie, with a disorderly heap of books and papers on his lap. Mary Ann stood glaring at him like a rebellious teenager.

"The question we need to answer," he told her, "is, Why did Poe write his detective stories?"

"Isn't that obvious?" she said. "It was his chance to kill off a few more women. Let an orangutan rip them apart, stuff their bodies up a chimney, rape them and toss them in the river, and if they're too powerful to kill, because they're the queen or something, blackmail them for daring to violate the patriarchal code of female chastity and sexual subordination."

She whirled out and slammed the door behind her.

"Perhaps that assignment will keep her busy for a couple of days," Borges said wistfully.

If serving the patriarchy had lost its charm for Mary Ann, the same could hardly be said for Señora Sanchez. No sooner had Miss Chalmers fled than the Señora pushed her cart in from the kitchen and began dispensing our afternoon cocktails, whisky and soda for Borges, Rheingold for me. She removed the books and papers from his lap and tucked a pillow behind his back. I was coming to enjoy these dialogues, in which my role, I thought, was not Watson-like at all, but more like one of Socrates's pals in Plato's dialogues.

"There's something I've been wondering about," I said. "What do you mean *why* did Poe write those stories? Are you asking about his psychological motivation?"

"You know very well that I don't believe in psychology."

I should have expected that. At every point in his career, from the surrealism of the 1920s to the postmodernism of the 1950s and '60s (which he practically invented), Borges had dedicated himself to a literature that eschewed psychology—emotions, self-awareness, unconscious motivations—in favor of universal archetypes of mind, myth and language. Critics (and many readers) have rejected his stories for their almost total lack of psychological insight. With one or two exceptions, his characters have no psychology. They are like chess pieces, fashioned to carry out specific functions directed by the author. And yet there is a kind of truth in those stories, the kind more often found in Homer than in Henry James.

"I don't believe in psychology," he repeated, "except, of course, for my conviction that everything we see, think and do is entirely psychological."

"Yes, there's that," I said, recalling his affinity for philosophical idealism.

"We know nothing about the world except our perceptions of it. And so, as far as we know, what we perceive is all that exists. Bishop Berkeley said that in the eighteenth century and I believe it to be true, provided that you don't put a narrow construction on *perception*."

He took a swipe at the air with his walking stick like a child swinging at a piñata. "Blindness, for all its hardships, has taught me that there is more to see in the world than visual impressions may lead you to believe."

I hesitated to ask. "Like what, for instance?"

"Archetypes."

Before I could demand an explanation, we were startled by a sharp knock on the door. It was Murray, waving a copy of that afternoon's *New York Post* and the headline on page three: MEDICAL EXAMINER REVEALS DEATH THREATS AS AUTOPSY FINDS PROBABLE HOMICIDE IN BROTHER'S DEATH.

"Did you see this?"

Murray handed the paper to me and I read it aloud for Borges's benefit. It confirmed what we already knew—that the second autopsy resulted in a finding of homicide. But for public consumption they were calling it "probable homicide," obviously to avoid embarrassment about the first autopsy. Something we didn't know was that Peter Netzer had been receiving death threats based on what the article called the "controversy over his alleged Nazi ties." The article concluded by saying, "The Mayor's office expressed full support for Dr. Netzer but reiterated its call for a full investigation of any alleged Nazi connections."

Murray looked tired and bedraggled from a day of interrogation by the NYPD, though his treatment by the police had been surprisingly humane. He hadn't been beaten, starved, humiliated or subjected to any of the other time-honored methods of extracting information from suspects. In fact Detective Foley had emphasized that he wasn't a prisoner or even, as yet, a target of the investigation. Murray understood that he owed this courtesy to Agent Harkins of the FBI, who needed him to be in one piece until the case against Bridget O'Hara could be firmed up, after which he would be thrown to the dogs. Agent Harkins had intercepted Murray as he left the precinct station and made him agree to spy on O'Hara at least until he gathered enough evidence to justify a search warrant. Murray didn't like playing the spy, but he had no choice. If he spurned the FBI, he'd be left to the tender mercies of the NYPD and the pro bono attorney they'd brought in for him, a nice enough young man whose practice to date had been limited to contesting parking tickets.

"What did they question you about?" Borges asked him.

"Oh, God, it went on all day," Murray said. "They wanted all the details of my visit to the hotel. Why I went—"

"What did you tell them?"

"The same thing I told you. To see if I could persuade Peter Netzer to give up the ring."

"Go on."

"What I said to the desk clerk, what he said to me. What I wrote down, how long I sat in the lobby. Where I sat. What I did next. Where I went afterwards. What time I got home. Did I go through the park."

"Did you?"

"Yes. I walked over to the west side to catch the subway. Where I was at ten o'clock."

"That must be the estimated time of death. What else?"

"Did I call Bernhard Netzer on the house phone? The answer is no; I tried to call Peter Netzer and didn't get an answer. From what I'd heard, it was Peter I wanted to deal with. Did I go to Bernhard's room? No. Peter's room? No. Did I go upstairs at all? No. Did I see anyone I knew? No."

"That's an interesting question."

"Especially in light of the next one: Do I know Bridget O'Hara?"

"Ahh!" Borges leaned back and sighed with satisfaction. "Then she was the 'lady' the clerk thought you might be with. She must have been there before you, looking for the Netzers."

"Evidently, but I didn't see her. If I had, I might have been in a fix. She knows me as Michael Forbis, the collector's representative, not as Murray Kellerman, the heir."

"And you gave the clerk your real name."

"Yes, I did. Which sort of proves I didn't go there to kill anybody, doesn't it?"

"Either that, or you're a very shrewd murderer."

"Murray is very shrewd," I pointed out. "So if he's a murderer, he's a shrewd one."

"Anything else?" Borges asked.

"They asked if I would submit to a physical examination, and I agreed. A doctor came in and examined my hands—"

"Looking for rope burns from the hanging."

"And dirty fingernails, apparently, like my mother used to do. He scraped the dirt out from under my fingernails."

"That will teach you to keep them cleaner," Borges said.

"With my shirt off, he made a thorough survey of my manly physique."

"Looking for scratch marks. Did he find any?"

"Not that I know of," Murray said. "Then they asked me if I made death threats to Peter Netzer. Have I ever talked to him? Did I send him anything in the mail? That kind of stuff. They showed me what looked like a couple of lines from a French poem and asked me to translate them, which I couldn't do."

"Did they seem to believe your answers?"

"Like I said, they're treating me with kid gloves until the FBI gets through with me."

"Was there anything else they asked you about?"

"Well, yes, there was," Murray said. "Detective Foley kept showing me a piece of paper with a mathematical symbol on it and asking if I knew what it meant. I can't imagine what it had to do with the case."

"What did you tell her?"

"I've studied math—I think I told you that—so of course I knew what it meant. It's a symbol used in set theory for the size of infinite sets."

Borges sat up and leaned toward Murray, suddenly alert. "Can you write it down?"

"Sure." Murray picked up a pen and drew a symbol that looked like this:

"Trace my finger over it," Borges said, and when Murray had done so he muttered breathlessly: "The *aleph.*"

"Right," Murray said. "That's the name Cantor gave it in set theory. What the hell does it have to do with Bernhard Netzer?"

I don't know when I'd seen Borges so excited. "*Aleph* is the first letter of the Hebrew alphabet, said to contain the entire universe," he muttered, his breath quickening. Beads of sweat glistened on his forehead. "It also stands for the number *One,* the number that includes all numbers."

"I still don't get it."

"*One* is a kind of infinity, isn't it?"

"To a crazy person, maybe," Murray laughed.

"Sometimes the very thought of infinity can drive a man mad. Cantor suffered a breakdown and died in a sanitarium."

Borges drifted into the luminescent cloud that was his version of space, where he seemed to lose the thread of the conversation. "Why did they do the second autopsy?" I asked, trying to bring the discussion back around to Bernhard Netzer.

"More to the point," Borges said, "what led the second medical examiner to a finding of homicide?"

"Detective Foley wouldn't tell me either of those things," Murray said. "Not that I didn't ask."

"And this piece of paper with the *aleph* on it—did they find that on the body?"

"She wouldn't tell me that either."

There was a long, uncomfortable silence before anyone spoke. "The *aleph* must have some significance," Borges finally said, "or they wouldn't have kept asking you about it."

"Could it be related to the curse?" Murray asked.

"Anything is possible."

A disconcerting swarm of thoughts buzzed in my mind as Borges and I settled in for our nightcap. Murray had returned to his apartment after Borges pledged himself and me— mainly me—to do whatever it would take to find Bernhard Netzer's murderer. "We will leave no path unexplored, no stone unturned, no conundrum unsolved," he had assured Murray, "until we find the killer and secure your vindication." The Señora appeared on cue with her cocktail cart, dispensed our drinks in silence, and withdrew. I sipped my beer slowly as I ruminated on Borges's theory of archetypes, which I didn't understand. Was it a corollary of his rejection of psychology? How was it related to his breathless interest in the *aleph*—an apparently meaningless Hebrew letter the police had interrogated Murray about—and the question I'd received that afternoon about the curse on the House of Atreus?

I could understand how a poet might dismiss psychology and focus his thinking on archetypes. But how could a *detective* succeed with such a method? Isn't the detective, by necessity, a master of psychology, who can follow the criminal mind through all the twists and turns of cunning, deceit and self-protection?

"My method of detection," Borges explained when I posed that question, "is to observe archetypes working their way into everyday life. Do you understand?"

"Not really."

"For example, consider the curse pronounced by Klaus Mannheimer on Matthias Netzer and his descendants. Curses have an ancient pedigree, as we've discussed, which was undoubtedly known to both Mannheimer and Netzer. The curse of the House of Atreus, as recounted by Aeschylus, is perhaps the best known."

Had Borges added mindreading to his repertoire of talents? I wanted to tell him about the letter I'd received at work—surely this couldn't be a coincidence?—but I held my tongue as I waited to hear what he would say next.

"When we see a curse in action," he went on, "what are we witnessing? Is it some supernatural intrusion from another world, such as we might read about in a ghost story or a gothic novel? Or is it rather a concrete part of *this* world, an archetype manifesting itself at the deepest, most essential level—as fear and hatred, cruelty, jealousy, an insatiable hunger for revenge, with consequences like the ones Aeschylus portrayed in the *Oresteia*: insanity, death, family extinction?"

"So then," I stammered, "do you think the Mannheimer curse could be real?"

He smiled and nodded. "The same might be asked about the *aleph,* which, as I mentioned, has been said to contain the entire universe. It is the ultimate archetype, the transfinite set that includes everything."

12. A Defense of the Kabbalah

As I slogged to work on Thursday morning in the pouring rain I amused myself by imagining, as Borges had claimed, that what I perceived was all that existed. It certainly made the world a smaller, drearier place, just a few rain-drenched city blocks crowded with pedestrians huddling under umbrellas as they waved desperately at disappearing yellow cabs; on the plus side it excluded Long Island and New Jersey, not to mention Siberia. There were no rocks to kick or I might have broken a toe trying to refute Bishop Berkeley's mad idea. By the time I reached my office I hoped that if I could avoid seeing Miss Kunkel she would vanish off the face of the earth. But I couldn't help wondering: If I perceived one thing and Borges perceived another (a highly likely scenario), which one really existed? And what about something neither of us perceived? Could it still exist?

Obviously Bishop Berkeley, like all philosophers, had too much time on his hands. I didn't have that luxury. I had fifty subscriber questions to answer, most of which, fortunately, were beyond the scope of our service. But there was one question that I could not avoid answering: the one I'd received about Atreus, the fellow who carved up his brother's children and served them to him in a stew. His family was definitely operating under a curse, which, as curses do, took on a life of its own in a cycle of fear and hatred, cruelty, jealousy, revenge and retribution. But as to its origin, the reference book consulted by Lucinda provided no guidance.

I decided to lay the question aside until I had time to do more research. Perhaps Borges would know the answer.

I still found it troubling that I'd received that question when I did, right after learning about the Mannheimer curse and just before Borges started talking about the curse on the house of Atreus. An uncanny coincidence, I told myself; but the next envelope I opened sent a shiver down my spine. It was from the same subscriber—Mr. G. Alfano, of Manhattan, N.Y.—and consisted of the following, paper-clipped to Coupon No. 2:

> *By what marks and signs on the body can suicide by hanging be distinguished from murder by strangulation? Please reference the leading paper by P. Netzer, "Varieties and consequences of ligature strangulation,"* Archives of Forensic Pathology, Vol. 32, No. 3 (1968).

Rushing out of the office, I splashed down to the New York Public Library—it was still pouring rain—where I found Peter Netzer's article in the biological sciences department. A scan of *Index Medicus* disclosed that it was the most cited article in the medical literature on how to distinguish self-hanging from "intentional ligature strangulation," otherwise known as garroting. Barely able to control my excitement, I xeroxed the article and jumped on a downtown train.

Borges and Murray sat playing chess in Murray's apartment, while Señora Sanchez flipped through a fashion magazine and Mary Ann Chalmers took notes from a biography of Poe she'd brought from the university library. They were all so immersed in their activities that no one seemed to grasp the enormity of my revelations about the Peter Netzer article. "It says here that real and fake suicides can be distinguished by the location and quality of ligature marks on the neck and throat," I said, waving my photocopy of the article in front of them, "as well as bruises, fractures, and burst blood vessels in various parts of the body, especially around the eyes. The determination of suicide or murder can easily be made by a skilled pathologist."

Mary Ann beamed up from her work with a triumphant smile. "Poe condemned at least six women to strangulation, suffocation or premature burial," she said. "He even hanged a cat."

"Doesn't it seem strange," I asked anyone who would listen, "that Peter Netzer wrote the leading article on the evidence used in his brother's autopsy?"

"Not at all," Borges said. "Obviously whoever murdered Bernhard Netzer read the article before deciding how to murder him."

"And even stranger," I went on, "that Peter Netzer—according to Dr. Mertz, who performed the second autopsy—arrived at the wrong result?"

"Ironic, yes," Borges agreed, "though not conclusive. It's one expert's word against another's. How can we know which one is correct?"

That was a point I hadn't considered. We were all assuming that the second autopsy was the correct one. If it wasn't—if the death was really a suicide—then Bernhard's choice of method to reflect his brother's article wouldn't be so surprising. "But isn't it strange," I pressed on, "that the article would come to light just now—"

"Not if it's the leading article."

"...because of a question posed by the same subscriber who sent in yesterday's question about the curse of Atreus?"

Borges seemed to be giving my last point some thought. "Indeed that would seem strange," he said, "without an awareness of how archetypes intrude into the sensible world *just at the moment when there is a meaning for them to take on.* If all these things had happened last week, no one would have noticed them. Isn't that right?"

"Especially all the women murdered by Poe," Mary Ann added.

"Amen," the Señora agreed without glancing up from her magazine.

I felt like I'd wandered into a madhouse. I turned to Murray, hoping to find some sign of sanity in his eyes, but he was transfixed by the chess game. He made his next move and announced it to Borges.

"Queen to King's bishop four," Borges replied without hesitation. "Checkmate."

The chess match having reached its inevitable conclusion, Señora Sanchez slipped over to Borges's apartment and returned with her refreshment cart. She dispensed an array of cocktails and we all sat back to enjoy them, Borges in the armchair with his whisky, Murray relaxing on the faux-Scandinavian couch with a piña colada, Mary Ann Chalmers scribbling manically into her notebook as she sipped her Dubonnet. Hoping to keep my head when all others were losing theirs, I contented myself with a cold Rheingold from Murray's refrigerator.

Murray reached behind him and pulled out that afternoon's *New York Post,* where the Netzer case had risen to the position of lead article on page three. "Wait'll you hear this," he said, and he read us the whole article.

KAHANE QUESTIONED AS FUROR RAGES OVER MEDICAL EXAMINER'S ACTIONS AND ALLEGED NAZI TIES
By Rachel Price

Rabbi Meyer Kahane, founder and leader of the Jewish Defense League, was questioned by police Wednesday in connection with alleged death threats against Dr. Peter Netzer, the city's new Chief Medical Examiner, and the death of Dr. Netzer's brother, Bernhard Netzer.

A police department spokeswoman disclosed that Bernhard Netzer's death is being treated as a "probable homicide" after a second autopsy found death resulted from "ligature strangulation," which can be caused by hanging or garroting. Mr. Netzer's body was found hanging in Central Park with injuries consistent with either suicide or homicide.

An earlier autopsy, conducted by Dr. Peter Netzer, ruled the death a suicide. The District Attorney's office, which ordered the second autopsy, said there is independent evidence of homicide and called it "outrageous" for Dr. Netzer to perform the autopsy on his brother, slamming the mayor and the Health Department for engaging in a "cover-up" to protect Dr. Netzer.

Jewish groups have raised alarms about Dr. Netzer's alleged Nazi ties and demanded a full investigation. Sources said Rabbi Kahane was questioned about a "mystical Jewish symbol" found on Bernhard Netzer's body, and about death threats to Dr. Peter Netzer based on allegations that the Netzer family stole art treasures from Jews during the Nazi era. Dr. Netzer has denied such allegations.

Rabbi Kahane issued a statement denying any connection to Bernhard Netzer's death. "I never heard of anybody named Netzer," Rabbi Kahane told reporters. "The Jewish Defense League does not condone or engage in violence of any kind. We also do not condone appointing a Nazi as the Chief Medical Examiner."

The Mayor's office declined to comment.

"What in the world is the Jewish Defense League?" Borges asked. "And who is this Rabbi Kahane?"

None of us had ever heard of them, except Murray. He said they were a bunch of fanatics from Brooklyn dedicated to protecting Jews at all costs. They had been accused of extreme tactics and implicated in a number of bombings.

"We know what the mystical Jewish symbol was," Borges said, "and we've learned something important: it was found on Bernhard Netzer's body. It was the *aleph,* which, as I mentioned, has been said to contain the entire universe. The delivery of the *aleph*—possibly by the Jewish Defense

League—suggests that the Kabbalah is the key to the mystery of Bernhard Netzer's death."

"Personally," Murray said, "I think this is getting ridiculous." He glanced at me in hopes of finding an ally, but I looked away. I knew better than to argue with Borges.

"Do you find all forms of mysticism ridiculous?" Borges asked indignantly.

"Is the Kabbalah mysticism," Murray said, "or just some kind of delusional superstition, like astrology?"

"What's wrong with astrology?" Mary Ann demanded, looking up from her notebook.

"To read deep meaning into the arbitrary arrangement of letters and words," Murray went on, "as if they determined the nature of reality—if that isn't ridiculous, even insane, I don't know what is."

"Insane?" she muttered. "You think astrology is insane?"

"The basic idea of the Kabbalah," Borges said, "is that God used *language*—specifically the ancient Hebrew language—in creating the universe, and that the words and letters of that language, and the precise order of their utterance, represent—no, constitute—the structure of reality itself. So the arrangement of words and letters is anything but arbitrary. The order and connection of ideas is the same as the order and connection of things."

"This is even crazier than I thought," Murray laughed.

Undaunted, Borges plunged ahead: "The *aleph,* the first letter of the Hebrew alphabet, is the beginning of all things—or better, perhaps, *before* the beginning of all things. It is not a sound in itself, merely the inhalation preparatory to uttering a sound. Before God could shatter himself into the differentiated universe, there was the *aleph.* It contained the whole of what he was about to say—every piece of the divine utterance was foreshadowed in it."

Borges shook a professorial finger in Murray's direction. "Which is why the *aleph,* being first, may be said to contain the entire universe."

"Then everything that ever happened was fated to happen," Mary Ann said, triumph rekindling in her eyes, "by the utterance of that first word..."

"Next you'll be talking about golems," Murray said.

"The golem is not a frivolous idea," Borges sniffed. "See Scholem's book on Jewish mysticism."

"And all those women murdered by Poe never had a chance!"

Señora Sanchez, who seemed amused by our conversation, let us carry on like this a while longer before she invited us over to Borges's apartment for dinner. She had prepared a roasted chicken, mashed potatoes and an assortment of vegetables, which she sliced up for Borges and arranged on his plate. Before she withdrew to the kitchen, she informed us—that is, Murray, Mary Ann and me—that as Señor Borges needed a respite from work, she would listen carefully and would whisk our dinners away and throw them down the garbage disposal if she heard any more talk about golems, the Kabbalah or God.

13. The Muse of Detection

We enjoyed a delicious meal, keeping the conversation within the bounds prescribed by Señora Sanchez. Borges talked about literature, mythology, and crime, while avoiding any mention of the Netzer case or (in deference to Mary Ann) the femicidal Edgar Allan Poe. After Murray had returned to his apartment, and Mary Ann (presumably) to her padded cell, Borges and I settled down for a nightcap, served by the kind Señora. It was getting late, and I was getting anxious. I had to walk over to West Fourth Street to catch the A train uptown before my bed filled up with Peruvians.

"Do you know the origin of the word 'clue'?" Borges asked me, as if entertaining an idle thought.

I should have known that idle thoughts were as foreign to him as brilliant thoughts were to me. "I don't know," I said. "I guess—"

"Guessing won't get you very far," he laughed. "'Clue' used to be spelled 'C-L-E-W,' and it meant a ball of thread or twine. Are you familiar with the myth of Theseus and the minotaur?"

"Vaguely," I said. Even that was an exaggeration. I took another sip of my beer and braced myself for the lecture.

"All right," he said. "Let me give you the background. Pasiphaë, the wife of King Minos of Crete, mated with a bull and gave birth to the minotaur—a monster half man, half bull, that fed on human flesh—which the king concealed at the center of an enormous labyrinth. Theseus, a young

Athenian sent to Crete to be sacrificed, succeeded in killing the minotaur: then he had to escape from the labyrinth. How did he do it?"

"Wasn't there some woman who helped him?"

"Yes. King Minos's daughter, Ariadne, gave him a ball of golden thread which he tied outside the labyrinth before he went in. After killing the minotaur he found his way out by following that thread."

"Sounds simple enough."

"What Ariadne gave Theseus was a *clew*—literally a ball of thread—which he attached to the entrance of the labyrinth before venturing inside. Then when he needed to find his way out, all he had to do was follow the clew. That's how English acquired its word for the steps a detective must follow to the solution of a crime."

"It's a good thing we're solving the Netzer murder in English," I said. "If we were solving it in some other language, we might not have anything to go on."

Borges ignored my little gibe. "Poe was well aware of this etymology," he said. "In 'The Murders in the Rue Morgue,' the decisive link in the chain of evidence allowing Dupin to solve the crime—the point where the clew terminated, as he said—was a certain nail in the window frame of the murdered women's apartment. And of course in France, where the story takes place, a *clou* is a nail. So the *clew* terminates with a *clue* that is in fact a *clou*—thus laying to rest your intolerable disregard for languages other than English."

"Very clever," I admitted.

"Poe, like Dupin, was always eager to demonstrate his brilliance and erudition."

Like somebody else I knew. But I kept that thought to myself.

"Dupin is the expression of an archetype that dates back to Theseus," Borges went on. "Groping his way to the light, Theseus experiences terror, rage, despair, and other emotions; but his psychology is of no interest to us. All that matters—his sole purpose—is his destiny: to find his way out of the labyrinth. In the modern world—since Poe—that is the archetype of the detective."

As always, I was troubled by Borges's inability to separate life from literature. Was he talking about real detectives or fictional ones? Real crimes or imagined ones? Was there any difference in his mind?

"The detective, like Theseus, has no psychology," he went on. "All he has is his intellect: he is a thinking machine, as some early writers of detective stories characterized him."

"Does that apply to you, then?" I asked, a little mischievously.

He hesitated—not from uncertainty, I sensed, but to suggest that my question scarcely merited an answer. "I have no psychology. I have always insisted on that."

It was true. Nothing infuriated Borges more than an attempt to delve into his motives or emotions, or even to suggest that he had any. You might as well look for psychological depth in his characters.

"The murderer also has no psychology," he said. "Once he has committed his crime, he has but one purpose, which is to evade detection and punishment. To the extent that he is driven by emotion—by guilt or fear or hatred, rather than by a single-minded dedication to escaping detection and punishment—he becomes unworthy of the detective's attention, and of ours as readers."

"We're talking about fiction, right?" I said. "Detective stories and the like? Because in the real world—"

Another thing he could not abide was any suggestion that a "real world" existed beyond his imagination. "The murderer," he said sharply, "like the detective, is an archetype, a chess piece. He can do only one thing: conceal his crime. And the detective can do only one thing: solve the crime and unmask the criminal."

I thought I had him. "If the murderer and the detective are chess pieces, who's moving them around?"

"Another captive of caprice," he said. "The author."

"Whose caprice?"

"God's, perhaps, or, in turn, some god beyond God in the dust of time."

That sounded far more metaphysical than any place I would care to inhabit. "Where does the lowly narrator fit into all this?" I asked.

"Ah, you still don't understand, do you? You're the only one who's free to make your own destiny. You said the other night that I had taken over your life—that's true—but when I release you you'll be a free man, who can write the story down, or not write it down, as you see fit."

"The narrator," I mumbled unenthusiastically.

"The narrator of your own story as well as of mine. But it's not time for that yet. There will be tests for both of us, ordeals, turning points we haven't even imagined."

All this sounded like crazy talk to me. At least it was clear now that he was talking about literature, not life. The problem was, we had a real murder on our hands. For which our friend Murray might be sent to a real electric chair with real electricity in it.

"I don't feel that all this literary talk is getting us anywhere," I said. "Are we any closer to knowing who killed Bernhard Netzer? All this stuff about Theseus... Does it really matter?"

"Theseus is everyman," Borges said. "And every detective, real and fictional. He is caught in a labyrinth—call it nature, time, reality, the world of appearances—that baffles him at every step. His purpose is to find his way to the light. For that he must rely on the clew—or clues—provided by Ariadne."

"Then if Theseus is the detective," I asked, "who is Ariadne?"

"Ah!" His sightless eyes glistened in the dim light. *"The eternal feminine draws us on.* For our purposes, you might say she is the muse of detection, perhaps of life itself."

The Señora, who had been hovering over him, as always, with careful attention, emptying his ashtray, refilling his glass, wiping away any drips that fell on his sleeve, registered her agreement with a sly, complicit glance, which told me she had already ascended to the status of muse. I found my jacket and said goodbye with a twinge of embarrassment at my own naivety, my own inability to see the real for the ideal. And that night and the nights that followed, I couldn't help but wonder if Borges and the Señora might be summoning into life the oldest archetype of all—I shuddered to imagine the details—as I made my solitary way home to toss and turn among the Peruvians.

14. The One and the Many

At work on Friday I struggled to answer—or mostly reject—my daily quota of questions, seeking assistance from Lucinda as often as possible without seeming a total idiot. Secretly (I did not share this with Lucinda), my main concern was the letter I'd received the day before from Mr. G. Alfano, of Manhattan, N.Y.—the same subscriber who'd asked about the curse on the House of Atreus—inquiring about how to distinguish various kinds of strangulation and referencing Peter Netzer's article on the subject. The question itself was easy enough to answer—questions seeking medical advice and information were beyond the scope of our service—but the bigger issue was why I was receiving these letters, and who was sending them. "Mr. G. Alfano" must have known something about Bernhard Netzer's murder, at least enough to ask these questions. Was it just a coincidence that he directed his inquiries to the *Anglo-American Cyclopedia,* and specifically to me?

My puzzlement only deepened when a third letter from "Mr. G. Alfano" landed on my desk that afternoon—the receptionist said it had been hand delivered—which contained, along with Coupon No. 3, the following question:

> *Albert Einstein said he believed in Spinoza's God. What kind of God did Spinoza believe in? Does that God exist?*

A pattern had been established—the first two letters were about the Netzer murder—and now it had apparently been broken. From the standpoint of the murder case, what difference did it make what kind of God either Einstein or Spinoza believed in, and whether that God exists?

"We can't answer whether God exists," Lucinda said when I showed her the question. "Check your Bible."

She meant the response manual, which specifically prohibited answering questions about the existence of God. "I forgot about that," I said, as if I'd ever known it.

"One of your memory lapses?" she asked with a friendly twinkle in her eye. By this time she must have realized that I used every imaginable pretext to seek her guidance, even on questions to which the response should have been obvious. Truth to tell, I had been fantasizing about her, imagining a relationship that went far beyond supervision or librarianship. With her superior intuition, she must have known about it before I did.

The ice having been broken, this was as good a time as any to skate across the pond. I asked her if she would like to go to a museum with me on Sunday.

"Not a date, right?" she smiled.

"No. No way. Not a date."

As I glided back to my cubicle, I felt lighter on my feet, more sure of where I was going, than I had felt in months. It seemed—of course that seeming was an illusion, it was way too early for anything real—that if I kept going where Lucinda was leading me, I might find my way out of the darkness I'd been wandering in.

There was still work to do before I could leave for the day. The first part of Mr. G. Alfano's question—What kind of God did Spinoza believe in?—seemed like something that could be answered with a little research.

I should have rejected that question too. It was, as I would learn, among the infinitude of things that are beyond the scope of my service.

I left the office early and went straight to Borges's apartment. He was alone, having sent Señora Sanchez to the market and Mary Ann to the library. He seemed in a flustered state, anxious, desperate to talk to someone. As soon as I arrived, that someone was me.

"That FBI agent," he asked me, "what is his name?"

"Harkins?"

"Yes, Harkins. Agent Harkins has bludgeoned Murray into meeting O'Hara at a restaurant wearing a surveillance device, whatever he calls it—"

"Wearing a wire?"

"Right. And Murray wants us to go along with him."

"Tonight?"

"Yes, he'll be here at six o'clock."

"I'm not wearing any wires," I said.

"Neither am I. I will not be a party to electronic surveillance."

Talking to me seemed to have calmed him down. He lifted his walking stick, which he'd been stabbing into the carpet, and laid it across his lap.

"Why does Murray want us to come along?" I asked.

"He has the mad notion that by passing us off as art experts he'll gain credence for his imposture as a collector's agent, and in the process we'll find out who killed Bernhard Netzer and keep him out of the electric chair."

"Can't blame him for that," I said.

"No, but neither can I spend all my time worrying about Murray's problems. I've got my Poe seminar to prepare for."

That seemed heartless to me, as if a seminar on some detective stories should take precedence over a real murder that could send Murray to the electric chair. But as Borges sat alone in his apartment that afternoon, it turned out, he'd given serious thought to Bernhard Netzer's murder and the literary tropes that dictated how it should be investigated.

"Before you know what's obvious," he said, "you've got to know what isn't obvious."

I had the sinking feeling that another assignment was coming my way, involving legwork on my part—which meant scouring the city for clues while he idled in his apartment listening to Mary Ann read nineteenth-century mystery stories.

"For example," he said, "we know that Bernhard Netzer checked into the Plaza Hotel, where his brother and sister-in-law were staying, on the afternoon of the day he died. We need to learn everything we can about his movements in and out of the hotel."

"Can't we leave that to the police?"

"We also know that Murray went there hoping to talk to Peter Netzer, unaware of Bernhard's presence, but he says he talked to neither of them. We need to confirm that."

"You don't trust Murray?"

"A detective trusts no one. It also appears that Miss O'Hara was at the hotel as well, before Murray, but the two didn't meet. You should confirm that."

"How am I going to do that?"

"In a luxury hotel the desk clerk—together with the concierge—knows as much about what goes on there as the doorman in an apartment building. You may be surprised to learn that Henri, the doorman of this building, keeps track of your comings and goings—along with those of Murray, Miss Chalmers, Señora Sanchez and myself—in a small notepad he carries in his hip pocket. He collects my mail, accepts delivery of my packages, and shares gossip he's overheard in the lobby. He knows everything, though he may require a generous tip to reveal it."

"All right, I'll go to the hotel."

"And what about the morgue? Do you think you could get in there?"

"I'm sure I could get in. The question is whether I could get out."

Borges grinned broadly. "Odysseus visited the land of the dead and came back to tell the tale; so did Aeneas. Any hero worth his salt—"

"Let's cut it off right there," I interrupted. "I'm not a hero and I'm not worth the tiniest grain of salt. Any way you could imagine of getting me into the morgue is out of the question. All they'd have to do is bundle me into one of those sliding drawers, and—"

"Nonsense! Remember, this is a detective story, not a thriller."

"Right. I forgot we'd left the real world."

"In a detective story," he went on, ignoring my gibe, "there are certain... I won't call them rules, but they recur often enough to be called archetypes. The detective must identify six suspects, no more, no less. The culprit must be a character who is present from the beginning. Accident, suicide and supernatural causes cannot be the solution (although, as in Chesterton, the tale may be enhanced by a whiff of the uncanny which proves to be a canard). And there is—for everyone but the victim—a surprising lack of danger. The detective never gets killed or seriously injured." He paused... "Although—I don't know whether to mention this or not, these are just stories we're talking about..."

"What?"

"Sometimes his assistant does."

With the help of Señora Sanchez, Borges put on a fresh shirt and tie, combed his wispy hair, and sat back down in his wing chair, poised to step out to dinner with Murray at six o'clock. The hour passed, and another half hour, with no sign of Murray. At 6:45 I stood Borges up and we traced a mincing path into the hall and across to Murray's door. I pushed the door open, only to find Murray standing in his shorts in the living room, as Agent Harkins and an FBI technician crouched around him attaching wires and gadgets to his arms, legs and torso. Luckily Borges couldn't see any of this or he might have beaten the FBI agents with his walking stick. I sat him down in his usual chair and told him we needed to wait a few minutes.

"Are you sure I have to do this?" Murray asked Harkins.

"You have no choice," Harkins said with an impish grin.

"What are you trying to accomplish?"

"I want to hear Bridget O'Hara talk to you about that stolen ring. I want to hear her say she has it and wants to sell it. I want to hear her admit that it's stolen. And if you can't get any of that, try to arrange a direct meeting with Peter Netzer."

"I still don't know why I'm doing this," Murray said. "When you get what you want, you're just going to throw me back in the clutches of Detective Foley."

"Not if you and your friends find the real murderer first. I'm with you on that."

"You don't think I did it?"

"Of course not. Why would you kill to get something you expect to inherit?"

"My analysis exactly," Borges said.

"And whoever killed Bernhard Netzer didn't get the ring," Harkins added.

"How can you say that?"

"We've had our eye on the Netzers for months, since you put us on to them. Through an arrangement with the customs and immigration service, we made sure that all three of them—Peter, his wife Helga, and Bernhard—and their baggage, were thoroughly searched at Kennedy Airport. I can assure you that none of those people brought the ring into this country."

Murray had left that afternoon's *New York Post* on the table. Page three featured another article by Rachel Price, with the headline, CHIEF MEDICAL EXAMINER WROTE LEADING PAPER ON STRANGULATION MURDERS DISGUISED AS SUICIDE.

I read the article aloud so everyone could hear it. It recited everything we'd already learned from reading Peter Netzer's paper, concluding that "real and fake suicides" can readily be distinguished by a skilled pathologist, and noting that the second autopsy was performed by Dr. Abraham Mertz, Chairman of the Department of Forensic Pathology at Columbia Medical School. That was obviously a dig at Peter Netzer, with the implication that he wasn't skilled enough to follow the directions in his own paper. The only new twist in the article was that the threatening letters Peter Netzer turned over to the police contained "mystical Jewish symbols" similar to the one found on Bernhard Netzer's body. This linked the killing of Bernhard Netzer to the threats against his brother, and linked both of them to the *aleph*.

"We come back to the Jewish Defense League," Borges said when I finished.

Agent Harkins disagreed. "There's nothing mystical about the Jewish Defense League," he said. "They're a bunch of violence-prone hotheads from Brooklyn whose main concern is the persecution of Jews in the Soviet Union."

"The leader is a rabbi, isn't he?" Borges asked. "I think of Rabbi Akiva, Rabbi Loew of Prague—"

"Rabbi Kahane isn't the type for arcane symbolism," Harkins interrupted. "More like a thug than a mystic. The Agency considers him a terrorist."

In this instance Agent Harkins's instincts were better than ours, as we would soon learn. Borges was so taken with the Kabbalah and its mystical overtones that we all missed the point of the *aleph,* which, as we knew, could stand for the number *One.* There are times when *One* has deep mystical significance—Spinoza's monism, the *unio mystica* of medieval Christianity, the Brahman of Vedanta— but sometimes it's just the first number in a series.

A series of dead bodies, for example.

15. Due Diligence

Bridget O'Hara was a fashionably dressed East Side divorcée, tall and elegant, with crystal blue eyes, a milky complexion, and the warm but slightly predatory smile of a high-end art dealer. Murray greeted her effusively—although they'd met only once and she thought his name was Michael Forbis—and she returned the compliment. She was just old enough to be susceptible to flattery from a good looking younger man like Murray. She had someone with her at the table when we arrived, a balding, stoop-shouldered man of about fifty with thin lips and dark, deep-set eyes, who was rising from the seat across from O'Hara as the waiter led us in. He wore a navy sports jacket, a dress shirt open at the neck, and a paisley ascot. His face was fat and shapeless and approximately the color of oatmeal. "Michael, I'd like you to meet... a friend of mine," O'Hara said, and the man reached out a pudgy hand.

"Boris Stossky," he said, with an accent that might have been French. "Very pleased to meet you."

"Boris just stopped by to say hello," O'Hara said, "and now he'll be on his way."

Boris smiled and ambled toward the bar.

"Not really a friend," O'Hara confided. "Quite frankly, I hate his guts." She was well into her third martini.

"I understand," Murray said.

She was taken aback when Borges and I sat down at the table. She must have thought we were part of the staff. "I thought it was just going to be the two of us," she glared at Murray.

"I hope you'll understand," Murray said with a gallant smile. "The item we discussed—for my client, for anyone really—would be a very substantial acquisition. That won't happen without due diligence by independent experts."

O'Hara eyed us skeptically. "These are your experts?"

"Nick Martin," I said as I reached across the table to shake her hand.

"I don't think I'd be exaggerating," Murray boasted, "if I said Nick's knowledge on this subject, on just about any subject, is positively encyclopedic."

"'Encyclopedic' is definitely the right word for my expertise," I agreed. Meaning whatever the question was, I would have to look it up in the encyclopedia.

She frowned at Borges. "And this gentleman?"

Borges bowed slightly. "Dr. Jorge Luis Borges, Director of the National Library of Argentina. If I am an expert on anything, it is early medieval heresiarchs, the image of time as a river, and the soughing wind of the pampas. I detest mirrors, identical twins and the man whose name I will not utter."

"And needless to say, he's one of the world's leading experts on ancient Near Eastern lapidary art," Murray added.

O'Hara leaned toward Murray and lowered her voice to a whisper. "But isn't he... you know... blind?"

"As I'm sure you'll come to realize," Murray whispered back, "that is a minor handicap." He raised his voice and continued, "Doctor Borges knows more about just about every subject than you or I or anyone we're likely to know. Including, I'm sure, your client."

"My client?" she tittered. "What client are you talking about?"

"The owner of the ring of Solomon."

"And who would that be?"

"The man I read about in the newspaper, Dr. Peter Netzer, whose family stole art treasures from Jews during the Nazi era."

"Are *alleged* to have stolen," she clarified. "I believe that's what the article said."

"Yes, of course," Murray agreed. "Alleged."

"If something were actually stolen, we wouldn't be having this conversation. I don't deal in stolen goods."

"Of course not."

She downed the rest of her martini and motioned to the waiter for another. "That's something I'm very particular about," she went on, "although in practice it isn't a simple matter. There was so much disruption and destruction in that tragic era that the documentation for many legitimate transactions has been lost. Private sales don't make it into the auction records. So the mere fact that an item had a Jewish owner who died in the Holocaust doesn't prove that it was stolen. The owner might have sold it before the war."

When the waiter returned with her drink, he took our orders and we proceeded to enjoy an excellent dinner. In those first few minutes Bridget O'Hara had shown herself to be a smooth operator worthy of her reputation in the art world. She'd made a record of her innocence (I doubt if she suspected that Murray wore a wire but she had no reason to trust Borges or me) and deftly sidestepped the attempt to identify her client as Peter Netzer. After that she steered the conversation in a benign direction, ignoring my encyclopedic silence and peppering Borges with questions about ancient Near Eastern lapidary art, which he answered with quotations from Herodotus. After our plates had been removed and the waiter took our orders for coffee and dessert, Murray brought the topic back around to the reason we were there. "The item we discussed," he said. "Is it in New York? Do you have it?"

O'Hara chose her words carefully. "I have reason to believe that it will be available soon. *Very* soon. If your client doesn't want it, there are others who will."

Murray gave her his most winning smile. "I'll need to talk to your client directly."

"That's impossible," she laughed. "Why would I let you do that?"

"I know his name, I know where he works. I could just call him up."

"At the morgue?" That was a slip—it was an admission that her client was Peter Netzer. Murray let it pass and she went on, a little rattled: "What makes you think he would talk to you?"

"I think he would," Murray smiled. He had switched into his irresistible charm mode, which I had witnessed before. The thought crossed my mind that Murray had missed his calling. If he wasn't an unemployed actor or an unemployed mathematician, he would have made a terrific con artist.

"You can trust me, Bridget," he said. "I'm not trying to cut you out of your commission. We'll guarantee that even if we deal with Dr. Netzer directly. But we need the kind of information and assurances that only the owner can provide."

"There are reasons why sellers go through dealers in situations like this," she said, shaking her head nervously. "They don't want to deal directly with the buyers."

"The Nazi allegations—which, I agree, are probably false—raise all sorts of issues. There's an FBI investigation, threatening letters, the death of Dr. Netzer's brother."

"Those are good reasons for what I'm talking about," she said.

"I hope you can work with me on this. I'm trying to keep my client from walking away."

"I could try to arrange something, Michael, but I doubt if the owner would want to meet with you."

Murray sighed. "Well, then, if you could just tell us when the item will be available."

"I wish I could be more specific," she said, twisting her napkin and dropping it on the table. "All I can say is what I've already told you. I expect to have it very soon."

"OK," Murray said, smiling. "Obviously there are some issues I don't know about. I don't want to put you on the spot. Just give me a call when it comes in. But if it's more than a couple of days from now, I don't know if my client will still be in the game."

The waiter returned with our coffee, and by the time we were all served, O'Hara had regained her composure. "I'm having a reception at my gallery tomorrow night," she said, "and I hope you all can attend. We'll be opening a very important exhibition of Poe and Dickens materials that's just come in from England as part of the Richard Gimbel collection—"

Borges, who had slumbered through the meal like a turtle on a rock, fixed his sightless gaze on O'Hara and rapped the table with his coffee spoon. "Did you say Poe?" he demanded. "Did you say Dickens?"

"Poe, yes," she stammered. "And Dickens. Most of Colonel Gimbel's collection is being donated to various libraries and museums and won't be exhibited together again in our lifetimes."

Borges bowed almost imperceptibly. "I'd be honored to accept your invitation."

"I'd be honored to see you there," O'Hara smiled. "A number of very interesting people have been invited." She beamed at Murray and let her smile linger a little longer than one might have expected. "People you will certainly enjoy meeting."

It seemed obvious that she meant Peter and Helga Netzer.

16. The Gangs of New York

Saturday! My day off—from the *Anglo-American Cyclopedia,* if not from the labyrinthine ways of Jorge Luis Borges. A springlike day drifted in through the usual stench of rotting garbage and bus exhaust, the kind of day which, in its triumph over expectations, seems more wonderful in New York than in a country meadow. That's the secret of life in New York, I'd already learned. Expect the worst and you will be pleasantly surprised, until the worst actually happens. Which in those days it often did.

I breakfasted at a lunch counter on Ninth Avenue where I left my greasy spoon standing straight up in a cup of coffee that could have beaten me at arm wrestling. Near the cash register a clipboard asked customers to rank the Greatest Villains of History: the winners, in order, were Hitler, Stalin, and Mayor Lindsay. I walked up to 42nd Street and across to Times Square, which was then at its peak as the porno and peep show capital of the world. For visitors with more elevated tastes, the neighborhood offered Tad's Steaks, Brazilian restaurants and Broadway musicals, the most popular of which at the time was *Man of La Mancha.* Seeing the title on a theater marquee, with a silhouette of the Spanish madman, naturally made me think of Borges. Intent on my detective work, I ambled up Broadway to Columbus Circle and across Central Park South to the Plaza Hotel, where Bernhard Netzer had checked in his first day in New York, not knowing that he would spend the night across the street, hanging from a tree in Central Park.

Outside the hotel stood a line of horse-drawn carriages and a doorman who looked like he belonged on a Beefeaters bottle. He allowed himself a curt bow as I stepped past him, on the odd chance that I might be an eccentric millionaire. The bellhop just inside the door—squeezed into a uniform that made him look like an organ grinder's monkey—was not so easily duped. He could tell at a glance that I didn't belong there: his smirk told me that he would keep my imposture to himself as long as I didn't leave his sight.

I stepped up to the desk and faced a nervous young man with rimless glasses and curly blond hair. "Can I help you, sir?" he asked.

"I hope so," I said. "Were you here last Sunday night when one of the guests was killed in the park? Bernhard Netzer?"

"Uh, no," he stammered. "I... wasn't here."

"That would be Sam you're looking for," a voice growled behind me. I turned to find a hatchet-faced, middle-aged man in a dark suit who looked like a moonlighting hit man. His name tag identified him as the concierge but something in his expression told me not to ask for an extra towel. "Who are you?" he demanded—and then suddenly polite: "If you don't mind my asking."

I played the eccentric millionaire card again. "You don't know who I am?" I bristled. "Let's keep it that way." I spun around and stalked out.

What was I thinking? I asked myself as I fled across 59th Street to the park entrance. Is this the way detectives operate? No, a detective would have softened the concierge up, slipped him a five spot, even a sawbuck, or bought him a gimlet in the world-famous Oak Room. And he would have gone in with a clearer idea of what he wanted to accomplish. We needed first-hand information about Bernhard Netzer, Bridget O'Hara—even about Murray, according to Borges. We needed to know what the hotel staff told the police and what they didn't tell them. For that, apparently, I would have to come back when "Sam" was at the front desk.

The fine weather had summoned all of humanity to the park and the wide path that led into it: loving couples, bewildered tourists, boom-box teenagers, irate old ladies, bicyclists, roller bladers, stroller pushers, dog walkers, pretzel vendors, soapbox orators, anti-war protesters, hippies, guitar strummers, bearded poets, head-shaven Hare Krishnas, and—I couldn't help noticing—lovely slender girls in jeans and T-shirts with flowers in their hair. Where was the climate of fear I read about every day in the *Daily News?* There were three murders a day in the city, they lamented; but as I gazed over the crowd I could only marvel that there weren't a lot more. Look at all these people! Every one of them must have rubbed somebody the wrong way, slept with somebody's spouse, gone somewhere they shouldn't have gone. Were they all living on borrowed time? In my guise as a detective I felt somehow privileged, as if I were above the fray, but of course that was an illusion. Borges said the detective can't be the victim, but in one of his most famous stories that was exactly what happened. A pond lay on my left; across it stood a thicket of trees. I couldn't help wondering which tree Bernhard Netzer had been found hanging from.

Then I noticed something even more disturbing. At the edge of the crowd, about thirty feet back, a familiar figure trailed along behind me: the smirking bellhop I'd met at the hotel entrance, still in the silly uniform that made him look like a performing monkey. Was he following me? Or just on his way home from work? I cut to my right, around the pond, and circled back down toward 59th Street, emerging from the park at Columbus Circle. The bellhop lingered behind me, pretending not to look in my direction. When I turned to stare at him he stopped and lurked, as bellhops do when they're waiting for a tip.

I hurried downtown, having promised Borges that I would escort him on a walking tour of the Bowery. That may sound odd, and it is, so I should explain. Unlike most visitors to New York, Borges had no interest in the Empire State Building or the Metropolitan Museum or Rockefeller Center. The only sight he was determined not to miss was the Bowery, owing to one of his favorite books, *The Gangs of New York,* by Herbert Asbury, as well as his own writings about Monk Eastman and other early New York gangsters. By that time the Bowery was no longer skid row, but it was a far cry from Soho or Nolita or whatever they call it now. Apart from some shabby buildings there wasn't much to see, but of course that didn't keep Borges from having a grand time as he rattled on about the saloons and brothels that once graced every corner and the brawls that left the sidewalks stained with blood. Our walking tour was like a snail's idea of a leisurely stroll, with Borges in his dark suit and tie, tapping along with his walking stick as he babbled on. I clutched his elbow and tried to keep from stumbling and pulling him down with me. He must have cut quite a figure for the few remaining winos who hadn't moved to more desirable neighborhoods. After about an hour of circling a three block radius, he needed a rest. I found a small bench where we could sit side by side and continue our monologue.

"So when will you be heading back to Boston?" he asked me.

"Who says I'm heading back to Boston?"

"Come on, Martin. I know you'll go back to that beautiful Icelandic girl. The raven's daughter."

I was amazed that he remembered Katie and even her last name—Hrafnsdóttir—and that her family was Icelandic. I confided a little about the issues I'd been dealing with after I got out of the Army, including my ups and downs with Katie and my reasons for coming to New York. He was surprisingly sympathetic and supportive—not that he'd ever been cold or uninterested. It was just that until then we had never talked about anything that touched on emotions, partly, I suppose, because he denied having any. I reminded him that he was with me when I first set eyes on Katie. We were sitting on a bench facing the Charles River in Cambridge when she climbed up the embankment in front of us as if she'd risen out of the water like a goddess. But of course Borges had never seen her. "How do you know she's beautiful?" I asked him.

"All Icelandic women are beautiful," he said. "That's the stuff Norse sagas are made of."

As he grew tired his mind seemed to spin in every direction. "I confessed to you and Murray, didn't I, that all my learning derives from two sources: the 11th edition of the *Encyclopaedia Britannica* and the *Arabian Nights?* I should have mentioned *The Gangs of New York* and the Icelandic sagas, and I suppose there are a few other books that have nourished my imagination. The *Arabian Nights* is a vast (some would say infinite) book, in its many compilations, recensions and translations—no two of which bear any resemblance to each other—and the numerous variant versions of each story, and the multitude of interpretations that can be given to each one. Over the years I have consulted it, as some consult the Bible or the Qur'an, for the illumination of whatever problem I'm facing at the moment. And I suspect that somewhere in that bottomless treasury of tales there must be one that will help us solve the Netzer case and save our friend Murray."

"How could a story from the *Arabian Nights* be relevant to that?" I asked.

"I recall a story—unless, like De Quincey, I have an inventive memory and the story never existed outside my own imagination—which I believe is called 'The Tale of the Unlucky Mirror.' The hero, I seem to remember, is a young nobleman, returned from the wars, who falls into the clutches of an old magician and a trickster who enlist him in trying to recover a magical mirror that was once used by King Solomon to conjure demons. The mirror has a curse on it, of course—that's why the story is called 'The Tale of the Unlucky Mirror.'"

"What happens? What's the plot?"

"It's probably been fifty years since I've thought about it. I can't remember any of the details. You might want to look into it yourself. And now, if you don't mind, it's getting chilly and I need to go back to my apartment."

I hailed a cab and took him home, frustrated by this tantalizing glimpse of some Arabian tale that may or may not have existed. "I'm sure you can find the tale in Burton's translation, possibly in one of the supplements," he said as I led him into his apartment. "That must be where I read it, if I read it at all."

Determined to find out if the story really existed, I ran over to Schneider's bookstore to see if I could find the Burton translation. As it happened, Schneider had a fine set, sixteen volumes in morocco leather, on offer for a tidy $300. He kept it in a locked cabinet along with his stock of antiquarian erotica. I asked him if I could look at it.

"You could get lost in there," he warned me as he unlocked the cabinet.

"I couldn't get any more lost than I already am." I opened the first volume at random and found myself in a magical world of tales within tales, entangled together in an infinite regress of narration. The table of contents at the beginning was as daunting as the stories: it listed hundreds of similar titles that included many unfamiliar Arabic names. Each of the six supplementary volumes contained its own table of contents listing dozens of tales and background articles. I must have spent fifteen minutes just scanning the tables of contents, and when I finished I read through them again, more slowly this time. I never found "The Tale of the Unlucky Mirror."

"Are you going to buy that set?" Schneider barked from his desk, where he sat watching me like a department store detective. "A library this is not."

"No," I admitted, returning the volume to the cabinet and snapping it shut. "Are there any more volumes? Anything that's not here?"

Schneider took his time answering. "Not in that set. You want other sets, other translations, maybe I can find you one."

I shook my head. "No, thanks. But there is something I'd like to buy. That copy you have of Borges's first book."

"I told you already it's not for sale."

"Then this must be a library after all."

He emitted a derisive snort and busied himself with a stack of books on his desk, occasionally aiming his crooked smile in my direction. As I headed toward the door, I noticed a collection of Crébillon's plays displayed where I couldn't miss it. Leafing through the collection, I confirmed that it contained *Atrée et Thyeste,* the play Poe quoted from in "The Purloined Letter."

"I hope you can read French," Schneider said. I assumed that Murray had told him I'd show up looking for Crébillon.

I paid an exorbitant price for the book and hurried back to Borges's apartment. The hour was getting late, I realized, and tonight was the night of the reception at Bridget O'Hara's gallery.

With any luck at all, we would finally come face to face with Peter Netzer.

17. The Reception

Bridget O'Hara's gallery occupied the first two floors of a corner building on Madison Avenue, with an ambience and decor calculated to make wealthy collectors feel at home. In the entrance lobby were a coat check closet, a temporary bar, and a desk where guests could obtain the prospectus for the new exhibit: "Dickens and Poe: Highlights of the Richard Gimbel Collection." Oil paintings and framed prints lined the walls, each with a descriptive placard beside it; a broad formal staircase led upstairs. In the gallery beyond the lobby, where a string quartet could be heard playing classical music, stood rows of glass cases displaying autograph letters of Dickens and Poe, original manuscripts, first editions, photographs and drawings of the writers and their circles, and various items of memorabilia. The larger memorabilia items, such as the mahogany desk where Dickens wrote *The Mystery of Edwin Drood*, could be viewed in roped-off alcoves along the walls. A good part of the collection would be auctioned off, but Colonel Gimbel had decided to donate some of the best items to libraries and museums. Those items were also on display; this would be the last chance to see the whole collection before it was broken up.

The Colonel himself—a portly, prosperous gentleman in his late sixties, the heir of the Gimbel's department store fortune—was something of a curiosity. He wore a neatly-trimmed goatee and carried a cane (which, unlike Borges, he didn't need for walking). It had a silver knob at the top in the shape of a skull and had once belonged to Charles Baudelaire. I don't know what the Colonel was a Colonel of, but something told me it wasn't the army. More likely a chicken franchising empire like Colonel Sanders, whom he resembled more than slightly. In an earlier era he might have been an African explorer or an Egyptologist breaking into tombs. He greeted the guests with the boyish—and in a man his age, insane—enthusiasm of the collector. His collecting interests were Poe and Dickens, but I suspected they might as easily have been baseball cards and balls of string.

We arrived early, before most of the other guests. Murray paid the taxi fare and hurried inside to greet O'Hara—cheerful, confident Murray, posing as Michael Forbis, buyer's agent and man about town. I guided Borges in at his usual tortoise-like pace as Mary Ann Chalmers held the door. Once we were inside she made a beeline for the bar, where she consumed one Dubonnet after another, keeping a wary eye out for Poe sympathizers. (I still didn't know what they put in Dubonnet—possibly eye of newt and toe of frog—and I made a mental note never to find out.) Borges clung to my arm as I led him past the effusive O'Hara and into the maze of display cases beyond the lobby, trying to give the impression that we had some reason to be there. Murray had told her we were experts, but I never thought she believed him. He felt Borges added to his credibility as the supposed agent of a wealthy collector, and he wanted both of us to meet Peter Netzer to see if we could learn anything about his brother's murder. Dr. Netzer, of course, had no way of knowing that the police regarded Murray as the prime suspect.

We headed back to the lobby when the Netzers arrived. Dr. Peter Netzer was more animated and athletic than I'd expected, not your typical forensic pathologist (if there is such a thing), but more like a rugged Swiss mountaineer who chopped up dead bodies in his spare time. He had dark, wavy hair, piercing blue eyes, and a mouthful of gleaming teeth that seemed to gnaw on his words as he talked, which he did in an accent that sounded more British than German. His wife Helga was quite beautiful, a pale blonde with a robust figure and a décolletage as deep as her eye shadow. As a couple they would have been perfect for a vampire movie. Slouching in behind them in a furry Russian hat was the stoop-shouldered man named Boris Stossky whom O'Hara had introduced us to the night before, now wearing, under his overcoat, a gray tweed jacket and a yellow ascot that circled his bullet neck a little too tightly. O'Hara, to judge from the way she glared at him when he walked in, would have liked to cinch it even tighter.

With that one exception she played the gracious hostess, greeting—often hugging, sometimes kissing—all the guests as they arrived. Such favors were dispensed on a sliding scale of potential financial gain. She hugged Murray, shook Borges's hand, smiled unenthusiastically at me, ignored Mary Ann, and had to restrain herself from kicking Stossky in the teeth. Kissing was reserved mostly for other women, including Helga Netzer, who rated a peck on both cheeks. Peter Netzer stepped sideways to avoid her touch. When she turned her back, he scowled at her as if he looked forward to seeing her in the morgue.

After the guests had been welcomed, O'Hara directed them to her assistant, a young woman named Janice, who checked their coats and handed out information about the exhibit. Servers in caterer's livery circulated balancing small trays laden with drinks and hors d'oeuvres. Colonel Gimbel wandered through the crowd with his death's-head cane, bragging about his collection to anyone who would listen.

"Colonel Gimbel!" I greeted him, as if we were old friends (in fact I had once bought a pair of socks at his department store). "I'd like you to meet Jorge Luis Borges. Doctor Borges is Director of the National Library of Argentina."

The Colonel greeted Borges with a bow. *"Mucho gusto en conocerlo!"*

He had evidently taken a Berlitz course in the 1930s. Borges was delighted. I left the two gentlemen propped on their canes and slipped away so I could keep an eye on Murray, who had just introduced himself to Peter Netzer (as Michael Forbis) and offered condolences on his brother's death.

"You've seen the news reports, I gather," Netzer frowned. "There seems to be no such thing as privacy in this country."

"Not when it comes to murder," Murray agreed.

"Evidently this is quite a dangerous city. Teeming with murderers and fanatics."

"You mean the Jewish Defense League? Have the police made any headway with them?"

Netzer glanced at his wife. "Not that we know of. It seems that the lack of privacy does not extend to the police."

"They've kept us completely in the dark," Helga said. "The newspapers know more about the murder than we do."

"And every day I get another death threat," Netzer said. "It's quite unnerving."

"Well, hopefully they'll make an arrest soon."

I admired Murray's audacity for saying that, especially the "hopefully" part, since he was the one most likely to be arrested. Before the conversation faltered he brought it around to his supposed representation of wealthy art collectors and a "certain item" belonging to Netzer that one of his clients might be interested in purchasing.

Netzer glowered at him with undisguised scorn. "I don't know what you're talking about. I suggest you speak to my agent."

"It's OK," Murray said. "Bridget knows I'm talking to you about this."

"I don't mean Bridget O'Hara," Netzer said. "I'm talking about Boris Stossky."

As it happened, O'Hara and Stossky stood exchanging insults about ten feet away, as they both listened with one ear to Murray and Netzer. When they heard their names mentioned they lurched toward the Netzers so abruptly that Murray had to dodge out of the way. "I'm your agent," O'Hara told Peter Netzer. "I'll be handling the sale. You don't need Mr. Stossky representing you."

"I just told you," Stossky said, "we're here to take the item back."

That was interesting, I thought. Taking it back implied that O'Hara had it, which she'd denied every time Murray asked her about it.

Glaring at Stossky, she lowered her voice. "We can't discuss that here."

"Where is it?" he demanded.

"I'll have it soon."

She'd have it soon—the same thing she'd been telling Murray. Now she was saying it in front of Peter Netzer, the owner. What was going on?

With his usual aplomb, Murray defused the situation with a joke. "Let's try to avoid bloodshed," he said, stepping between O'Hara and Stossky like a boxing referee. "At least in the first round."

"Soon isn't soon enough," Stossky snarled. He looked and sounded like a gangster.

"I couldn't agree more," Murray said. "As I've told Bridget—and I'll tell all of you—time is of the essence. Isn't it in everybody's interest for my client to stay in the game?"

O'Hara was cornered. "Everyone please bear with me," she pleaded. "I've got half of New York trooping in to see Colonel Gimbel's collection." She motioned to her assistant, who came running. "Janice, when these people are done looking at the collection, please escort them upstairs to the conference room." She smiled at Murray and the Netzers and backed away. "Just give me thirty minutes."

18. Birds of a Feather

I grabbed a glass of wine from the bar and searched for Borges, whom I found in one of the alcoves along the wall, listening to the string quartet. Twenty feet away, halfway up the staircase, I saw O'Hara and Colonel Gimbel confronting each other in what looked and sounded like a heated argument, with the Colonel shaking his cane in O'Hara's face, though I couldn't understand a word either of them said. Borges had been left propped on his walking stick in front of Dickens's mahogany desk. He didn't seem to mind. He gazed toward it as if giving it a thorough examination. "Just imagine," he said when I joined him. "Dickens worked at this desk the day before he died."

A dour woman in a slinky black dress—she was later identified as a collector named Constance Volpe—sidled up and pushed her way in front of us. "Don't waste your time looking at that," she said. "It won't be in the auction."

"Why not?" Borges asked.

"He's donating all the best stuff. Just to keep me from bidding on it." She eyed Borges suspiciously. "Are you a collector?"

"Yes. I collect paradoxes, conundrums, and heresies."

"Well, you won't see any of those here, no matter how hard you look."

"I assure you, madam," he said with a slight bow, "I am quite blind."

Just then Colonel Gimbel, gasping and red in the face, rumbled back from his argument with O'Hara. The dour woman in the black dress ducked away at the sight of him and melted into the crowd.

"Keep your eye on that one!" he told Borges, pointing toward her with the skull-shaped knob at the end of his cane. Then he laughed: "I'd better get rid of this cane before I beat somebody over the head with it!"

"Yes, you'd better!" O'Hara laughed as she appeared beside him. She seemed eager to let bygones be bygones as far as their argument was concerned, but anxious to disarm him in case it revived. "Give that cane to me and I'll leave it for you at the front desk."

Borges assumed she was addressing him. "This is not a cane," he informed her. "It's a walking stick, and I'm not giving it to you."

"So sorry," O'Hara fluttered. "I was talking to the Colonel."

Somewhat sheepishly, the Colonel handed her his cane.

"You can pick it up on your way out." She flashed an unfriendly smile and took the cane out to the lobby, pushing her way past Stossky as she went.

"Now," the Colonel said, taking Borges by the arm, "let me show you my collection."

Inching along at Borges's usual pace, Colonel Gimbel guided him from one rarity to the next, talking nonstop about the significance and provenance of each. Only a mad collector would try to show his collection to a blind man, but Borges's eccentricities were the perfect complement to the Colonel's. Having lived in his bluish cloud for so long, he seemed as excited to imagine the collection as he would have been to see it. At any rate he enjoyed the tour a lot more than I did, which isn't saying much. I minced along behind them, thirsting for another drink. Lurking behind us, to add to my annoyance, were Boris Stossky and Mary Ann Chalmers, who had struck up an unlikely friendship. They pored over each of the Colonel's treasures like tax appraisers, as Mary Ann lectured about Poe's femicides and Dickens's infidelities. Stossky seemed to find her amusing.

The Colonel's voice dropped to a low, reverential tone as we approached the Holy of Holies. "In this display case," he told Borges, "is the original manuscript of one of Poe's most famous works: 'The Murders in the Rue Morgue.'"

"Ahh!" Borges gasped, bending over the case as if praying for a miracle that would enable him to see into it. "The world's first detective story."

"Unfortunately, my biggest collecting coup couldn't be here tonight." The Colonel paused to ensure that we would await his next words with bated breath: "Poe's raven."

"Poe's raven? Did Poe really have a raven?"

"Well, not exactly. But Dickens did. It inspired Poe to write his masterpiece."

"His masterpiece?" Borges's voice fairly dripped with scorn. He hated "The Raven," as he'd told me many times.

"I have the actual bird—his name is 'Grip'—that Dickens put in *Barnaby Rudge* and Poe made the centerpiece of 'The Raven.' *Once upon a midnight dreary, as I pondered, weak and weary—*"

"I am familiar with the poem," Borges cut him off.

"And just think! I have the actual bird!"

The actual bird would have been a hundred and fifty years old. "I assume," Borges said, "that your raven, like the poem, is a musty confection of sawdust, glue and empty plumage."

"Indeed, he is," the Colonel agreed enthusiastically.

"A perfect fit for the greatest piece of doggerel in the English language."

"Yes, indeed!" There was no limit to Colonel Gimbel's enthusiasm for Poe. "I wish Grip were here tonight so you could meet him."

The Colonel must have been crazier than I'd imagined, if he thought Borges would regret missing a chance to meet a stuffed raven. But there were more surprises to come.

"Why isn't he?" Borges asked.

"There are those"—the Colonel's eyes darted suspiciously around the gallery—"who have designs on Grip."

"Designs?"

"Do you see that woman over there?" He shot a glance at Constance Volpe, who peered at us from a nearby alcove. "That's Constance Volpe. She's one of them. She follows me around from one auction to another trying to keep me from getting what I want."

"Does she bid?"

"Yes, but she can never outbid me. That's why she followed me here, all the way from London. To steal what she couldn't afford to buy."

"She wants Grip?"

"Of course she wants Grip. Everybody wants Grip. They're all beside themselves because he's not here."

The Colonel leaned forward, closer than Borges liked to be approached. I grabbed Borges's elbow so he wouldn't stumble backwards.

"I knew they were after him," the Colonel went on in a low, rasping voice, "so I removed him from the exhibit and put him where they'll never find him. I refuse to bring him back here under any circumstances. I plan to donate him to the Free Library of Philadelphia. He belongs in the city where Poe met Dickens."

"The city where he buried the most women," a voice croaked in my ear. It sounded like a raven but it was only Mary Ann Chalmers, who went on to list the hapless females Poe sent to their graves in the City of Brotherly Love. She and Stossky had drifted up behind us without making a sound. I had no idea how much of our conversation they had overheard.

Stossky gawked at us with a look of bemused satisfaction—gloating, I assumed, at Borges's capture by the mad collector and his rebuff by the even madder graduate student. Before Borges could say anything, O'Hara's assistant, Janice, arrived with Murray to summon Stossky and me upstairs to the conference room. Stossky complied without a word, and with some misgivings I left Borges alone with Colonel Gimbel and followed them up the stairs.

Another tense scene was playing out in the second-floor conference room, where Peter and Helga Netzer sat across a long rosewood table from O'Hara sipping white wine. They did not appear to be enjoying O'Hara's company, in spite of her desperate efforts to ingratiate herself. As I walked in behind Murray and Stossky, she pointed at Stossky and said, "There's something you need to know, Peter. Boris Stossky is not a legitimate art dealer."

Netzer coughed out a dry laugh. "Whatever that is."

"He has a reputation as a swindler, but he's worse than a swindler. He's a thug."

Stossky smirked at Netzer. "I'm offended."

"He approached me yesterday," O'Hara went on, "and tried to get me to split my commission with him. Did he tell you that? Since I won't do it—and why should I?—he's urging you to take the item back so he can sell it to Mr. Forbis's client himself. Or more likely, steal it."

Stossky's smirk faded to a snarl. "Now I am offended. I told Dr. Netzer to take it back before *you* steal it, which it looks like you've already done."

"That's absurd."

"Where is it then?"

"I've told you, I'll have it very soon."

"Well, whoever ends up with it, please give me a call," Murray laughed, trying to defuse the situation. "My client might actually want to buy it."

Netzer rose wearily to his feet and offered his hand to Helga, as if she needed help standing up. "When I spoke to you on the telephone in London," he said, addressing O'Hara in a low, grating voice, "you gave me a specific date when the transaction would be completed, and that date has passed."

"There's been an unforeseeable delay."

Netzer's air of quiet control vanished. Hatred flashed across his face, and for a fleeting moment I caught a glimpse of the family curse. "You gave it to my brother, didn't you?"

"No, of course not. I never talked to your brother."

"Or maybe you killed him for it. Is that what happened?"

She stared back at him, wide-eyed, holding her breath.

Helga squeezed Netzer's hand and tugged him away. "Let's get out of here, darling. This is going nowhere."

"I'll give you until noon on Monday to produce that ring," he said, and followed Helga out the door.

"Or what?" O'Hara taunted him.

"You think I'm a thug," Stossky said, "maybe you'd like to find out what a thug can do to a face like yours."

Stossky and the Netzers trooped down the stairs, with Murray close behind them. I followed them into the lobby. The Netzers retrieved their coats from the coat check and stepped outside without putting them on. Stossky didn't seem to mind making them wait in the cold. He took his time wrestling himself into his overcoat, selecting the right angle for his Russian hat, winding his scarf around his neck and pulling on his white kid gloves. He even stood by the table leafing through the brochures advertising upcoming auctions.

I motioned to Murray and the two of us went in search of Borges. We found him gazing blindly into a display case as Colonel Gimbel hovered over him with a look of mad intensity.

"Here is another priceless gem," the Colonel said in a hushed tone. "An exceedingly rare copy of Poe's first book."

"Tamerlane," Borges murmured.

"I plan to donate it to the Free Library of Philadelphia." The Colonel glared at Murray and me as if he'd spied a pair of potential thieves. "Along with Grip."

19. Two Versions of Solomon

Sunday morning. A light drizzle captured the mood as the city awoke with a collective hangover, listless and depressed after the frenzied excesses of the week before. I had asked Lucinda out for coffee and a visit to a museum. When I called her that morning she said she'd already had her coffee, and as for the museum, she had a better idea. "How about a library?"

The library was the Pierpont Morgan Library, a museum-like edifice on Madison Avenue built by J. P. Morgan to house his private collection of rare books, illuminated manuscripts, and medieval and Renaissance art. Lucinda breezed past the security guards—she was a member—and led me to a special exhibition she'd read about: a series of allegorical German woodcuts from the sixteenth century depicting scenes from the life of Solomon. The prints were decorated with alchemical and Hermetic symbols that emphasized their allegorical character. A placard on the wall behind the display case summarized the legends surrounding Solomon, most of which I'd already heard from Borges. But what I saw in these prints struck me as new and important, probably because it was Lucinda showing them to me.

According to the Bible (the placard explained), the Lord appeared to Solomon in a dream, and like a genie in the *Arabian Nights,* offered to grant him one wish. Solomon didn't ask for a long life, worldly riches, or the death of his enemies. Instead he asked for wisdom, and God rewarded him by granting this request, along with all the things he didn't ask for. And so Solomon became not only the wisest but also the richest and most powerful ruler of his time.

"In Renaissance art," Lucinda said, "Solomon is typically shown sitting in splendor on his throne, applying his proverbial wisdom to the two women who claimed the same baby. But there's another ancient tradition—transmitted in occult sources outside the mainstream of Christianity or Judaism—of Solomon as a sorcerer and magician, talking to animals and commanding demons to construct the Temple of Jerusalem."

I had heard about that from Borges, without giving it much thought beyond its relevance to the ring that Murray hoped to inherit. The woodcuts turned the occult legend into an allegory—which, like most allegories, I sensed was beyond my grasp.

In the first print, Solomon was shown in his sumptuous bed gazing up through clouds representing a dream sent by God, whose presence was indicated by a fiery sword hovering over Sophia, wisdom personified as a beautiful woman. In the second print he is presented as a great magician, building the temple with the aid of demons, which he commands by raising his signet ring displaying the divine seal. Sophia still floats in the sky, but in the third print Solomon has turned his back on her and the demons have seized control of him, leading him down through a dark, labyrinthine passage into Hell, where he is lured on by women worshipping false gods. In the fourth and final print he is rescued by the beautiful Sophia, who sweeps down to embrace him and carry him back up to the light.

"Solomon chose wisdom over wealth and power," Lucinda said, "but that wasn't enough to build the temple. For that he needed to command the demons." She pointed to the hideous, defiant creatures in the second print. "He needed the energy of the demonic."

"The demonic..." The word fell haltingly from my lips.

"As understood in the sixteenth century," she said. "Today we would probably call it something else. The id, the unconscious, the instincts. Jung called it the shadow."

Her equation of the instincts with the demonic caught me by surprise. I tried to hide my reaction by directing her attention to the third print. "And after the demons are done working for you," I mumbled, "they drag you down to hell."

"Unless you're rescued," she smiled, "by a wise and beautiful woman."

That smile, I realized later, was a turning point in our relationship. Lucinda had become more to me than a mentor and friend: she had found her way into my dream life as a woman. Among the Peruvians, boasting and teasing and jostling far into the night, it wasn't easy for a woman, even one as strong as Lucinda, to hold her own against the psychic debris that slipped past the dream censor. Yet there she was, night after night, guiding my sleepwalking through a maze of corridors, tunnels and caves to some destination I couldn't foresee. In my dreams, though not yet in waking life, she displayed a tenderness, a vulnerability, and increasingly, a tinge of sadness, that both exhilarated and terrified me.

How could I not shape my dreams to the instinct that made me follow in her path? Borges would have called it an archetype, and that was true—it was the oldest story in the world. But only in my dreams did I dare to ask: What is love? Fact or fiction?

20. Borges Finds the Ring

I arrived at Borges's apartment a little after two o'clock, opening the door to the sound of Mary Ann Chalmers's croaking voice as she read from a book that lay open in front of her. It was something about an old necromancer who looked like the embodied spirit of evil biding his time, and if I hadn't seen the book I might have thought she was talking about Borges. He sat beside her in rapt attention.

I cleared my throat and Mary Ann stopped reading. "Sorry to interrupt," I said. "I thought you'd be preparing for your seminar on Poe."

"That's what we're doing," Borges said.

"What are you reading?"

"Barnaby Rudge."

I knew all about *Barnaby Rudge,* having read the Cliff Notes summary in graduate school. "Isn't that novel by Dickens?"

"Of course it's by Dickens. I got the idea from Colonel Gimbel last night."

"I don't see the connection."

"Like all collectors, Colonel Gimbel is mad, and he gave me a mad idea," Borges said. "That *Barnaby Rudge* is the key to Poe's detective stories."

"But there's no detective in *Barnaby Rudge,"* I pointed out.

"Exactly."

We heard a tap on the door and Murray let himself in. Cheerful greetings were exchanged all around, except by Mary Ann, who seemed resentful that her croaking recitation had been interrupted.

"Murray," Borges said, "I can't play chess this afternoon. I have a hypothesis about Dickens and Poe that I'm exploring for my seminar—with Miss Chalmers's help, of course. That must take precedence. You and Nick will hear about it at the seminar."

"No problem," Murray said. "We can play chess another day."

Borges shot one of his blind but intimidating glances in my direction. "You are planning to attend the seminar, I presume?"

"When is it?"

"Thursday afternoon."

"I'll be at work."

"Nonsense. There's nothing going on at the *Anglo-American Cyclopedia* that's more important than that seminar. I'm going to reveal the murderer of Bernhard Netzer."

"Do you know who it is?"

"Not yet. But by then, I trust, we will have figured it out."

I started to stammer a response but he cut me short: "I almost forgot—while you're both here: I'm quite sure I know why Miss O'Hara is unable to produce Solomon's ring."

"This I've got to hear," Murray said, settling down on the couch.

"Last night at the reception," Borges said, "when you both left me alone to attend the meeting upstairs, Colonel Gimbel confided what he and Miss O'Hara had been arguing about on the stairs. As I suspected, it was Grip."

"Grip?" Murray asked.

"The raven—now stuffed—that once belonged to Charles Dickens, which Colonel Gimbel is convinced was the inspiration for Poe's inexcusable versification. He acquired it at an auction at O'Hara's gallery in London. The gallery was responsible for crating it up and shipping it to New York, to be exhibited along with the rest of his collection."

"But the raven wasn't in the exhibition," I pointed out.

"No, it wasn't," Borges agreed. "Colonel Gimbel, as you may have noticed, is not of a trusting nature. He became convinced that a woman named Constance Volpe, who bid against him at the auction in London, would steal the raven if it was exhibited in New York. And his fears may not be unfounded. Constance Volpe attended the reception."

"You talked to her," I said, recalling the sour-faced woman in a slinky black dress. "She warned you that conundrums and paradoxes wouldn't be included in the auction."

"Ah, yes," Borges nodded. "She slipped away when the Colonel arrived to show me his collection. He's quite sure that she would steal his raven if she got the chance. So when it arrived in New York, he demanded that it be turned over to him immediately so he can donate it to the Free Library of Philadelphia. Miss O'Hara tried to resist, but he took it home before she could stop him. Ever since then she's been hounding him to bring it back, on the pretext that she needs it for final customs clearance, tax declarations, and so forth, but the Colonel has stoutly refused. That's what they were arguing about on the stairs.

"Meanwhile, as you know, Miss O'Hara has been unable to produce Solomon's ring, which she confidently agreed to do just a week ago. She's been telling Murray and now Peter Netzer that she doesn't have it but expects to have it soon.

"Thus, two extraordinary events occurred at the same time which have no apparent connection with each other—the unexpected seizure of the raven by the Colonel, and the disappearance of the ring. The only logical inference is that these two events are related. I believe—indeed I am all but certain—that the ring was concealed inside that raven, and remains there. Colonel Gimbel, of course, knows nothing about it."

"Now it all makes sense," I said. "O'Hara's inability to produce the ring, her claims that she would have it soon, the argument on the stairs...."

"A great piece of detective work," Murray agreed. "Unfortunately it doesn't solve Bernhard Netzer's murder, which I'll probably be charged with as soon as Agent Harkins realizes O'Hara doesn't have the ring. And don't forget where all this started. Assuming I don't go to the electric chair, I'm still hoping to inherit that ring. I don't want it to be permanently stuffed inside some raven in Philadelphia."

"If my hypothesis is correct, Miss O'Hara knows where the ring is," Borges said. "I wouldn't be surprised if she stole it from Colonel Gimbel."

Again I was incredulous. "Really?"

"I was quite emphatic about the danger of a theft when I talked to Colonel Gimbel," Borges said. "I told him he was in mortal danger from Constance Volpe, and possibly other collectors, and from Miss O'Hara, all of whom would stop at nothing, including robbery and murder, to get his raven."

We all laughed, even Mary Ann, who until then had seemed uninterested in our conversation.

"Did he believe you?" Murray asked Borges.

"He seemed delighted that I shared his assessment of the danger from Constance Volpe. But until then he had done nothing to protect himself. He lives in a brownstone at 467 West 35th Street. I asked him if there was some other place he could stay for a few days, and he said, yes, his daughter lives a block away, and he could stay there. Don't go home, I warned him, the danger is imminent—and he agreed. He promised to go directly to his daughter's."

"Leaving poor Grip at home to fend for himself," Murray said with a pensive expression.

"Fortunately a stuffed bird's needs are minimal."

"O'Hara doesn't strike me as the breaking and entering type," I observed.

"No," Borges agreed, "but perhaps someone else might carry out the raid for her. By proxy, as it were. Someone for whom it is especially important that O'Hara regain possession of that raven, so she can remove the ring and attempt to sell it, thus satisfying Agent Harkins, and when that unlawful transaction is foiled by the sting operation, the ring can be returned to Switzerland, where it will be subject to certain inheritance claims. I will say no more."

"I think he's telling you to steal it," I said to Murray, whose broad grin told me he'd already got the message.

"Tonight?" he wondered aloud.

"I'd suggest you wait until tomorrow," Borges said. "Peter Netzer's ultimatum for return of the ring expires at noon. It's possible that O'Hara will carry out the operation herself before then, or—who knows?—the Colonel will have a change of heart."

21. Playing at Dice with the Universe

Señora Sanchez spent Sunday afternoon visiting her sister in the Bronx. She returned in time to prepare an excellent dinner of fried plantain, tamales, and Chilean sea bass. After dinner, Mary Ann Chalmers flew off to where she usually roosted for the night. Murray retreated to his apartment about nine o'clock after a bruising chess match that Borges won in eight moves. As soon as the others left, Borges and I settled down for our nightcap—whisky for him, beer for me, dispensed by the Señora from her indispensable cocktail cart—before I would have to subway home to the land of horizontal Peruvians.

I usually didn't bring my work home from the office, but over the weekend I'd had some nagging thoughts about the question I received on Friday concerning Einstein, Spinoza and God. Those three gentlemen, when you think about them, can occupy a good deal of mental space, so I'd put off dealing with the question until, Rheingold in hand, I could give it the attention it deserved, with the assistance of Borges, that collector of heresies, paradoxes, and conundrums.

"Albert Einstein said he believed in Spinoza's God," I said casually, as if commenting on the weather or some sports team. "What kind of God did Spinoza believe in? Does that God exist?"

"There is much to admire in Spinoza," Borges said without missing a beat. "He said that God and nature are one, and thus refuted the notion that there is some external principle—whether it be God, natural law, or Platonic form—that governs the universe. The universe does not exist twice, once as theory and again as fact."

"Then you agree with Spinoza?"

He shook his head. "Spinoza was a strict determinist. There is no contingency—no chance, no freedom—in his universe, and as a poet I must reject it."

"Einstein said God does not play at dice with the universe," I pointed out.

"Einstein was misinformed."

Half an hour later I caught the A train at West Fourth Street, from which my stop was the next one, thirty blocks uptown. Fighting drowsiness, I thought about my nightcap discussion with Borges and remembered that the next morning I would need to address the question about Spinoza, Einstein and God, a daunting trio at any time but even more so on a Monday morning. The train clattered ahead and I tried to gather my thoughts, but they kept slipping away as I floated in and out of drowsiness. It struck me that Borges had used the same phrase in describing the Kabbalah that he'd attributed to Spinoza during our lunch at O. Henry's: *The order and connection of ideas is the same as the order and connection of things.* And the order and connection of things, according to Spinoza, was strictly deterministic, with no contingency, no chance, no freedom, regardless of how it appears to us. That was Spinoza's God, and Einstein's, and strangely enough it was also the God of the Kabbalists. Borges, as a poet, had rejected the pitiless connectedness of Spinoza's universe and chosen freedom. In one of his poems—I think it's called

"Chess"—he imagined human beings as chess pieces, subject to the whims of the players, and the players likewise as the captives of caprice by an infinite regression of gods beyond God, playing at chess, if not at dice, with the universe. Even that unnerving image, in his poet's mind, was preferable to the rigidity of Spinoza's universe.

The lights flickered as the train lurched to an unscheduled halt in the tunnel. I closed my eyes and drifted a little farther, praying that I wouldn't miss my stop. So much for Borges's views as a poet, I thought. What kind of universe did he believe in as a detective? It almost had to be one where the order and connectedness of ideas is the same as the order and connectedness of things—isn't that the assumption that any detective makes as he fits the clues together in his mind? But even with that assumption, where should he search for the clues? In Einstein's universe or in the Kabbalah?—in the real world or the ideal one (or are they one and the same)? Or could a detective do his work in the kind of universe envisioned in Borges's poem, a universe of facing mirrors, infinite regressions, destinies captured by caprice? That, I'd begun to suspect, was the universe conjured into being by the *Anglo-American Cyclopedia,* with the complicity of readers like Mr. G. Alfano and librarians like Miss B. Kunkel and reference assistants like me. Glancing at the seat across from me, I saw a vision of Miss Kunkel, unaccountably wearing a Mets cap and reading the *Daily News* as she sipped an R.C. Cola.

My train screeched into the station and I awoke in a panic of consciousness. The phantom Miss Kunkel had vanished. It was almost too late to be admitted to Sloan House. The Peruvians lay in wait in our room, chattering in Business English as I slid in beside them and drifted back to sleep.

22. A Narrow Escape

I arrived at the office on Monday morning troubled by two unanswered questions from the week before: the origin of the curse on the House of Atreus, and the nature of Spinoza's God. The questions were oddly complementary, and since they'd both been sent in by Mr. G. Alfano, I hoped to be able to answer them in one response of six to ten xeroxed pages. Spinoza's God (and Einstein's) was identical to nature and his universe strictly deterministic, while for Atreus the invariable depredations of Fate had been modified by his outrageous conduct, a gesture of freedom for himself which determined the fate of his descendants. Such is the nature of a curse. It defines a place where morality and destiny intersect. In just this one place, the pitiless universe is altered to become even more pitiless.

I found the answer to the Atreus question—at least I thought I did—in the *Agamemnon* of Aeschylus. And then, while in the library, I started looking for the story Borges had told me about on Saturday. The *Cyclopedia,* in a surprisingly comprehensive article, listed all the editions and translations of the *Arabian Nights,* including translations of translations, and—with the caveat that there are many variant texts and titles—it listed all the titles of all the stories. And there I found the title Borges had remembered—"The Tale of the Unlucky Mirror." The article didn't reveal where the story could be found.

When I returned to my cubicle I was in for a shock. Mr. G. Alfano had sent in coupon No. 4 with another question. As I opened the envelope I wondered: What will it be this time? A question about King Solomon or the *Arabian Nights?* But it was far more disturbing than that. First came a clipping of a recent news story by Rachel Price, and then the question: *Who killed Bernhard Netzer?* Just like that—the Rachel Price article, Coupon No. 4 and *Who killed Bernhard Netzer?* My hand shook and I had to check my breathing to keep from hyperventilating. I'd thought of my job at the *Cyclopedia* as a safe harbor, a place where I could hide out until I got my bearings. The reference service was just a marketing gimmick, nothing for anyone to take seriously. I was a peon who made $90 a week. But Mr. G. Alfano had apparently set his sights on me. He was stalking a reference assistant.

I hurried over to Lucinda's cubicle and read her the question: *Who killed Bernhard Netzer?* She could tell how upset I was and tried to calm me down. "A lot of people are talking about that case," she said. "It's on the news all the time. So this might not be as bizarre as you think."

"I don't know, I—"

"Maybe Rachel Price sent it in," she laughed. "Hoping you can give her a scoop."

"Why me?"

"She's probably seen you hanging around the investigation. Didn't you say you went to Bridget O'Hara's gallery the other night?"

"How should I answer this?"

"Well, obviously, the question is beyond the scope of our service. We're not running a detective agency."

I remembered—and in some deranged corner of my mind must have believed—Borges's dictum that the Arabian tale I'd been searching for would help us solve the Netzer case. If I could find that tale, maybe it would somehow lead me to the solution. So I told Lucinda about my quest for the tale and pretended that it was prompted by a subscriber's question. "Did you look in the *Cyclopedia?*" she asked me.

"The title's listed in there. What I need is the story itself. I looked for it in the Burton translation and couldn't find it."

She peered at me skeptically. "Do we have the Burton translation?"

"It was in a book store," I explained, which only made her more skeptical.

"'The Tale of the Unlucky Mirror,'" she murmured, with an ironic smile, as if she wanted me to know she was humoring me. "I'll do some looking of my own and let you know what I find."

On my lunch hour I decided to go back to the Plaza Hotel in hopes that Sam the desk clerk might be there. Slipping past the doorman, I nearly collided with the smirking bellhop just inside the door. He was still smirking—apparently that was the natural condition of his face—but he gave no sign of recognition. A line of clerks hovered behind the main desk attending to other customers. I joined the longest line so I'd have time to squint at their name tags, and by the time I reached the front I'd concluded that the elusive Sam was nowhere in sight. Turning to leave, I noticed the Mafia concierge scowling at me from across the lobby. I gave him a jaunty wave and ducked out before he could intercept me.

Heading west on Central Park South, I found my way blocked just before the entrance to the Oak Bar. A man stopped right in front of me to light a cigarette, forcing me to a dead halt to avoid knocking him over. He turned to face me and I realized it was the smirking bellhop, minus the smirk, which had morphed into a sinister sneer. He jumped forwards; I jumped back; and a heavy clay flower pot full of soil and foliage sailed past my face and shattered on the sidewalk. The bellhop ducked into the Oak Bar and disappeared.

I looked up, assuming the pot had fallen off a ledge, which might have been a reasonable assumption if there'd been any other pots on ledges up there. There weren't even any ledges.

Across the street I caught a glimpse of a man walking hurriedly away. He was on the heavy side, wearing a raincoat, with his shoulders hunched and his hat pulled down, as if to block his face.

23. Scheherazade

Arriving at Borges's apartment about six o'clock that evening, I found my way inside blocked by a large package which evidently had just been delivered. When Borges traveled he had most of his belongings shipped to him rather than carrying them along, though for whatever reason he never opened most of the packages they were shipped in. Instead he let a pile of unopened packages accumulate near the door. This new delivery made the entry all but impassable. I was glad to find Señora Sanchez relocating the pile to a less obstructive location, in the corner behind the ancient TV.

Borges greeted me and went back to his work with Mary Ann, listening eagerly as she squinted down at a book on her lap and read from it in a determined monotone. I recognized the turgid, convoluted prose of Edgar Allan Poe, sprinkled with references to "Barnaby" and "Mr. Dickens" and "the raven," and concluded that she was reading something Poe wrote about Dickens's novel *Barnaby Rudge*. "Stop there," Borges interrupted about every ten seconds. "Read that sentence again." And when she repeated what she'd read, he mumbled "extraordinary" or "astonishing" and told her to go on.

"This is the first of two reviews Poe wrote of *Barnaby Rudge*," he told me when Mary Ann stopped reading. "The novel came out in installments, and he wrote this after reading just the first few chapters." He aimed his gaze at Mary Ann. "Now read me the second review."

When she had finished, he again spoke to me. "The remarkable thing about these reviews is that Poe, even before he'd read the whole book, knew exactly why *Barnaby Rudge* would not succeed as a mystery story. He wrote 'The Murders in the Rue Morgue'—the world's first detective story—partly in response to the deficiencies he perceived in Dickens's novel."

Señora Sanchez wheeled her cocktail cart in front of us and requested our selections. Since I was living dangerously now, practically a hardboiled private eye, I skipped my usual beer and asked for a gimlet, though I had no idea what was in one. The Señora knew. She mixed one up without a second thought, as if she served cocktails to Philip Marlowe twice a day. The gimlet was a bracing experience, seemingly pure gin with a spot of lime juice. A fitting cap, I thought, to a day of detective work that included an attempt on my life by a flower pot—though not conducive to deep literary/historical analysis, I realized as the alcohol flooded my brain.

"And the main deficiency in *Barnaby Rudge* is exactly what you said last night," Borges told me. "It lacks a detective."

"An editor, you mean?"

"No, I mean a detective. The book has a murder and a mystery, even a talking raven, but it doesn't have a detective. That's why Poe had to invent the detective story."

Luckily Murray burst in just at that moment, exuding his usual practicality and common sense. He gave us two important updates on the Netzer case, the first of which came from Agent Harkins. When Bridget O'Hara called Boris Stossky a thug, she knew what she was talking about. The

FBI had staked out both the restaurant where we first met Stossky and the reception at O'Hara's gallery, and one of their agents recognized him from a photo which had been circulated by Interpol. He was a suspect in several art heists in Rome, a murder in London and the bombing of two galleries in Paris. The other news came to Murray in a call from Bridget O'Hara. She had been unable to obtain the ring before Peter Netzer's noon deadline expired, and thus any sale to Murray's supposed client would be impossible. "Are you sure?" Murray had asked her. "Maybe a little more time—"

"No, I've been told definitively that I won't be able to get it," she replied.

In other words Colonel Gimbel had called her, as Borges suggested, and given her the last word on whether the raven would be returned. "Which means the FBI's sting operation goes down the drain," Murray said. "Leaving me at the mercy of Detective Foley, the NYPD, and the Manhattan District Attorney's office."

"Not to worry," Borges said. "I'm confident we can find the real murderer before you are electrocuted."

That seemed as good a time as any to report my progress on the case. I described my two trips to the Plaza Hotel, my walk through Central Park dogged by the smirking bellhop, and now the attempt on my life by a falling flower pot. "I didn't see who dropped it, but I think I saw the man who directed it from across the street, hurrying away with his back turned. I couldn't see much of him. He had on a raincoat and his hat pulled down over his head."

"Could it have been Stossky?" Murray wondered.

"I'm afraid that's a possibility."

"Let me ask you one question," Borges said after a moment. "Did you notice this man when you went to the hotel on Saturday, or only today?"

"Only today."

"Which indicates that it was something you did or said since then that put him on your trail."

Señora Sanchez served another round of drinks and we all leaned back to enjoy them, except Mary Ann, who never enjoyed anything. My second gimlet was at least one too many, and I will admit that it—and those that followed—may cast into doubt my account of what happened next.

Borges waited for Murray to finish his drink and sent him back to his apartment. "If you'll excuse me and my two scribes," he said, "we have reading to finish before we can call it a day."

The reading was light—a short note from Dickens to Poe, a few passages from the 11th edition of *Britannica,* a fable from the *Arabian Nights*—and it was made still lighter by further dispensations from the Señora's cart. Mary Ann and I took turns reading and taking notes of Borges's interruptions. It almost seemed as if he'd kept us there merely to prolong his dominion over us, like the sultan who forced Scheherazade to entertain him with stories until dawn. When I made a joke about that, he laughed but didn't contest the aptness of my simile. "In Islam," he said, "every believer is attended by two recording angels, one of whom writes down his good actions, the other, his evil ones." He aimed his glaucous eyes at me. "Which one are you?"

"Ask me when the book comes out," I teased him.

"I know which one I am," Mary Ann said, scowling as she scrawled something on her note pad.

"Luckily I'm not a Muslim," Borges smiled.

"What are you?" she pounced, bracing her pen to record his answer.

"A Catholic, of course," he said. "Also, I might add, an aspiring Protestant, and a philo-Semite."

"Do you believe in God?"

"Not in His existence," Borges said. "But in all His other attributes—yes, of course."

Mary Ann gawked at him, her lips quivering.

"Infinite goodness, omniscience, omnipotence—in those, my faith is unshakable."

She found the words she needed: "But if God doesn't exist..."

"A God who must exist in order to be believed in is hardly worthy of belief."

He was teasing her—trying to loosen her up, to make her see, as he always did, that everything we know is a metaphor for something that can only be conceived metaphorically. It was more than she could bear—I saw desperation, even madness, in her eyes. She packed up her things and without another word hurried out the door.

"Glimpsing the first light of dawn," Borges said with an impish smile, "Scheherazade lowered her eyes and discreetly fell silent."

24. The Purloined Raven

At Sloan House the first light of dawn was agonizingly slow in coming. The Peruvians amused themselves far into the night translating all the dirty jokes they'd ever heard into Business English. When I finally drifted off, the night flashed by in alternating episodes of elation and panic. I awoke to the realization that an important turning point lay ahead.

My dreams about Lucinda seemed more real than the life I was living. I felt ready to bridge the gap, to bring the feelings she had aroused into the real world. The tenderness, the vulnerability, the tinge of sadness—I saw them in her eyes now, not just in my imagination. Yet something held me back. It was as if I foresaw that coaxing her out of her hiding place might bring her harm, strand her in a place she couldn't live. Was she too true to go where I needed to go? Borges, confounding life and literature, had bewitched my intelligence with myths, archetypes and paradoxes. What I needed was not a life of abstraction fabricated by old men on sticks but one that unfolded as a concrete part of nature. Could Lucinda lead me to that life? If so, could she be part of it, or only my guide?

It never occurred to me that she might have a destination of her own.

When I arrived at work, Lucinda summoned me to her cubicle to inform me that the other reference assistants had complained about my absences from the office. Further complaints could have dire consequences, she said with a wry smile, including being locked in the file room with Peg.

I threw myself on her mercy. "Borges will announce his solution to Bernhard Netzer's murder at the seminar on Thursday," I told her. "I have to be there. And until then I'm probably going to need more time off."

"All right," she said, trying to look stern. "This ordeal will be over soon."

"Thanks, Lucinda."

As I stood up to leave, her supervisory sternness melted into friendly concern. She motioned for me to sit back down. "I stopped at the New York Public Library on my way home last night," she said. "And I found this." She reached behind her desk and handed me a thick scholarly tome that appeared to be in Russian.

"I can't read Russian," I confessed, handing it back to her.

"It's called *The Thousand and One Nights: A compendium of universal story archetypes,* by Vladimir Propp, published in Moscow in 1923. And here, on page 354, in a footnote, there's a reference to 'The Tale of the Unlucky Mirror.'"

She showed me the cited page, on the bottom of which was a footnote in tiny Cyrillic print. I couldn't even read the book's title, much less the footnote, so I had to take what she said on blind faith.

"The footnote at least proves that the story exists," Lucinda said. "All it gives is some of the story elements. There's a hero, an old magician, a trickster, a doctor, a thief and a merchant, and they're all searching for a magical mirror formerly used by Solomon to command demons. And there's a raven, who appears as a portent of death."

"No wonder Borges thought it might be relevant to the case."

She frowned and looked away. "That's why you've been searching for this story? I thought it was for a subscriber."

I was embarrassed by my deception and vowed never to deceive Lucinda again.

She closed the book and set it down on her desk. "Nick," she said, "I want to help you with this, if I can." There was warmth in her voice, and in her eyes a touch of the tenderness I'd seen in my dreams. "This story might have a hidden meaning—that's common in folk tales. But why does it have to be about the Netzer case? Couldn't it be about something else?"

"Like what?"

She smiled back at me as you might smile at a querulous child insisting on an answer he couldn't understand. "I'll go back to the library tonight and see what I can find."

I ducked out of the office before noon, obeying Borges's summons to lunch with him and Murray at Murray's apartment. When I arrived they were immersed in a chess game, Murray hunched disconsolately over the board—there were only a few pieces left on it—while Borges, enthroned near the window, studied the bluish mist that illuminated his world. "We are approaching the stage of the investigation which in chess would be called the endgame," he said as I sat down.

"The investigation or the chess game?" I asked.

"Both," he smiled. "The opening has led where the textbooks said it would lead. The middle game has exhausted our favorite tricks; and we find ourselves contemplating an almost-empty board. The most powerful pieces—the knights and the bishops, the rooks and, tragically, the Queen—have been eliminated. On the field of battle a strange social leveling plays out as the King—formerly weak and immobile, like a blind man with a cane—stands his ground, hectored by upstart pawns."

"That would be me," Murray muttered, frowning at his remaining pieces.

I struggled to understand how all this applied to the investigation. "If the most powerful pieces have been eliminated—"

"In most cases," Borges cut me off, "the fight comes down to the *Zugzwang,* in which a player is forced to make a move, even if that move is not to his advantage and will lead inevitably to his defeat."

"Uh, oh," Murray said.

"Pawn to Queen's bishop three. Checkmate."

There was a knock on the door, and Murray opened it, probably assuming it was Señora Sanchez with our lunch. Instead he found himself face to face with Detective Bernadette Foley, wrapped in her Burberry raincoat and crimson scarf and holding up her NYPD badge like a crucifix in front of a vampire. "May I come in?"

Murray hesitated as if he had a choice. "Sure," he said, then stepped aside to let her in. He didn't seem the least bit nervous or alarmed. "Have a seat?"

"I'll stand." She nodded grimly as she sized up Borges and me, keeping her hands near her weapon in case we tried anything rash.

"Something new on Bernhard Netzer?" Murray asked.

"No, I'm here about your latest victim."

"What are you talking about?"

"Colonel Richard Gimbel." She glanced again at me and Borges. "He was found dead this morning in his house on West 35th Street."

I was shocked. Borges sunk his face into his hands and groaned. Murray looked rattled. Worse than rattled—he looked like he might run out the door. "How did he die?"

"Why don't you tell me?" Foley pulled out a pen and a pocket notebook and stood poised to record his answer.

"Why would I know anything about it?"

"You were probably the last person to see him alive."

I assumed she was referring to the reception at O'Hara's gallery. Murray admitted that he'd met Colonel Gimbel there, and she smirked as if she and Murray shared a secret. Then she turned her withering gaze on Borges, who still sat groaning with his face covered, leaning forward and rocking back and forth in his chair.

"You seem to be deeply affected, Señor Borges."

"Yes." He lowered his hand and sat up straight. All the color had drained from his face. "Please pardon me."

"Had you known Colonel Gimbel for many years?"

"I met him for the first and only time on Saturday night, at the reception. We spent the whole evening together. We walked around together as he showed me his collection."

"Was he using a cane?"

"I don't believe so."

I spoke up for the first time. "By the time he showed us his collection he wasn't using his cane," I said. "He was helping Señor Borges maneuver with *his* cane—his walking stick, excuse me—so he handed his own cane to Miss O'Hara. Apparently he didn't need it for walking."

"Did you see the cane?" Foley asked me. "What did it look like?"

"It was black with a silver knob at the top in the shape of a skull. He said it had once belonged to Charles Baudelaire."

She gave me a smile that was mocking and menacing at the same time. "Charles who? Should I write that down?"

"It's not important."

"That's what I thought. What did Miss O'Hara do with the Colonel's cane after he handed it to her?"

"She walked out to the lobby with it. I don't know what she did with it after that."

"You didn't see it again that night?"

"No," I said.

"But you saw Miss O'Hara after that, didn't you, and you saw Colonel Gimbel, and neither of them had it?"

"I didn't notice one way or the other."

Detective Foley set her sights back on Murray and jotted something in her notebook.

"Why are you asking us about the cane?" Murray asked. "Was that the murder weapon?"

"We'll come to that."

"I can tell you a few things you need to know," Borges said. "Colonel Gimbel was especially proud of one recent addition to his collection, which was not on display that night: a stuffed raven named Grip that once belonged to Charles Dickens. The reason that item was missing was that he feared it would be stolen. He had snatched the raven away from Miss O'Hara, and she had been hounding him to return it. This was during precisely the same period when she'd been telling Murray, and also Peter Netzer, that she didn't have the ring but expected to have it soon."

"What are you suggesting?"

"I believe the ring was inside that raven. The Colonel didn't know that, but I warned him that he was in danger. I realize now that I should have told him the whole story, warned him about the ring. I shall never forgive myself."

"If it wasn't the ring, what did you warn him about?"

"By his own account there were other collectors—one in particular—who wanted the raven and would stop at nothing to get it."

"Was that other collector Constance Volpe, by any chance?" Foley asked.

"Yes, that was her name. I spoke to her but of course I didn't see her."

The usually debonair Murray had grown increasingly anxious. His face was flushed and beads of sweat glistened on his forehead. "There's something I need to tell you," he said. "I went to Colonel Gimbel's house yesterday afternoon."

"Now we're getting somewhere," Foley gloated. "Why did you go there?"

"To try to persuade him to return the stuffed raven to Bridget O'Hara. The idea was to get the transaction with Netzer back on track so the ring would end up back in Switzerland and I could inherit it."

"You knew the ring was inside the raven?"

"Yes, and I feel terrible for the same reason as Señor Borges. I should have told him about it."

"I confess I gave Murray the idea that the ring was inside the raven," Borges said. "I wish I had kept the suspicion to myself."

Detective Foley smirked at Murray. "So that's why you were carrying that big brown satchel?"

"Yes," he said, without missing a step. "I offered to take the raven to O'Hara and bring it right back. Colonel Gimbel wouldn't hear of it. He didn't trust me. In fact he asked me if I was working for Constance Volpe."

"Was the raven there?" Foley asked.

"Oh, yes. Standing on the coffee table with its eyes twinkling as if it were still alive."

"And his cane?"

"I didn't see the cane."

"Really?"

"When he escorted me back to the front door, I'm sure he didn't have his cane with him."

"And you met Constance Volpe outside?"

"She was at the bottom of the steps when I came out the door. She waited for me to come down. I assume she went up to the door but I didn't notice."

"We've already talked to Ms. Volpe," Foley said. "That's how I knew you were there."

"I figured as much."

"She saw you leaving with your satchel."

"The satchel was empty," Murray said. "Do you realize how big that raven was? I didn't until I saw it standing on the coffee table. I couldn't have fit it in that satchel if I tried."

"I'd like to see your satchel, if you don't mind."

"Sure." The prospect of showing her the satchel didn't seem to trouble Murray. "What did Constance Volpe say?" he asked. "She must have talked to Colonel Gimbel after I did."

"No, he didn't come to the door," Foley said. "Probably because you had just killed him."

When Detective Foley had finished questioning Murray, she asked him to come to the precinct station to sign a statement, which he readily agreed to do. She didn't arrest him—in fact she had no real evidence against him. If being at the Colonel's house made him guilty, then Constance Volpe was just as guilty. Murray ducked into his bedroom and emerged with a brown satchel, which he handed to Foley. "I'll bring this along," he said, "in case you want to check it for raven dust."

Was the satchel big enough to hold a raven? None of us—including Detective Foley—had ever seen the Colonel's raven—or, in all likelihood, any other raven. How big is a raven? I could only guess.

"Ravens have always been seen as omens of death," Borges observed. "The Icelandic bards, for example—"

"Did the Icelandic bards mention whether a raven would fit in this satchel?" Foley interrupted. "If not, I don't want to hear about them."

"May I ask a couple of questions before you leave?" Borges said.

Detective Foley sighed and rolled her eyes. "Señor Borges, with all due respect—"

"Was the Colonel beaten with his cane?"

"Bludgeoned almost beyond recognition," she said quietly.

"When they found the Colonel's body, where was it?"

"It was in his living room."

"Along with the cane?"

"Yes, the cane was on the floor, caked with blood and hair."

"And was the stuffed raven there? The one Murray said he'd seen on the coffee table?"

"No, of course not. He took it with him in his satchel. This satchel."

"Miss Volpe was at the house after Murray was," Borges said.

"Colonel Gimbel didn't let her in," Foley said.

"You have only her word for that. She had a strong motive to steal the raven even without knowing what was inside it. Miss O'Hara also had a strong motive. I suggest that you check the fingerprints on the cane."

"Obviously we're doing that."

"You won't find any of mine on it," Murray said.

"Because you wiped them off?"

"No, because I never touched it."

After Murray left with Detective Foley—it was after two o'clock—I sat with Borges as he sank farther into existential gloom. "I shall never forgive myself," he muttered. "I shall never forgive myself for letting Colonel Gimbel spend the night in the same house as that raven."

"You tried to warn him."

"I could have done something to stop him."

There was nothing I could say. I said my good-byes and hopped on an uptown train, hoping I wouldn't have to explain to Miss Kunkel why I wasn't at my desk refusing to answer subscribers' questions. Colonel Gimbel's death had unnerved me, especially when I tried to understand it in terms of "The Tale of the Unlucky Mirror." I had taken the merchant for O'Hara, but of course Colonel Gimbel, scion of

the department store fortune, might have fit the role of the
merchant just as well. And who was the thief?—that was the
all-important question. I desperately needed to talk to Lucinda, but she'd left for the day, possibly to continue her research on the story. I huddled in my cubicle the rest of the
afternoon, asking myself whether I really wanted to go down
this road. Had I been infected by Borges's inability to distinguish fantasy from reality?

Sometimes I wondered if I'd been sleepwalking ever since
I arrived in New York, or at least since I fell under Borges's
spell. The Peruvians told me I often went missing in the night
and they had to find me before a security guard brought me
back and discovered how many people we had in our room.
Needless to say I couldn't remember anything about those
forays. What conclusion can you draw from that? Just the
night before, after leaving Borges's apartment, I'd walked the
thirty blocks uptown to 34th Street, slipping into Sloan
House just before they locked the doors for the night. I
remembered that walk, but of course I couldn't remember
every step I took, every traffic light, every deviation from my
usual route—all told I probably couldn't remember more
than ten percent of what I saw, heard or did along the way. I
know I was the one there for that ten percent. But who was I
the rest of the time?

25. Six Suspects

Borges's dark night of the soul lasted only until cocktail hour. When I arrived back at his apartment he was sipping a whisky and chatting affably with Murray, who had returned from the police station in time to join us for an early dinner. Señora Sanchez prepared an excellent chicken dish with lots of garlic and green peppers, served over a bed of saffron rice. She had bought some French pastries for dessert and a nice bottle of Sandeman port which we drank after our coffee. Nobody had much to say until the first glass of port had been sipped and savored. "Miss Chalmers will be coming over later to work on the seminar," Borges said. "We still have some important reading to do."

"Do you know what you're going to say?" Murray asked him.

"Not quite yet, though it's coming into focus. I expect to be able to announce the solution to both murders at the seminar."

Murray and I exchanged indulgent but somewhat derisive glances. I knew what Murray must have been thinking: What possible connection could exist between the Poe seminar and the solution to these murders?

"I guess I should feel important," Murray said. "Not everybody can be the prime suspect in two unrelated murders."

"They're not unrelated," Borges said. "I'm quite sure there's a connection between them."

I thought I should try to help Murray look on the bright side. "It was lucky that you spoke up about going to the Colonel's house," I told him.

"I had no choice when Detective Foley mentioned Constance Volpe."

Did that mean he would have kept it a secret if he thought he could get away with it? "And showing her the satchel, that was a big help," I added.

He burst out laughing. "Yeah, it's a good thing I didn't show her the other one I have in my closet."

"A big brown one?" I asked nervously.

"Yep. That's the one I took with me to the Colonel's. Do you have any idea how big a raven is?"

A few awkward moments passed. I was starting to feel like an unindicted co-conspirator.

"Fortunately you're not the only suspect," Borges said. "It's far too early in the case for that."

"Bridget O'Hara is a suspect," Murray said. "The police know she was seen arguing with the Colonel at the reception and then walking off with his cane."

"That makes two suspects," Borges nodded.

"And don't forget Constance Volpe."

"That's three. We need three more."

Murray smiled at Borges naively (he still didn't know that literary conventions trumped reality). "Does there have to be six suspects?"

Borges reacted with a dismissive snort. "With any fewer than six, the solution is obvious. With more than that, the denouement becomes unwieldy and unconvincing."

"We're not writing a story," Murray said, even more naively.

"Not yet," Borges said. "Presently we're just sketching it out." He shot an encouraging smile in my direction. "The writing will come later."

Murray looked at me. "Where are we going to find three more suspects?"

"We've got to keep looking," Borges said. "Was there anyone who could have overheard what Colonel Gimbel and I were talking about and made the same inference—that the ring was hidden in the raven?"

A light bulb flashed on in my mind. "Yes, as a matter of fact, there were two of them," I said. "Bruno Stossky and our very own Mary Ann Chalmers. They were following close behind you and they probably heard everything the Colonel said."

"Harkins says Stossky is a gangster," Murray observed.

"That's four, then," Borges said.

"Mary Ann probably saw Colonel Gimbel as an accomplice to Poe's femicides," I pointed out. "And she was here in your apartment on Sunday when we were talking about the ring being inside the raven."

"Miss Chalmers is at the very least a mental defective," Borges said. "Quite possibly a lunatic. Such a person can't be a proper suspect."

"There's always the Jewish Defense League," I said.

"A secret society can't be a suspect either."

"What about Nick?" Murray asked with a sly smile, avoiding my eyes. "He knew the ring was in the raven. Why isn't he a suspect?"

"The narrator can't be the murderer," I said with a nervous laugh.

"Obviously you're not familiar with the Ackroyd case," Borges said, taking a sip of his port.

"And if he was the murderer," I added, "he could cover it up and blame someone else."

"No one would believe him."

"I'm innocent."

"That's what they all say," Murray chuckled.

"That makes five," Borges said with an air of finality.

Murray shot a triumphant glance in my direction. "Then who is Number Six?"

I was offended to be on the list of murder suspects. "What about you?" I asked Borges. "You know everything I know."

"Yes, but the converse is not true," he smiled. "I know some things you don't know. Some things I can't share with either of you, which would cancel out whatever motive you might suppose me to have. At any rate, I can't be a suspect. That would violate one of the most time-honored rules of the detective story."

"Which is what?"

"The detective can't be the murderer."

26. The Borges of Crime

Before he went back to his work, Borges asked me whether I'd had any success finding "The Tale of the Unlucky Mirror."

"Just some of the story elements my supervisor found in a book by Vladimir Propp," I told him. "There's a hero, a magician, a trickster, a doctor, a thief and a merchant, and they're all searching for a magical mirror once owned by Solomon, but we haven't been able to find the actual story."

His brow darkened. "She found that in Propp?"

I was amazed (though I shouldn't have been) that Borges had heard of Propp. "One of his early works," I said, as if I'd heard of him. "There's also a raven who appears as a portent of death."

"This young librarian—Lucinda, is it?—is helping you with this?"

"Yes. She had to translate what I just told you from a footnote in Russian."

"Do you read Russian?"

"Not a word."

He chuckled as if at some private joke. "Keep working with her until you find the whole story. And keep me informed of your progress."

At eight o'clock Mary Ann arrived to work with Borges on the seminar. She sat on the couch with her notebook recording his pronouncements as he sipped another glass of port. Murray amused himself by flipping through an outdated *Time* magazine he found on the end table. I stared out the window at a pair of pigeons standing watch on the window ledge. Señora Sanchez brought me another glass of port.

"We've identified how Poe wrote 'The Murders in the Rue Morgue' as a corrective to the flaws he discovered in *Barnaby Rudge,"* Borges said. "But he didn't stop there, did he? He wrote two more stories chronicling the investigations of C. Auguste Dupin: 'The Mystery of Marie Rogêt' and 'The Purloined Letter.' The first of those is a botched-up job of trying to predict the outcome of a real criminal case, but 'The Purloined Letter' is a masterpiece that defined the detective story for a hundred years. Do you have it there, Mary Ann? Read it to us."

As I watched the pigeons mechanically marching back and forth on the window sill, Mary Ann picked up a collection of Poe stories and read the one about Dupin and his credulous sidekick, the prototype for every dim-witted Watson up to and including myself. The plot is ingenious but completely absurd. A French government official identified only as "D" steals a compromising letter sent to an "illustrious personage" (presumably the Queen of France) by her lover, and uses it to blackmail her on important matters of state. The blackmailer's identity is known to the police, yet they are unable to find the letter. After months of futile searching, the Prefect of Police visits Dupin and asks for advice. Dupin questions him closely about his methods and concludes that the letter must be hidden in plain view— where the police would have neglected to search. He goes to D's "hotel" (which is apparently where high government officials lived in those days) and finds the purloined letter, turned inside out to disguise its identity, in a hanging letter holder. Diverting D's attention, he steals the letter and replaces it with a facsimile copy, in which he has written a quotation found in Crébillon's *Atrée*. Hearing that reference gave me an uneasy feeling. I stood up and walked over to the cabinet where I had shelved the volume of Crébillon's plays I'd purchased at Schneider's on Saturday and quickly leafed through it. The full title of the play cited by Poe was *Atrée et Thyeste*. Atreus and Thyestes.

"Dupin knew D," Borges said, "well enough that he had an old score to settle with him. And well enough that he knew D would recognize his handwriting. He wanted D to know who had foiled his blackmail scheme by purloining the purloined letter."

"The play Poe quoted from was about the curse on the House of Atreus," I said, my voice a little weak.

"Of course," Borges said. "That's one of the reasons I've become so interested in the Netzer case. The two brothers linked by a curse."

"I received a question at the encyclopedia about the curse on the House of Atreus," I said.

"Probably just a coincidence," Murray told me.

"I can assure you," Borges said, "that quotation and my involvement in this case are not a matter of chance, if that's what you mean by coincidence. Until we heard about Bernhard Netzer's death, I was only mildly interested in your predicament. But I had been thinking about 'The Purloined Letter' for my seminar, and when you were named as a suspect, and Nick received the question about the curse on the House of Atreus, I could not resist involving myself in the case. As I said the other day, archetypes intrude into the sensible world at just the moment when there's a meaning for them to take on. That is when the detective must follow their lead. Chance has nothing to do with it."

"So what's the story on Atreus and Thyestes?" Mary Ann asked, setting the collection of Poe stories down on the couch beside her.

"They were brothers," Borges said, "infamous for their escalating acts of revenge against each other, which culminated in Atreus slaughtering Thyestes's sons and serving them to him in a stew."

"There must have been a major payback for that one!" she laughed.

"Thyestes put a curse on Atreus and his descendants, which of course is what led to all the unpleasantness when Agamemnon returned from the Trojan War."

"In light of all that," I pointed out, "'The Purloined Letter' ends with an odd twist. By putting that Crébillon quote in the letter, Dupin seems to be identifying himself with Atreus."

"Both brothers were equally depraved," Borges said. "But you raise a good point. We should look more closely at that quotation. Please read it again, Mary Ann."

Her pronunciation was so bad that I had to take the book from her and read it in my own halting French:

> —*Un dessein si funeste,*
> *S'il n'est digne d'Atrée, est digne de Thyeste.*

"What does it mean?" she asked.

"It means," I translated, "'So infamous a scheme, if it's not worthy of Atreus, is worthy of Thyestes.'"

"And what does *that* mean?"

We all thought about it for a moment, and Borges said: "Admittedly it doesn't make much sense. The 'scheme' must be the trick Dupin played on D, so why would he describe it as infamous?"

"And," I said, "why would he identify himself with Atreus?"

Murray had picked up the collection of Poe stories, which remained open to the last page of 'The Purloined Letter.' He stared at it for a long moment and raised his eyes to meet mine with an air of uncanny incredulity. "Speaking of coincidences, or archetypes, or whatever," he said, "you're not going to believe this. These French verses that Poe quotes at the end of the story are the same ones Detective Foley kept asking me about during my interrogation. She seemed to think I'd seen them before and would be able to translate them for her."

"They must have been in the suicide note," I said, "and they're trying to see if you wrote it."

"They did make me give them a sample of my handwriting."

"Or perhaps those lines were included in one of the threatening letters to Peter Netzer," Borges said, "along with the mystical Jewish symbols." He let that possibility sink in for a moment before completing his thought: "In which case we may be dealing with a criminal mastermind such as the world has never seen. Not the Napoleon of crime—as Sherlock Holmes described Professor Moriarty—but the Kafka."

"Or maybe even the Borges," I teased him.

He flicked that possibility away with a wave of the hand. "Nick," he said, "I want you to read that play by Crébillon and find the quotation so we can see exactly what Dupin meant."

Dupin didn't mean anything, I wanted to say: he was a fictional character. But what difference would that have made to Borges? And who was I—in light of the path I was going down with Lucinda—to insist on a distinction between fact and fantasy?

27. The Third Victim

Wednesday dawned, or I suppose it did: the sun was high in the sky by the time I arrived at the office, my head still throbbing from the port wine I'd imbibed the night before. We didn't have a radio or TV in our room at Sloan House, so if anything important happened during the night—which it did—I didn't hear about it, and I didn't notice the headlines on the newspapers as I walked to work. Lucinda had left a note on my desk; I hurried to her cubicle.

"I found a little more about the Arabian tale," she told me, holding up a writing tablet. "Some more story elements in a different commentary. It picks up where Propp left off."

"Do you have the book?"

"No, just my notes," she said, leaning over her writing tablet. "In some versions the hero finds the magical mirror, gazes into it, and is attacked by powerful demons who drag him down to hell for a fight to the death."

"I'm glad I'm not the hero."

"Which character would you rather be? The thief?" She sounded serious.

"What do you mean?"

"Well," she said with a furtive smile, "if you're determined to read this story as a commentary on the Netzer case, the magician would have to be Borges, and the trickster your friend Murray."

"That's about right," I laughed. "Murray's turning out to be sort of a slippery character. And Borges is like a magician who expects everybody to believe in the illusions he creates."

"Then what's your role in the drama?" she asked. "Why not be the hero?"

"A fight to the death with demons doesn't really appeal to me."

"Maybe you're already in one and you don't know it."

At lunchtime I strolled down 57th Street to Fifth Avenue and then a couple blocks up to the Plaza Hotel, hoping to find the clerk they called Sam. It was a warm, sunny afternoon but my doubts about Borges and Murray made the world look a few shades darker than it had looked the day before.

Plucking up my nerve, I dodged past the horse-drawn carriages and the costumed doorman and kept my eyes open for falling pots, striding into the lobby as I'd done before, insanely expecting a different result. It must have been my lucky day. The smirking bellhop and the menacing concierge were nowhere in sight, and the fellow who welcomed me at the front desk wore a name tag that said Sam.

"Sam," I greeted him, keeping my voice down. "I was hoping you'd be here. I want to ask you about the guest who got killed. Bernhard Netzer."

"You a cop?" he murmured, leaning closer. "I already talked to the cops."

"Reporter," I lied.

His furtive eyes flitted from side to side. "I can't talk to you now."

"You get a break? I'll sit down and wait for you."

I found a seat in the lobby and leafed through that week's *Time* magazine. After about fifteen minutes Sam walked past and motioned for me to meet him outside. I followed him out and across the street to the park entrance, where we blended into the crowd. I slipped him a ten dollar bill and looked away as he shoved it in his pocket. Sam's appearance could most charitably be described as unfortunate. His black hair tapered to a widow's peak that descended toward an equally pointy nose and a pair of pouty lips; a single eyebrow stretched across and between his dark, wary eyes. In short it was a face only a ferret's mother could love.

He lit a cigarette and took a long drag. "All right, get to the point. I'm on my break."

"I just wanted to follow up on what you told the cops about the guy who came to the hotel the night Bernhard Netzer was killed," I said.

"Yeah?"

"Who did he ask for?"

"I don't remember. There were two brothers staying here. I buzzed them both and nobody answered."

"And you gave him their phone numbers?"

"Yeah, I shouldn't have done that, but I did. I got in a lot of trouble for it."

"Then what happened?"

"The guy sat in the lobby for a while, then he started dialing one of the courtesy phones. He must have reached somebody. I saw him talking on the phone."

"He talked to one of the Netzers?"

"I don't know who he talked to. It must have been somebody in the hotel. You can't call out on those phones."

"Did you tell that to the cops?"

"I don't remember," he smirked. "I just answered what she asked me."

"Female detective?"

He nodded. "I can't remember her name."

"Detective Foley? What did she ask you about?"

"She wanted to know if you can tell the room number from the phone number, and I told her yes, you can, if you know the system. So when the guy got the phone number, he could have gone up to the guest's room. That's all she wanted to know."

"She didn't ask anything else?"

He tossed his cigarette down on the sidewalk and crushed it, indicating that the meter had run out on our conversation. I reached into my wallet and pulled out another tenspot.

"She just kept asking me about that," he went on. "About whether you can figure out the room number from the phone number. I don't think she asked me if I saw the guy talking to anybody, or about the note, so I might not have told her about that."

"The note? What note?" I must have sounded excited. That triggered another awkward pause, which ended only when I handed over the ten dollar bill.

"Before the guy left," Sam said, "he dropped a note off at the desk."

"For one of the guests?"

"Dr. Peter Netzer, it said on it. I didn't read it. I just put it in his slot."

"Did Dr. Netzer pick it up?"

This time the smirk was on me. "That'll cost you another ten," he said, looking away.

I forked it over without a whimper of protest. It was Borges's money, I told myself, though I could have used it to keep from starving.

"He must have picked it up," Sam said. "It wasn't there the next time I looked."

"You didn't see him pick it up?"

"I wasn't the only guy on duty. Listen, I gotta get back."

We walked across the street toward the hotel. "That was the guy that got blown up, right? Peter Netzer?"

"What are you talking about?"

"Don't tell me you didn't hear about that?" His voice sizzled with anger. "Who the hell are you? You're no reporter."

28. Murder in the Morgue

I stopped at the first news stand I could find and picked up that afternoon's *New York Post*. The front-page headline told it all: MURDER IN THE MORGUE – MEDICAL EXAMINER DIES IN BLAST. I slipped into a phone booth and called Lucinda to tell her I wouldn't be coming back to the office that afternoon. Then I headed to Columbus Circle to catch the subway downtown.

I read the story—which carried the byline of Rachel Price—as I waited for the train. Peter Netzer had been blown up in his office at the morgue at eleven o'clock the night before. Police refused to speculate, except to say that they were searching for a man who was seen entering the building with a parcel about an hour before the bombing. Rabbi Meyer Kahane of the Jewish Defense League had been brought in for questioning.

When I arrived at Borges's apartment, I found him working calmly with Mary Ann, aware of this latest development but seemingly untroubled by it. "At least they haven't accused Murray," he said. "Though it's possible they'll claim he was the man seen entering the building with a package—in which case we may be his alibi. He was here last night until what time?"

I had already done the math on that. "He left here about nine," I said, "a little before I did. The bomber was seen entering the morgue an hour later. So that alibi wouldn't stand up."

"Still I refuse to believe that Murray is a murderer."

"I hope you're right," I hesitated, "but... there are some pretty incriminating things you need to know."

"Whatever you think I need to know," he said with a dismissive wave, "it can wait until Murray is here to defend himself. I don't like the idea of trying my friends *in absentia*. Right now Mary Ann and I must finish our preparations for the seminar. We were about to read Poe's famous essay, 'The Philosophy of Composition.' After that you're going to read Crébillon's *Atrée et Thyeste*. There's no time to waste."

The brush-off I'd received from Borges put me in a negative, self-pitying frame of mind, from which Señora Sanchez tried to rescue me with a freshly mixed gimlet—the one bright spot in what was shaping up as a depressing evening. I was getting heartily sick of Poe and, frankly, sick of Borges too. Sick of humoring him and catering to his fantasies, sick of helping him play detective based on the conventions of outdated mystery novels, sick of trying to grope my way out of the labyrinths he dreamed up for everyone around him. Now he'd tapped me for another pointless exercise: reciting this French play that nobody but Poe had read in a hundred and fifty years. My relationship with Lucinda had taught me some things I could never have learned from Borges, and I was hoping it would teach me more. But first I had to free myself of subjection to his vanities and conundrums. That's what Lucinda seemed to be telling me; maybe that was even what the Arabian tale about the unlucky mirror was trying to tell me. I resolved that when the seminar was over I would say goodbye to the old magician and his paradoxes and get on with my life.

Just as Mary Ann finished reciting Poe's essay—in which he explains in ludicrous detail every purported step of his thought processes as he wrote 'The Raven'—the door clicked open and Murray walked in carrying a copy of the *Post*. For a few minutes all the talk was about Peter Netzer and his violent death. "It looks like it was the JDL after all," I said. "They're questioning Rabbi Kahane. Which means the JDL probably killed Bernhard Netzer too."

"Nonsense," Borges said. "The JDL had no motive to kill Colonel Gimbel."

"Then you're sure the murders are related?"

"Of course they're related. That's the key to solving this mystery."

"Then wait till you hear this," Murray said. "There was a Hebrew letter painted on the wall in the Colonel's living room."

"The *aleph?*"

"No, the next one. The second letter of the alphabet. I forget what it's called."

"*Bet,*" Borges said. "I suppose they'll find the third letter—*gimel,* which also means three—on the wall at the morgue."

"Somebody's counting off the murders?" I gasped.

"And they've arrested Bridget O'Hara," Murray said, "and charged her with the murder of Colonel Gimbel."

"Is she in jail?"

"She's got a fancy lawyer and he expects to have her out on bail in a couple of hours."

Borges gripped his walking stick and leaned toward Murray. "How do you know all this?"

"Agent Harkins. We just had a long conversation on the phone. He told me O'Hara's fingerprints were on the cane the Colonel was bludgeoned with—"

"Yes, of course. She had it in her hands at the reception."

"And the police found the remains of the stuffed raven in the trash behind her gallery. Whoever killed Colonel Gimbel ripped out the inside to get the ring and threw the rest away."

That silenced all of us for a long moment. Even Borges seemed at a loss for words.

"The police also have a theory that O'Hara killed Bernhard Netzer," Murray finally said. "They think she figured out his hotel room number from the phone number the clerk gave her, went up to his room while he was out, took down the curtains, and used the cord from the curtains to strangle him and hang him in the park."

Borges shook his head incredulously. "That's their theory?"

"It's more complicated than that,' Murray said, "but that's it in a nutshell."

"That scenario would apply equally to you," Borges observed. "You got the phone number from the desk clerk and could have done all the same things."

"Agent Harkins pointed that out," Murray said. "I think he's disappointed that I wasn't the one who got arrested. This puts the kibosh on his sting operation. But he told me I'm still a suspect as far as the cops are concerned. If the lawyer gets O'Hara off, I'm next on Foley's list." He dropped into a chair and ran the back of his hand over his forehead. "Luckily they don't have anything on me."

"Maybe not," I said. "But we do."

He gave me his most innocent—I should say most disin-genuous—smile. "What are you talking about?"

It was time to confront him about what I had learned that afternoon at the Plaza Hotel. "I stopped at the Plaza this afternoon and finally got to speak to Sam the desk clerk. The one who was there on the night Bernhard was killed."

"So?"

"He says you talked on one of the phones in the lobby."

"That's right. Didn't I tell you that?"

"You told us you tried to reach the Netzers and neither answered," Borges said.

"You must have misunderstood me," Murray said. "I talked to Peter Netzer on the phone."

"What about?"

"I wanted to try to convince him that he should just re-turn the ring and avoid all the complications it was getting him involved in. I told that to the police."

"What did he say?"

"He didn't want to hear it. He wouldn't listen to what I had to say."

"And then you left him a note," I said.

That caught Murray off guard. "Yeah, I did," he said, a little embarrassed. "So what?"

"You didn't tell us that," Borges said sharply. "Did you tell the police?"

Murray grinned. "I think I might've forgotten to do that, just like I forgot to tell you."

"What was in the note?"

"When he said he wouldn't return the ring, I told him about the curse. I was hoping it would scare him into going through with the sale. But you know, curses have become sort of passé. So I talked up the conspiracy theory. The secret society sworn to destroy anyone who has the ring. I sort of hinted that such a group might be gunning for him."

"Did that scare him?"

"He laughed at me. So I told him I'd leave something at the desk for him to think about. I had no idea what I meant when I said that. But after he hung up I took a piece of hotel stationery and wrote the JDL slogan *Never again!* on it and signed it with the *aleph*—I'm familiar with that symbol from math—and left it at the desk. That's what was in the note."

"But you didn't tell that to the police?"

"It made me look guilty. I'm innocent and I didn't want to be the center of attention."

Borges stared at Murray as if he could see right through him. "Now I want to focus on something that's very important," he said. "Whose name did you write on the note? To whom was it addressed?"

"Peter Netzer. He's the one I had talked to."

"Are you sure?"

"Sure I'm sure."

"And you left it at the desk for him to pick up?"

"Yes. I folded it over and wrote his name on it and left it at the desk. How many times do I have to tell you that?"

When Borges reminded Murray that we had work to do, he took the hint and headed home, annoyed at the way we'd treated him. He was even more vexed when Borges insisted that he attend his seminar the next day.

"Why would I want to do that? I'm not the least bit interested in Poe."

"You need to be there," Borges declared, thumping his walking stick. "No excuses. It starts at one o'clock."

After Murray left—he winked at me as he sidestepped out the door—Borges turned his full attention to the subject of his seminar. Mary Ann sat, pen in hand, with her notebook poised on her knee, in case Borges revealed any new examples of Poe's depravity which she could add to her bill of particulars.

"Nothing is random or unintentional in Poe's writings," he said, "as Poe himself told us in his 'Philosophy of Composition.' Each of his three detective stories begins with an epigraph, and two of them end with French quotations. 'The Purloined Letter' ends with the Crébillon quote we have looked at before. For its full context, we must read Crébillon's *Atrée et Thyeste.*"

He insisted on hearing the whole play, even though the lines quoted by Poe come near the end, as Atreus gloats over the cannibalistic meal he is preparing for his brother. The gimlets—by this time I'd had two or three—had taken their toll. Yawning and rubbing my eyes, I tried to concentrate on my reading, without thinking much about the play, a poetic tragedy from the eighteenth century. It was formal, stilted, boring, and yet there was something subliminally disturbing about it that kept me awake and even made my heart beat faster as I read on.

As I approached the climax I noticed Borges's face stiffening into a mask of horror, as if he'd been invited to witness the horrible feast. And when I came to the lines quoted by Poe, he let out a gasp and muttered, "I see it all now."

I stopped reading and he said, breathlessly: "Don't stop. Read on to the end."

By the time I finished, Borges, ghastly pale, sat hunched forward with his head in his hands. "Mad!" he murmured. "Utterly mad. How could I have been so blind?"

Mary Ann nodded with satisfaction, whether at Poe's madness or Borges's blindness I could only guess. I sat in silence, mystified as to what would happen next. "Nick, get the phone and dial Detective Foley," Borges rasped, still pale and short of breath. "Tell her it's essential that she come to the seminar tomorrow and bring at least two uniformed policemen with her. She must also bring Bridget O'Hara, Bruno Stossky, Constance Volpe—"

"Constance Volpe?"

"—and Helga Netzer."

"Helga Netzer may not be available. Her husband just got blown up in the morgue."

"All the more reason why she'll want to be there when I reveal the name of his murderer."

I found Detective Foley's card and started to dial. "And when you're done talking to Detective Foley," Borges said, "I'll need you to dial Inspector Fritz Egli of the Swiss Federal Police. He called earlier and I believe Señora Sanchez wrote down his number by the phone."

"Call Switzerland at this hour?"

"Oh, no," Borges said. "Inspector Egli is in New York."

After Mary Ann had gone home to her grave or her padded cell or wherever she spent the night, Borges and I settled down for our nightcap. Señora Sanchez brought our drinks—

whisky and soda for him, another gimlet for me—and retired
to the kitchen, leaving her cocktail cart behind. The color
returned to Borges's face as he sipped his whisky, and in a
few minutes he had recovered his usual sang froid.

"So," I said, affecting a nonchalant tone, "you know who
the murderer is?"

"Murderers," he said cryptically. "Plural."

A few silent moments drifted by, making it clear that he
had no intention of telling me more. "And how did you
figure it out?" I asked.

"In a word: Crébillon."

What had he heard in my recitation of *Atrée et Thyeste* that
gave him this sudden insight into the mystery we'd been
struggling with for almost two weeks?

"Frankly," I said, "your methods of detection make no
sense to me. How can you solve a crime with fiction instead
of facts?"

"I'll tell you exactly how I can do that," he said in an ex-
asperated tone. "The commission and concealment of a crime
amount to a staged event very similar to a novel or play,
authored by the criminal with the purpose of creating a false
representation of reality. The detective must be an expert
critic who knows the tropes of storytelling and can see
through the stagecraft to the hidden truth. Is that so very
hard to understand?"

"No," I admitted. "But—"

"In any event," he cut me off, with an intensity I had seldom seen in him, "the distinction between fact and fiction is
vastly overrated. 'Knowledge' is the name we give our pet
fantasies. For that reason, the more knowledge we think we
have, the more it baffles us; we need a guide to find our way

through even a small part of it. The mind itself—a mirror of the world that contains itself—can only lead us in circles."

"Then how—"

"We need archetypes: poems, stories, images. Don't you see? We need Poe—madman that he was—before we can solve the murders of Bernhard Netzer, Peter Netzer and Colonel Gimbel."

After he finished his drink, Borges asked Señora Sanchez to turn on the radio so we could listen to music. That was a surprising request, as I had never known him to show any interest in music. Classical music filled the air—I think it was a Beethoven string quartet—and we listened for a few minutes.

"I've been meaning to ask you something," he said. "When we were at that reception at Bridget O'Hara's gallery, a string quartet was playing a piece that sounded something like this."

"Yes," I said. "I remember that. I think it was by Mozart."

"You know something about music, then?"

"I took piano lessons for five years."

"I heard the leader of the group say to the others: 'Take the second ending.' What did he mean by that?"

"Well," I said, "in classical music, a section often has a first and second ending. You play the whole section through and take the first ending, which leads back to the beginning. Then you play it through again and take the second ending, which leads to the next section, which might also have a first and second ending, and so on to the end."

"Can you imagine if stories were written that way?" he laughed. "If some diabolical author—Edgar Allan Poe comes to mind—made you read almost to the end and then said: ˝ That was only the first ending! Now you must go back to the beginning and read it again to find out what really happened."

29. The Oracle

I spent a restless, all but sleepless night, my mind churning as I tried to make sense of what had happened in the past few days. To add to my distraction, the night manager kept tapping on our door on one pretext or another in an attempt to discover how many people slept in our room. By then the number was up to six, with a pair of starving Chilean jugglers, both fortunately very thin, stretched out on the floor beside the bed. In my insomniac fantasies I was as suspicious of Borges and Murray as the Sloan House management was of the Peruvians.

At the office I confided my worries to Lucinda, who as always was supportive and understanding. The Arabian tale was now irrelevant, since Borges had supposedly solved the Netzer case and would announce his solution that afternoon. Still I wanted to find the text—or discover why I couldn't find it—because I needed to know if Borges had been leading me down a rabbit hole. Lucinda had arranged a meeting with Miss Kunkel, preliminary to consulting the Authoritative Source, on the pretext that my interest in "The Tale of the Unlucky Mirror" was prompted by a subscriber's question. As she guided me through the maze of cubicles to Miss Kunkel's office, wary-eyed reference assistants peeked over their partitions like creatures in a forest and a rumor of awe and excitement buzzed around us. She tapped on Miss Kunkel's door and was granted admittance; the curtains were drawn, the room almost dark. The old librarian sat erect behind her desk, hands folded in front of her, in a pose of receptivity. Lucinda briefed her on what our research had uncovered—a reference to the title in the *Cyclopedia,* the footnote in Propp, the mentions she'd found in other scholarly works. Miss Kunkel took notes and asked us to step outside, where we waited on a wooden bench along the wall that was as hard as a church pew. From behind the door we heard a low moaning and occasional indistinct exclamations—was Miss Kunkel talking on the phone or to herself?—until she appeared in the doorway and invited us back inside. She seemed out of breath, her eyes dull and glassy.

"Unfortunately the Arabian tale you've been searching for probably doesn't exist," she murmured, collapsing back in her chair. "It has been said to exist, assumed to exist; purported fragments have been published in scholarly treatises. But those fragments, you understand, are not conclusive proof that the complete story has ever existed. Among the fragments are countless variant versions and redactions, which in their permutations give rise to a vast number of possible reconstructions of the complete story they are presumed to be fragments of, or possibly—and you must count this as more than a possibility—of some other story. Indeed, there is an immense literature of commentary and disputation concerning whether any complete story exists or has ever existed, and in what form it exists or has existed. Some say the fragments are all that has ever existed, others that they are remnants of a lost tale, or series of tales, of enormous length and great antiquity. Some maintain that the fragments are forgeries, and even those who acknowledge their authenticity don't agree on the correct interpretation."

Miss Kunkel rose and glided toward the door, signaling that our meeting was over. Before we left, Lucinda was able to extract some details about the variant versions of the story. In some, the magician joins with the trickster to frame the merchant and the doctor; in others the hero is captured by demons and tortured for killing their master. And in one version—said by some to exist, Miss Kunkel cautioned, though a full text of it has never been found—the hero wanders in a cave until a wise and beautiful woman takes his hand and leads him to the light.

That image captured my imagination. "So in other words—"

"There are no other words to express what I just said," Miss Kunkel cut me off. "If there were, I would have used them."

Wending our way back toward Lucinda's cubicle, I made no effort to conceal my disappointment. "Your Authoritative Source is the Wizard of Oz," I said. "Just an old man—in this case an old woman—hiding behind a curtain pulling levers to mystify the public. A lot like Borges, in fact."

"I doubt if that Arabian story—assuming it exists—would shed any light on the Netzer case," she agreed. "Or any story, for that matter. All this nonsense about archetypes and stories, Poe and Crébillon and the *Arabian Nights*—Borges is just using it to manipulate the truth and control people."

"People like me, you mean."

She smiled and turned away. "There is something you should know, if you haven't thought of it already. It's about your friend Murray."

"What?"

"Isn't it obvious that he submitted all those seemingly uncanny questions, about the curse on the house of Atreus and Spinoza's God and Peter Netzer's article about ligature strangulation? The last one should have tipped you off: *Who killed Bernhard Netzer?*"

I leaped to Murray's defense. "How can you be so sure?"

"Who else could have sent them in? You don't believe in Mr. G. Alfano, do you?"

I had to admit that I didn't.

"Then someone you know must have done it. Someone who knows a lot about the case. Who else could it have been?"

"Not Mary Ann," I admitted. "Or Señora Sanchez. And certainly not Borges."

"That leaves Murray," Lucinda said. "He's been sending in the questions to keep you and Borges working on his case."

It was so embarrassingly obvious that I could hardly glance in her direction. By this time we had reached her cubicle, and when she stepped in I remained outside, anxious to get back to my desk. "It would be just like Murray to do something like that," I admitted. "Just in order to see how long it would take me to figure it out."

"Something like that," she smiled.

"Which without you, I guess, would have been forever."

"Don't forget that ending to the Arabian story—I think it's the real one. Where the wise and beautiful woman leads the hero to the light."

By the time I arrived at the seminar, my outlook had faded to black. I'd been duped by Murray, a man I'd liked and trusted from the moment I met him. He sent in those questions to the encyclopedia, lied to me and Borges, lied to the police and the FBI; there was an excellent chance that he was a murderer. I'd lost my faith in Borges and now saw him as a charlatan peddling a bogus elixir of paradox and obfuscation. His brilliance at crime detection was a fantasy if not a fraud, based on literary tropes that had no application to the real world. Even if he was not an impostor (which at one point he had admitted to being), he had nothing important to teach me. I thought back to one of the variants of the Arabian tale related by Miss Kunkel... Wait a minute! Had it come to this? Did I imagine that an Arabian tale scattered through a thousand sources could lead me anywhere near the truth? I would have gone back to Sloan House to sleep off my confusion if Lucinda hadn't insisted that I attend the seminar. "You've got to finish what you started," she said. And at that moment I trusted Lucinda as I trusted no one else.

30. The Seminar

The seminar took place in a small auditorium in one of the university's classroom buildings. Its wide entrance opened from a foyer where groups of students and professors chatted in small groups, waiting for the great man to appear. I was astonished to see Borges being led through the foyer, arm in arm, by a woman I'd never seen before. She was a tall brunette in her late thirties, very well dressed, with an eager, acquisitive gaze. An expensive camera dangled around her neck. Ignoring the crowd, she ushered Borges into the auditorium with a proprietorial air and led him to the dais, where she seated him at the table between Mary Ann and a haggard, white-bearded gentleman who looked like he might have been stranded on a desert island. Then, stepping back, she aimed her camera at Borges and snapped his picture. The flash must have sent a shock through his bluish haze: he responded with a censorious frown.

"Señor Borges doesn't permit photography," I said, stepping up on the dais.

"Ah, Martin!" he said, recognizing my voice. "I'm glad you're here. I'd like you to meet Rachel Price of the *New York Post*. We've just come from the morgue."

I recognized her name from the articles in the *Post*. What on earth had they been doing at the morgue?

"Nick is writing a book about the case," Borges told her.

"Well, then," she said with a sly smile, "I'll leave you in his capable hands." She stepped off the dais and took a seat in the first row next to Murray, who seemed to know her.

By this time the whole cast of characters sat in the auditorium, except for the ones who'd been murdered. Detective Bernadette Foley, flanked by two uniformed officers. Agent Harkins, still firm in his conviction that he was the smartest person in the room. Bridget O'Hara, wedged into her seat beside a spindly, wooden-faced man who turned out to be her lawyer. Constance Volpe, Colonel Gimbel's collecting rival, in the second row a few seats to the right of Bridget O'Hara. Helga Netzer, a widow for just over thirty-six hours, seated by herself in a black dress and hat. Murray Kellerman, of course, chatting amiably with Rachel Price. And another man I didn't know, but would meet later, who looked like a plainclothes cop. He was a square man with a square head covered with thick gray hair, who sat apart from the others on the far end of the first row, clutching a leather briefcase on his lap. Needless to say there were also dozens of faculty members and a large crowd of bespectacled graduate students. I found a seat on the aisle in the third row where I could keep my eye on everyone I wanted to watch.

On the dais, Borges was flanked by Mary Ann, who had erected a row of white posterboard placards on the table, and the white-bearded department chairman, Professor Alexander Selbourne. Professor Selbourne must have been what the feminists of that era had in mind when they complained about Dead White Males in the English department. If, on rare occasions, his body temperature rose into the low 90s, it was owing more to his tweed suits and cable-knit sweaters than to any metabolic processes going on inside him. Nevertheless, his meandering introduction of Borges was met with enthusiastic applause, which Borges obviously enjoyed.

From where I sat I couldn't tell what purpose Mary Ann's placards served: I assumed that they were visual aids meant to illustrate the lecture. It was only after Borges started talking, when she arranged small votive candles in front of each of the placards and began lighting them, that I felt the first hazy suspicion of what they might represent.

"Although today's event was billed as a seminar on Poe's detective stories," Borges began after a few preliminaries, "intended for the literature faculty and graduate students, I intend to go beyond abstract literary analysis and apply my thinking to a recent series of murders which have been much in the news. Specifically the murders of Bernhard Netzer, Dr. Peter Netzer and Colonel Richard Gimbel, all of which I believe are closely related. To that end I've invited a number of people who don't usually concern themselves with literary matters. We have police officers, an FBI agent, and an art dealer, Miss Bridget O'Hara, who has been named as a suspect in those murders and in a conspiracy to sell stolen art treasures, including the fabled Ring of Solomon."

"All of which she unequivocally denies," O'Hara's attorney interjected, rising in his seat. He was a thin man with a dull, cadaverous face, whose name, I later learned, was James Stewart MacNeish, Esquire.

"And her attorney," Borges nodded, "as well as Mr. Murray Kellerman, a neighbor and friend of mine, who claims Solomon's ring by right of inheritance, and who has also been named a potential suspect in the murders; Miss Constance Volpe, a collector of literary manuscripts and memorabilia; and Frau Helga Netzer, the widow of Dr. Peter Netzer, to whom I extend my most heartfelt condolences. Most of the other people involved in the events I will discuss are, unfortunately, dead.

"You have all heard about the 'Murder in the City Morgue,' as the bombing death of Chief Medical Examiner Peter Netzer two nights ago has been called by the newspapers, in an allusion to Edgar Allan Poe's famous detective story. As if by coincidence (if you believe in such things), the alleged conspiracy to sell stolen art—and the morgue murder itself, I believe—involve a taxidermically preserved (which is to say, stuffed) raven by the name of Grip, who, in his brief lifetime, was the pet of Charles Dickens, and in his afterlife was immortalized in Dickens's novel *Barnaby Rudge* and later in Poe's 'The Raven.'

"Colonel Richard Gimbel, whom I had the privilege of meeting shortly before his untimely death, was a great collector who acquired Grip in England last year. In doing so he bested his perennial rival, Miss Constance Volpe, who, as I mentioned, is here with us today. Colonel Gimbel arranged to have the raven crated up and shipped to New York by the O'Hara auction gallery, with the intention of donating it to the Free Library of Philadelphia. He permitted part of his collection to be displayed in the O'Hara gallery in New York, but the stuffed raven Grip was not among the items on display. The Colonel, fearing that the raven would be stolen by one of his collecting rivals—specifically, Miss Volpe—retrieved it from the art dealer, Bridget O'Hara, when it arrived from London and took it to his home on West 35th Street. What he didn't know was that Miss O'Hara had hidden the Ring of Solomon inside the raven in order to smuggle it into the United States. Two nights after I spoke

with Colonel Gimbel, someone—possibly Miss O'Hara—
went to his home, beat him to death with his cane and stole
the raven."

Attorney MacNeish leaped to his feet, his face suddenly
alive with indignation.

"And now the raven has disappeared," Borges went on,
blissfully unaware of the lawyer, "though I understand that a
quantity of black feathers was found in an alley behind Miss
O'Hara's gallery."

"I object!"

"And who are you, sir?"

"James Stewart MacNeish, Esquire, representing Bridget
O'Hara."

"Can we stipulate that you will find everything I say today
objectionable? I'm sure the feeling is mutual."

MacNeish sat down and whispered something in his client's ear. By this time Mary Ann Chalmers had lighted all her
votive candles. She stared across them at the audience with a
gleam of deranged solemnity in her eyes.

"The only reason I've outlined the facts of the current
case," Borges resumed, "is to introduce the topic of Poe and
his detective stories. As you will learn, the tragic events of
the past few days are closely related to that topic. Those
events, I believe, were the reflection—or, better to say, the
recapitulation or re-enactment—of a relationship, the relationship between Poe and Dickens, that was of enormous
consequence to literary history. Please allow me to sketch that
out for you."

31. Nevermore

A puzzled but tolerant mood had settled over the audience. The students and faculty were doubtless aware of Borges's reputation for eccentricity—hadn't he said the goal of his writing was to astonish?—and they seemed to enjoy following him into unexplored territory (except for Professor Selbourne, who had fallen asleep). But those who would rather have been somewhere else—Detective Foley and the two uniformed cops, Agent Harkins, Bridget O'Hara, Constance Volpe, and even Murray—had started yawning, shifting in their seats, and glancing at their watches. Rachel Price whispered to Murray and peered around the room jotting notes on a steno pad. Detective Foley kept her eyes fixed on Murray as if she expected him to sneak away. The two uniformed cops glared at Borges with the kind of bemused disdain they ordinarily reserved for the homeless. None of them had the slightest idea of what was in store for them.

"Edgar Allan Poe was engaged in a fierce, though one-sided, quasi-fratricidal rivalry with Charles Dickens," Borges resumed after a long drink of water. "I say one-sided because Dickens, though he must have sensed Poe's envy, had no idea of its madness and intensity. Poe considered himself Dickens's peer if not his superior; he was older by three years, but Dickens had achieved an early success that Poe could never equal. I call it quasi-fratricidal because on Poe's side it reached the archetypal level epitomized by Atreus and

Thyestes in the Greek myths. There can be no doubt of its importance. It gave us three landmarks of literary history—'The Raven,' 'The Murders in the Rue Morgue,' and 'The Purloined Letter'—and led to the creation of a whole new genre: the detective story."

"Is there any reason why we need to know all this?" Detective Foley called out.

"If you'll bear with me, Detective"—Borges must have recognized her voice—"its relevance will become clear. By the time Dickens made his first trip to America in 1842, at the age of thirty, he was the most famous writer in the world, acclaimed wherever he went, while Poe labored in obscurity and poverty in Philadelphia."

"When he wasn't murdering women," Mary Ann interjected.

"Of course," Borges smiled, making a show of tolerating her interruption. "During the year before that, Dickens's novel *Barnaby Rudge* had been published in serial form. Poe read the first few chapters as they came out and wrote a favorable but condescending review, the thrust of which was that yes, Dickens was a literary genius, but he, Poe, was an even greater genius, because he could deduce the entire plot (which he did with impressive accuracy) from the first few chapters. Nevertheless he doubted that the overall conception of the book would succeed. It was a tale of mystery, with a murder at its secret core, but the mystery was conveyed by intimations, dark hints and portentous glimpses of the truth which would either baffle the reader or overshadow the denouement."

"There was nothing baffling about the death of Morella," Mary Ann said, printing the name on one of her placards with a felt-tipped marker. The placards, I realized, were meant to look like headstones. She had set up a miniature graveyard for Poe's female victims.

"No, of course not," Borges agreed affably. "At any rate, Poe elaborated these ideas in a second review published around the time Dickens arrived in the United States, by which time the complete novel had been published. In that review, Poe congratulates himself for having correctly predicted the entire plot—in fact, he boasts that his predicted plot was, in some ways, better than the actual plot written by Dickens. The problem with the book, he says, is that Dickens, in order to preserve the aura of mystery, couldn't tell the story in the order in which it actually happened. He had to maintain the secrets of the murder and the identity of the murderer until their revelation at the end of the book. This was because the whole interest of the narrative was in *curiosity*. The story had to be arranged so as to perplex the reader and whet his curiosity with an accumulation of details that would remain incomprehensible until the solution was revealed.

"As he wrestled with these ideas, Poe perceived the fundamental problem of the mystery genre, which he was then in the process of inventing. The mystery is created by presenting a series of baffling facts, the meaning of which must be preserved until the end; but the author cannot, in his own voice, deceive the reader or use any artificial means of concealing the secret. As long as the story is conceived as the story of the murder itself, it cannot be told without anticipating the denouement or withholding critical facts. What was needed was a new conception of what the story is."

Borges raised his hand to ward off any interruption. "What was needed," he said, "was a *detective*. The story could then be the story, not of the murder itself, but of its investigation. The Chevalier C. Auguste Dupin was born."

"And who, may I ask, is that?" Detective Foley called out.

"The world's first detective," Borges said. "Without whom, you—and I, and everyone else in this room—would not be here today."

"If only wishing made it so," Agent Harkins quipped, and the audience laughed nervously.

Professor Selbourne, awakened by the laughter, called for order and Borges continued: "Poe wrote the world's first detective story, 'The Murders in the Rue Morgue,' to put this thinking into practice, in the process demonstrating that his understanding of how to write a mystery was superior to that of Dickens."

Mary Ann had printed two more names on her headstones. "Rest in peace, Madame L'Espanaye and her daughter, Mademoiselle Camille L'Espanaye," she intoned, facing the headstones toward the audience. "Strangled and horribly dismembered by an orangutan."

"Yes," Borges said, shaking his head, "those two Parisian ladies made the supreme sacrifice so that Poe could invent the detective story. But his rivalry with Dickens did not stop there. In his first review of *Barnaby Rudge* he had praised Dickens's introduction of Barnaby's talking raven as a character, anticipating how Dickens planned to use the bird in the rest of the uncompleted novel."

"Ah, the raven-haired Lenore," Mary Ann sighed. "And next to die—Lady Rowena!"

"Unfortunately Dickens did not live up to Poe's expectations in the completed novel. In his second review Poe expresses his disappointment that Dickens has not made better use of the raven, along the lines he had prescribed. He faults Dickens for not using the raven's croakings *prophetically* as a musical accompaniment to the fantastical hero.

"And so 'The Raven' was conceived as a corrective to the perceived flaws in *Barnaby Rudge*. Poe uses the raven in his poem exactly as he thought Dickens should have used it in the novel, teaching the world a lesson about who was the greater genius. But Poe's obsession still could not rest. A year later he published his famous essay, 'The Philosophy of Composition,' which purports to be a description of how he composed 'The Raven.' His procedure, he says, was strictly rational, with the precision of a mathematical problem, and owed nothing to accident or intuition. The writer should start by determining the overall *effect* he wants to achieve and then choose the best means of achieving it. Each facet of the projected work—length, theme, diction, incident, tone, plot—should be selected by an abstract process of deduction from the desired effect."

"And what theme did he select?" Mary Ann demanded, raising her voice. "The death of a beautiful woman—which he called *the most poetical topic in the world!* How rational!"

The audience laughed again, and when Borges joined in the laughter it occurred to me that Mary Ann's bizarre performance must have been part of the script. So this is what they were working on in his apartment when I wasn't there! But what did it have to do with the murders of the Netzers and Colonel Gimbel?

"In his account of how he wrote 'The Raven,'" Borges went on, "Poe brings this rationality down to a ludicrous, utterly fantastic level of detail. He claims to have selected the word 'nevermore'—before knowing how he would use it—

based on the sonority of the 'r' and 'o' sounds. He claims to have considered using a parrot before deciding on a raven. He claims to have selected the theme—the death of a beautiful woman—after he concluded, as Miss Chalmers has stated, that it is the most poetical topic in the world."

"How much longer are we going to have to listen to this nonsense?" MacNeish demanded, rising to his feet.

"The thrust of the essay, once again," Borges said, as if answering the question, "is to demonstrate his superiority to Charles Dickens. In his review of *Barnaby Rudge* he accuses Dickens of what he identifies as the cardinal sin of the incompetent storyteller. In order to write a good story, he says, one must start at the end and work backwards to the beginning—exactly the method prescribed by Dupin for solving a crime. Dickens's failing was that he operated on intuition and genius, not by analysis and rational calculation."

"I don't have all day," MacNeish grumbled, nodding at other audience members to enlist their support. "None of us has all day."

"On the contrary," Borges smiled, "everybody has all day." The audience laughed.

The laughter jolted Professor Selbourne awake once again. "Señor Borges," he said, "perhaps you could wind up this part of the presentation?"

"I suppose I'm not the first reader who breathes easier with the knowledge that Edgar Allan Poe became a fiction writer rather than a criminal mastermind," Borges went on, ignoring the professor, who drifted back to sleep. "He had unusual insight into the minds of certain kinds of criminals: the kind who would dismember an annoying old man and bury him under the floorboards of his apartment, or brick an enemy into a disused wine cellar, or hang a black cat from a tree in his garden—in each case providing a lengthy and detailed account of the rational thought processes that led him to his crime. In his philosophy of composition Poe sounds like nothing so much as the narrator of 'The Tell-Tale Heart,' determined to convince us, in his utterly mad way, that every insane thing he ever did made perfect sense."

"Ah, Berenice!" Mary Ann said, adding another head-stone to the collection. "Her teeth still chattering in the grave!"

"Poe chose writing instead of crime, but what if he had taken the opposite path? He would have gone about his criminal activity in the same way he wrote a story, with the goal of outwitting the detective instead of the reader. He would have constructed the narrative of his crime as he claimed to have constructed 'The Raven.' That's what every criminal does, isn't it, in his battle of wits with the detective? He would have conceived the ending first—the dead woman brutally beaten and stuffed in a chimney, the purloined letter concealed by the blackmailer, the cigar girl's bound body retrieved from the river—and then, working backwards, constructed the fictional chain of events that led inexorably to that end point *with a logic that is impervious to the detective's intelligence.* He would plant false clues and false interpretations of real clues at every turn, diverting the detective from the true path and instead guiding him toward the predetermined false conclusion. His aim—any criminal's aim—would be to outwit the detective in the same way that a chess player outwits his opponent. And, I might add, in the same way that a writer of detective stories seeks to outwit his readers—not unlike a magician, and with same goal: astonishment—until the moment when, after endless indirection and procrastination, and usually at a moment like this, with the police and all the suspects gathered in one room, the solution is unveiled."

Detective Foley raised her wrist and pointed to her watch. "I will be here for exactly two more minutes," she declared. "If you don't unveil the solution—"

"The detective, for his part," Borges cut her off, as if anxious to meet her deadline, "must read the criminal's narrative as if he were writing a story of his own. He must assume that the criminal's conclusion—which is usually the one reached by the police—is false and that the truth has been cunningly concealed. Then, like Theseus, he must grope his way back through the labyrinth of time to find the truth. He must work backwards, from the crime to the past events that led up to it, bypassing all the false branchings—all the might-have-beens—until he comes to daylight. Unfortunately he has no Ariadne to show him how to escape from the labyrinth. Or does he?"

A few throats were cleared, a few papers shuffled, but no one in the room ventured to answer Borges's question. Professor Selbourne opened his eyes and twisted his gaze toward Borges, searching desperately for some sign that he'd come to the end.

Mary Ann rose to her feet and faced the audience.

"Poe thought he did," Borges went on blithely. "Poe thought a detective could use his brilliant analytical mind— the kind of mind Poe had, or thought he had—to solve even the most difficult crime. That's why he invented the detective story. To show us how it can be done."

If he had finally made his point, nobody seemed to grasp it, except perhaps Mary Ann, who stood behind him and recited from Poe's "Annabel Lee":

> *And the stars never rise, but I feel the bright eyes*
> *Of the beautiful Annabel Lee;*
> *And so, all the night-tide, I lie down by the side*
> *Of my darling—my darling—my life and my bride,*
> *In the sepulcher there by the sea,*
> *In her tomb by the sounding sea.*

The audience looked for guidance to Professor Selbourne, who appeared ready to join Annabel Lee in her grave by the sea. "Let's take a short break," he said.

32. The Least Likely Suspect

The second half of the seminar began on an anxious note as Professor Selbourne called it to order, and Borges announced, to a chorus of groans and catcalls, that he would now turn his attention to the murders of Colonel Gimbel and the Netzers—"as an illustration," he said, "of the methods pioneered by Poe in his detective stories." The students and faculty, their patience sorely tested by Borges's exposition of irrelevant and highly questionable theories about Poe and Dickens, seemed ready to leap to their feet and confess to the murders themselves if that would bring the punishment to an end. There was dread in their eyes, as if they feared he would veer into a discussion of German idealism or knife fights in Buenos Aires. Some of the professors had vanished, along with a fair number of graduate students. But Agent Harkins and Detective Foley and her two uniformed officers remained in their seats, as did Murray Kellerman, Bridget O'Hara, Constance Volpe, and Helga Netzer—each of whom would soon be called into the limelight. Rachel Price—to whom Borges must have given a preview of the spectacle he was putting on—kept her eyes glued on them and took notes whenever one of them spoke. The square man with the square head still sat by himself at the far end of the first row, clutching his briefcase and talking to no one.

Mary Ann sat quietly, having replaced her headstones with different posterboard placards intended to represent the suspects. She seemed hardened in her determination to have the last word.

"In a detective story," Borges began, "there must be six suspects, no more, no less. I will ask you to bear with me as we examine each of the six suspects. At the outset we can dismiss the Jewish Defense League and its leader, Rabbi Meyer Kahane. They have been red herrings from the start, introduced by other suspects, then by the police, for the sole purpose of misdirection. A secret society cannot be a suspect in a murder case—see the rules laid down by S.S. Van Dine— any more than a professional criminal can be. The first true suspect in this case, I'm sorry to say, is my friend and neighbor, Mr. Murray Kellerman."

Mary Ann had written a big number "1" in magic marker on one of her placards. When Borges identified Murray as the first suspect, she wrote his name under the number and held it up, turning it from side to side for the audience to see. Murray acknowledged this tribute with a bashful smile. I half expected him to stand up and take a bow.

"Let's review the evidence against Mr. Kellerman," Borges said. "It is undisputed that he went to the Plaza Hotel, where both Peter and Bernhard Netzer were staying, on that fateful Sunday night. Why did he go there? He says it was to attempt to persuade Peter Netzer to relinquish the ring of Solomon in the name of truth and justice. But he has admitted to me that it was for a different purpose. His aim was to frighten Peter Netzer with the curse his grandfather had pronounced on the ring. He wanted Dr. Netzer to complete the sale to his alter ego, Michael Forbis, which he had arranged through Miss O'Hara. That transaction was a trap set by the FBI (Agent Harkins, I must beg your pardon for my unauthorized use of this metaphor), which would have resulted in the ring being returned to Switzerland for continuation of the inheritance proceedings initiated by Mr. Kellerman.

"When Mr. Kellerman stopped at the hotel desk—it was about eight o'clock—he asked for Dr. Netzer, and the clerk said, to Mr. Kellerman's surprise, 'Which one? There are two Netzers here, Peter and Bernhard.' The clerk tried to reach both of them unsuccessfully. Then he gave Mr. Kellerman both Netzers' phone numbers and suggested that he wait in the lobby and try calling them on a house phone. Mr. Kellerman sat down and in a few minutes he reached Peter Netzer. He gave his name as Murray Kellerman—as he had done to the clerk—and told Dr. Netzer about the curse on the ring, explaining, however, that it was no mere curse—an idea which is easily dismissed—but in fact the mission of a secret society sworn to destroy anyone who wrongfully gains possession of the ring. (I confess that he got this idea from my discussion of *The Moonstone*.) Dr. Netzer reacted scornfully, and Mr. Kellerman said he would leave something at the desk for him to think about. What he left was a small piece of hotel stationery inscribed with the motto of the Jewish Defense League—'Never again!'—and a single Hebrew letter: the *aleph,* the first letter of the Hebrew alphabet, which is also a mystical symbol, said to contain the entire universe. Although Mr. Kellerman had no connection with the JDL, he knew of their slogan and reputation from news articles and hoped they would strike fear into the heart of Dr. Netzer. And in case that wasn't enough, he hoped that Peter Netzer would perceive the *aleph* as the sign of the secret society sworn to protect the ring."

"But that note was found in Bernhard Netzer's pocket," Detective Foley objected. "It wasn't directed to Peter Netzer."

"Yes, that was the assumption when the body was brought to the morgue," Borges said. "Remember that—it will become important later."

"What are you suggesting?"

"As I said, that detail will become important later. Meanwhile there's something we must notice. Mr. Kellerman gave his name to the clerk and to Dr. Netzer, and left a note for Dr. Netzer at the desk. You might ask: Why would someone implicate himself in this manner? The answer is, of course, he didn't know he was implicating himself in anything. He didn't know a murder was about to be committed."

"We hear that line all the time," Agent Harkins objected. "I couldn't have done it, because if I had done it I wouldn't have made that mistake. You can see where that leads: the more incriminating the evidence, the less it proves."

"A clever paradox!" Borges snorted. "Almost worthy of Zeno himself."

"Who the hell is Zeno?"

Borges dismissed him with a wave of the hand. "We come now to the heart of the police case against Mr. Kellerman. Evidently the hotel's telephone system assigns phone numbers that correspond to the room numbers. From this, since Mr. Kellerman was given Bernhard Netzer's phone number by the clerk, the police conclude that he knew what room Bernhard Netzer was in and therefore had the opportunity to go there and kill him. We are told that the curtains were taken down in that room, and the cord removed from the curtains, and that it was with this cord that Bernhard

Netzer was both strangled and hanged. I say 'both' because the second autopsy showed that the victim was strangled—and already dead—before he was hanged. That is the basis of the finding of homicide."

"How do you know what the second autopsy showed?" Detective Foley demanded, rising to her feet. "The report hasn't been made public."

Rachel Price spoke up: "I've seen it, and he's right."

Foley scowled at her and sat back down.

"But the hanging," Borges said, "if not the prior strangulation, took place in Central Park—about a quarter mile from the hotel. So the murderer would have required access to Bernhard's room, without his knowledge, to take down the curtains and remove the cord, in order to strangle and hang him a quarter of a mile away. Is there any way Mr. Kellerman could have done that?"

No one—not even Foley—would venture an answer to that question.

"Which brings us to the murder of Colonel Gimbel. I take it as a given that the strangulation in Central Park and the bludgeoning of Colonel Gimbel were related; in fact I am certain that the same person committed both of them. As we review the suspects, we must look for the one who had the motive, means and opportunity to commit both murders. And I will go further, and add the bombing in the morgue to the list of related crimes. All three murders were part of a single pattern."

I happened to be watching Helga Netzer when Borges said that. The grieving widow had betrayed no emotion until then. Her eyes were puffy, her lips pale, her face heavily made up. Understandably she seemed to be in a state of shock.

When Borges mentioned the bombing in the morgue, she lowered her eyes and stifled a chirping cry with her handkerchief, with which she quickly covered her face.

"Mr. Kellerman was present at Colonel Gimbel's house shortly before he was murdered," Borges said. "Isn't that a bit too much of a coincidence—being at the hotel and then at Colonel Gimbel's house before each murder?"

Murray shook his head dismissively, as if again the existence of evidence against him proved his innocence. Rachel Price, sitting beside him, craned her neck to see his face.

"But we must be rigorous in our analysis," Borges said. "Mere proximity to the murder scene doesn't prove anything. Murray Kellerman had no motive to kill Richard Gimbel or either of the Netzers. Yes, he disliked the Netzers and he wanted the ring, but—assuming his inheritance claim is sustained—he has every expectation of obtaining it without killing anybody. Though he was present at the hotel, he had no practical opportunity to kill Bernhard Netzer. And there is no evidence whatsoever linking him with the death of Peter Netzer. We must conclude that the person who killed the three victims was not Murray Kellerman."

The crowd stirred, coughed, shifted in their seats, the way people do between movements of a symphony. There was grumbling, surprise, but no protest; most seemed to agree with Borges's conclusion. Murray beamed his relief with little shakes of his head, as if trying to awaken from a bad dream. You might have thought it was his trial and the judge had just set him free. Detective Foley shot a glance in his direction that was not nearly so reassuring.

"This logic doesn't apply," Borges went on, "when we look at the second suspect: Bridget O'Hara."

Mary Ann had prepared a placard for the second suspect. She quickly wrote O'Hara's name under the "2" and held it up for the crowd, this time eliciting a few laughs. There was no way of knowing whether Borges knew what she was doing.

"Miss O'Hara had a much more palpable motive to kill the first two victims," he said, "and some important knowledge that no one else had. She knew where the ring of Solomon was hidden. She'd expected a handsome commission for selling it, and after it slipped out of her grasp and fell into the hands of Colonel Gimbel, she was under intense pressure to produce it. She went to the Netzers' hotel in an attempt to buy time. We can only speculate as to what happened there. Did she meet with the brothers together, or with Bernhard Netzer alone, by some prior arrangement they'd made before he left Zurich? Did they threaten to terminate her contract, call in the police, or use less savory elements—such as Boris Stossky—to get the ring back from her?"

"I didn't meet with either of them," O'Hara said, standing up. Her lawyer grabbed her arm, trying to keep her quiet, but she ignored him.

"But when you stopped at the front desk," Borges countered, "you were given Bernhard Netzer's phone number, weren't you? From which you could infer his room number?"

"I called his room and got no answer. That's all that happened."

The lawyer jumped up beside her, shaking his finger at Borges. "I object to this! You have no right to interrogate my client!"

Borges ignored him and pressed his case against O'Hara. "When we come to the death of Colonel Gimbel, the evidence against you is more damning. You argued with Colonel Gimbel at the reception on Saturday night and walked off with his cane. You knew the ring was inside the raven and that Colonel Gimbel had the raven in his house. The murder weapon had your fingerprints on it, and the stuffed raven's feathers were found in the alley behind your gallery."

"I never went to his house," O'Hara said.

"You wanted to persuade Colonel Gimbel to go through with the sale which Mr. Kellerman, in the guise of Michael Forbis, had arranged as part of the FBI sting operation. Yes, Miss O'Hara, I'm sorry to have to tell you, you were being played. But the pressure was real, wasn't it? When Colonel Gimbel wouldn't give you the raven, did you resort to violence?"

"No, I—"

"Don't answer any of his absurd questions," the lawyer insisted.

"And later, when you heard that Peter Netzer had been blown up by a bomb, did you see that as an opportunity to keep the ring for yourself? Or perhaps—since the JDL isn't really a serious suspect—I should ask you: Did you set that bombing up yourself, with the assistance of Bruno Stossky, in order to eliminate your last rival for possession of the ring?"

"Do you think I'd be that stupid?" O'Hara asked. "To throw the feathers in my own garbage? Or leave that cane with my fingerprints on it?"

Borges laughed out loud. "There's your paradox again, Agent Harkins. If there's compelling evidence against me, I must be innocent!"

Harkins shrugged and shot a glance at O'Hara. "Sometimes it's true," he said. "Much as I hate to admit it."

"Then you don't think Miss O'Hara is the murderer?"

"No, I don't. She's going to be charged with conspiracy to receive stolen art objects, but I don't think she's a murderer."

"I must agree with Agent Harkins," Borges said. "Although her ethics may be non-existent, Miss O'Hara is not a fool. But those two bits of evidence—the cane and the feathers—are too damning to be disregarded. If they do not prove Miss O'Hara's guilt, they may prove someone else's. They point to the person who planted them to incriminate her."

"Bruno Stossky," O'Hara said bitterly.

"Ah, yes!" Borges sighed. "Suspect No. 3. I knew he would make an appearance."

Mary Ann's next numbered placard shot up and the crowd began to chant: "Stoss-ky! Stoss-ky! Stoss-ky!" She egged them on, waving the placard from side to side like the ring-card girl at a boxing match. There was laughter, a few shouts and foot stomps. A graduate student behind me started taking bets on who the murderer was. Professor Selbourne slept through it all without a twitch.

"We have no idea where Stossky is," Detective Foley said. "He's disappeared."

"We'll come back to that later," Borges said.

"Stossky knew the ring was inside the raven," O'Hara said. "He figured it out the same way you did, as he followed you and Colonel Gimbel around at the reception. He called me to boast about it."

"When was that?"

"Monday afternoon, after Peter Netzer's ultimatum had expired. Stossky called and asked whether I'd be getting the raven back from Colonel Gimbel, and I had to tell him no."

"Perhaps the two of you forged an alliance—"

"I hated Bruno Stossky. I would never—"

"But he double-crossed you. Killed Gimbel and took the raven, left enough evidence to incriminate you, and ended up with the ring."

"He framed me, all right," O'Hara said, "but I wasn't in any kind of alliance with him. Are you kidding? He killed Colonel Gimbel and probably both Netzers too, then he framed me and disappeared with the ring."

Crowd sentiment seemed to run in O'Hara's favor and against the absent Stossky. The graduate student behind me was laying three-to-one odds on Stossky as the perpetrator.

In the midst of this hubbub, Constance Volpe stood up and addressed Borges. "Señor Borges," she said, "I am Constance Volpe. There's an important fact I told the police, but they didn't seem to believe it, or care about it."

"What was that?"

"I saw Bruno Stossky take that cane when he left the reception. I was standing by the bar and I saw Stossky pick up the cane and walk out the door with it wrapped in his raincoat."

"That proves it!" O'Hara shouted. "That proves Stossky killed Colonel Gimbel."

"Of course it does," her lawyer said. "Let's stop this circus right now."

"Not so fast," Borges said. "The crime scene in Colonel Gimbel's house was a stage set, equipped with the props of a play that didn't take place. The cane was obviously a planted clue, meant to incriminate someone other than the real murderer. Since Miss Volpe is using it to incriminate Stossky—and she is the only one claiming to have seen him take it from the gallery—we are entitled to wonder if she planted it there to incriminate him. And we must note that she was seen at the Colonel's house the afternoon before he was murdered."

"Are you accusing me of killing Colonel Gimbel?" Constance Volpe demanded.

Mary Ann's hands shot up with placard No. 4 and the crowd cheered. The student behind me dropped the odds on Stossky to 5 to 3 and quoted 2 to 1 on Volpe.

"Colonel Gimbel told me you would stop at nothing to get your hands on that raven," Borges said, waving the crowd back into silence. "Not because of the ring—neither you nor Colonel Gimbel knew anything about the ring—but for the raven itself, because it had once belonged to Charles Dickens."

"I don't care a fig about Dickens. I'm a Poe collector."

"You're a collector, and as such you are mad—and a Poe collector must be the maddest of all. The law will take that into account if you enter an insanity plea."

"I've never heard anything so insulting in my life."

"Like it or not, you must be counted as the fourth suspect."

"Who is the fifth one?" she demanded, eager to move on.

"The fifth suspect?"

The question hung in the air as Mary Ann raised the next placard and waited with her magic marker to add the suspect's name. No one in the audience took a breath or moved a muscle. "For this one," Borges went on, "we must tread warily." He wagged his head from side to side in a movement quickly copied by Mary Ann with her ring card. "For it is none other than the grieving widow: Helga Netzer."

Shock and anger rumbled through the crowd as Mary Ann added the widow's name to the placard. "No!" people shouted. "You wouldn't dare! This is an outrage!"

Borges waited for the commotion to die down before he went on: "Frau Netzer—to avoid confusion with her late mother-in-law, I will call her Helga, with apologies—had been married to Bernhard Netzer before Peter seduced her away from him. The ring was probably the only reason she attached herself to either of them. She believed—and still believes—that it is truly the fabled Ring of Solomon, with all the mystical powers attributed to that holy artifact, including the power to command demons. She married Bernhard, and later Peter—compounding her schemes, as we shall see—to get possession of that ring. Their mother, Elisabeth Netzer, saw the truth about her and ended up under a tram."

Detective Foley was on her feet, practically climbing on top of her seat. "So what are you saying? Helga killed Elisabeth Netzer and then Bernhard so her husband would be the sole owner of the ring? And then she killed Colonel Gimbel to get the ring her husband already owned? That's beyond ridiculous."

"Only if you think Peter Netzer really owned the ring, even after those others were out of the way. If you think of him as a thief—or the heir to a thief, which Helga knew he was—then her behavior becomes more understandable, doesn't it?"

"What you're doing is a disgrace," Foley said. "You seem to have a preconceived notion that there has to be six suspects—"

"It's not a notion," Borges cut her off. "It's an iron law observed by all the best writers."

"—and you're accusing everyone in the room just to fill out your list. We've already questioned Helga Netzer. She has an alibi for every one of those murders. She was with her husband when Bernhard was killed, at a dinner party the night Colonel Gimbel was killed, and in a restaurant when the bomb went off. Leave her alone."

"Very well," Borges said, apparently chastened. "In deference to those alibis, which appear to be rock solid, I will proceed to Suspect No. 6. But let's not forget what we've said about Helga Netzer."

"And who is this Suspect No. 6?" Foley demanded.

"It seems that we've eliminated all the obvious suspects," Borges said. "Murray Kellerman, Bridget O'Hara, Constance Volpe, Boris Stossky, Helga Netzer. That's only five, not counting the police department's favorite, Rabbi Kahane, who isn't a suspect in my opinion."

"Then have you finished this preposterous exercise?"

"By no means. I believe this is one of those cases, popular in detective fiction though rare in real life, where the least likely suspect is actually the one who committed the crime."

"And who might that be?"

Borges gestured toward the left end of the first row, where the square man with the square head sat by himself with his leather briefcase, as he had since the seminar began. At this signal the man stood up and turned part way around to face Detective Foley.

"I'd like to introduce you to Inspector Fritz Egli of the Swiss Federal Police," Borges said.

Inspector Egli bowed slightly to acknowledge this introduction to a fellow police officer. Foley stared back at him as if he were a homeless man accosting her on the street. The uniformed officers who flanked her seemed ready to arrest him.

"Inspector Egli has been investigating the Netzer family for some time," Borges continued. "It was his impending arrival from Zurich that triggered the tragic attack on Colonel Gimbel and the explosion in the morgue. Now Detective Foley, I'm going to ask Inspector Egli to show something to Miss O'Hara. Miss O'Hara, would you stand up, please?"

O'Hara glanced at her lawyer, then at Foley, and rose slowly to her feet.

"Herr Egli, would you kindly show Miss O'Hara the photograph we discussed earlier?"

Inspector Egli opened his briefcase and pulled out a file. From the file he removed a black-and-white photographic print. He stepped toward O'Hara and handed it to her. "Do you know who that is a picture of?" Borges asked O'Hara.

"No, I don't. I've never seen that man in my life."

"Who is that a picture of, Herr Egli?" Borges asked.

"That's Dr. Peter Netzer."

"How do you know that?"

"As a forensic pathologist, Dr. Netzer is well known in Zurich police circles. I've worked with him several times."

"That's not Peter Netzer," O'Hara said, shaking her head. "I've met Peter Netzer."

"Show her the other picture, please," Borges said.

Inspector Egli reached back in his file, found another photograph, and handed it to her.

"Now you've got the right one," O'Hara said. "That's Peter Netzer."

"I must beg your pardon," Inspector Egli said. "That is Bernhard Netzer."

Borges spoked up before anyone could interrupt. "Maybe we should ask Helga," he said. "She's been married to both of them."

Helga turned away and buried her face in her handkerchief.

"The man in that photograph is the murderer," Borges said.

Detective Foley yanked the picture out of Inspector Egli's hand and eyeballed it fiercely. "Bernhard Netzer had been dead for a week when Colonel Gimbel was killed," she said. "And even longer when his brother was killed. And—wait a minute! Are you saying Bernhard Netzer killed... Bernhard Netzer?"

Borges held up the palms of his hands and shrugged. "I told you it would be the least likely suspect. Who could be a less likely suspect than a dead man?"

33. Ragnarök

The auditorium froze in silence. Everyone and everything stopped moving, like Achilles's arrow suspended in mid-air. Vision sharpened to a photographic stillness. Gasps begun remained ungasped. Time itself struggled against the spell the old necromancer had cast over the room.

Professor Selbourne, jolted awake by Borges's astonishing revelation, must have felt obliged to speak for the spectators in their shock and confusion. "Perhaps," he began—but his voice trailed off and the rest of the sentence never reached the audience.

Borges, blind and indifferent to his effect on the crowd, plunged blithely ahead. "I'm afraid—for those of you who came here today for a seminar on Poe's detective stories— that we seem to have wandered rather far afield. I owe it to you to bring the discussion back around to Poe."

The audience relaxed a little. Inspector Egli slipped back into his seat on the end of the first row. I glanced at Detective Foley and found her unchanged: skeptical, contemptuous, defiant. O'Hara remained disoriented from her attempt to identify the photographs. Helga sat unmoved in her widow's weeds, like a dummy planted in the auditorium. Borges seemed to think that even after his spectacular accusation of Bernhard Netzer, the audience—even the police and the other suspects—were desperately eager for him to bring the discussion back around to Poe.

"More specifically," he added, "to his rivalry with Charles Dickens."

"Doctor Borges," Professor Selbourne grumbled, "perhaps—"

"For that," Borges interrupted, "is what led me to the solution of the Netzer murders."

Say what you will about the old fabulist, he was a master of suspense, and as he had shown, an enthusiastic stickler for form. Now that he had the crowd's attention, he would hold them—especially the police—in his grip until he had forced them to listen to a full account of how he had arrived at his ingenious solution. Such an explanation, as he'd told me on more than one occasion, was an essential component of any detective story.

"By the time Poe wrote 'The Purloined Letter,'" Borges said, "his obsessive rivalry with Dickens had risen to the level of madness. Fortunately it was the madness of a poet, who murders on the page and not in some dark alley. Poe found his inspiration in the 18th-century French playwright Crébillon, concluding 'The Purloined Letter' with a quotation from Crébillon's play about Atreus and Thyestes, the brothers famous in Greek mythology for their murderous rivalry.

"It was in listening to this play that I grasped the solution to the Netzer murders. Until then I had thought of Atreus and Thyestes as fraternal rivals, each equally depraved in his thirst for revenge against the other, and I accorded Poe's quoted lines the meaning which has become conventional among commentators on the story. But when I actually had the Crébillon play read to me, I was horrified by the character of Atreus—the central character in the play—and I realized that I'd met this man before: he is the prototype of Poe's mad narrators. He is the narrator of 'The Tell-Tale Heart,' 'The Cask of Amontillado,' and 'The Black Cat.' The diabolical, hyper-rational madman who confesses to a grisly murder while explaining how it all makes perfect sense. In the play, Thyestes's only crime is to seduce Atreus's wife. But Atreus—the character Dupin identifies himself with, just as Poe identifies himself with Dupin—is a bloodthirsty monster.

"I will not attempt to explain all the details of my reasoning, lest I sound like one of Poe's mad narrators myself. My thoughts on the subject could fill a book, though I am unlikely ever to write it. Suffice it to say that the lines from Crébillon's *Atrée* quoted by Poe have been misunderstood and misconstrued for over a hundred years, even by French critics, including Lacan in his famous seminar. 'The Purloined Letter' is a tale told by a madman, like those other famous Poe stories. But the madman is not Dupin—it is Poe. And the 'D' in the story is Dickens, the 'brother' whom Poe was determined to destroy."

Borges stopped for a sip of water, and Detective Foley took this opportunity to steer him back to reality. "I'm a little disappointed, Señor Borges," she said in a surprisingly mild tone. "You had us all glued to our seats, anxious to hear how you solved the murders. Now you've gone off on one of your tangents."

"If you recall your trigonometry," he said, "the tangent can be a useful tool in a complicated proof. Nevertheless, I take your point. Stay glued to your seats and I promise you won't be disappointed.

"First I must account for the presence of Inspector Egli, who has already had a crucial impact on the case. He first became involved when the FBI, investigating Murray Kellerman's inheritance claim, asked the Swiss Federal Police to interview the Netzers. When Elisabeth Netzer, upon returning from a trip to London, was killed by a tram in suspicious circumstances, Inspector Egli began to investigate her death. Thanks to his careful work, we are now in a position to sketch out what happened. Elisabeth Netzer became alarmed by Murray Kellerman's inheritance claim and the resulting investigations. She and her sons disagreed about what to do with the ring, as they disagreed about everything. She and Peter favored continuing to keep it a secret, while Bernhard insisted on an immediate sale. In this he was seconded by his young wife, a former model who dabbled in witchcraft named Helga, who confided to a friend that she coveted the ring and would do anything to get it. She had married Bernhard hoping to gain access to the ring, and when that failed—because his mother kept him from exercising any control over it—she divorced Bernhard and married Peter.

"When Peter was offered the job in New York, Elisabeth plotted with him to smuggle the ring into the United States and sell it without Bernhard's knowledge. She engaged Miss O'Hara to transport it to New York to sell it secretly to a collector. If, as I believe, Helga was in on that plot as Peter's wife, she was a double agent, secretly in league with Bernhard and presumably still his lover even while married to Peter. We know what happened to the ring when it reached New York inside Colonel Gimbel's raven.

"While Miss O'Hara was frantically attempting to retrieve the raven, Peter Netzer arrived here, accompanied by Helga, to assume his duties as Chief Medical Examiner. Shortly afterwards Bernhard also arrived in New York. He checked into the hotel where Peter and Helga were staying, and the next morning his body was found hanging from a tree in Central Park.

"At least that is what we have been led to believe. But Inspector Egli brings us irrefutable proof that the man who for more than a week served as Chief Medical Examiner was in fact not Peter Netzer, but his brother Bernhard. No one in New York knew either of them. It was a simple matter for Bernhard—with the connivance of Helga—to fake his brother's suicide and assume his identity. Then, after a quick, no-questions-asked sale of the ring through Miss O'Hara (this is what Bernhard intended) and the apparent murder of Peter Netzer, they would vanish.

"It was an ingenious plan which the inherent chaos of our universe began to disturb almost immediately. Faking the suicide seemed to be the easy part. Bernhard was in a position to identify his own body and perform his own autopsy, after leaving a suicide note in his room. It was Murray Kellerman who inadvertently foiled the plan when he left a note for Peter Netzer at the hotel desk—a note that contained the mystical *aleph* and the slogan of the Jewish Defense League: *Never again!* On his way out to dinner, Peter Netzer picked up that note and stuck it in his pocket; it was found on his body (supposedly Bernhard's body) and its ominous tone raised the suspicion of foul play. 'Peter Netzer'—actually Bernhard—read the note when the body was brought to the morgue; it gave him the idea for the fake threatening letters and the murder scenes decorated with the Hebrew alphabet. But when he insisted on conducting the autopsy and made a finding of suicide, the District Attorney's office cited Mr. Kellerman's note in rejecting that autopsy and demanded another one.

"By the way, has it occurred to anyone in the police department to look at the handwriting on the suicide note? If you'd like to do that now, Inspector Egli has brought a sample of Bernhard's handwriting, which of course is the handwriting on the suicide note—after all, he was the one supposedly committing suicide. The note gave strong support to the suicide theory that was confirmed by the first autopsy. But as soon as the second autopsy found homicide, Bernhard's handwriting on the suicide note proved—or would have proven, if anyone had bothered to examine it—that he was the murderer. To the police, that was an impossible thought, since Bernhard was the victim. To me it was obvious, because poets, unlike the police, are in the business of thinking impossible thoughts.

"It was clear to me that Bernhard was both the murderer and the victim, based on consideration of the facts, even before Inspector Egli arrived with his handwriting samples. My eyes would have been of no use in making a comparison in any event. But for you doubting Thomases who can only believe your own eyes, I suggest that you examine those writing samples and judge for yourself whether Bernhard Netzer was the author of the suicide note.

"Every misstep made by the police can be traced to their erroneous belief that the dead man was Bernhard Netzer. In this they relied on the identification of the body by his 'brother'—actually himself—and his sister-in-law, also his ex-wife. The falsity of that identification proves beyond all doubt that they were the murderers. But again, once the mind is set spinning in a certain direction, it takes a miracle or a poet to turn it back around. Instead of looking at the obvious suspects, the police focused their attention on the Jewish

Defense League—a fool's errand, since an organization of that type can never be a suspect in a murder case—and on Miss O'Hara and Mr. Kellerman, neither of whom had a plausible motive to commit the murder, or could in fact have committed it. The necessary logistics of the crime, as committed by either of them, would not bear scrutiny in the most far-fetched detective novel. And how could any one person have strangled a man in the prime of life and hoisted his dead body into a tree? Such a crime clearly required two murderers working in tandem.

"Bernhard and Helga never anticipated a murder investigation. They expected the fake suicide to be accepted as such, and but for Mr. Kellerman's note it would have been. But that note, though it triggered the investigation, also suggested tactics to defend against it. The Jewish Defense League, the manufactured death threats against Peter Netzer, the Hebrew letters—all inspired by Mr. Kellerman's note—were used for purposes of misdirection and sleight of hand to deflect the investigation of Bernhard's murder away from them, as well as to lay the groundwork for the bomb attack on Peter Netzer.

"Nevertheless their plan began to go seriously awry thanks to the unfortunate Colonel Gimbel, when he refused to give up his raven. For this Colonel Gimbel too had to die. Again we have been bombarded with unbelievable evidence of Mr. Kellerman's or Miss O'Hara's supposed culpability. The Gimbel murder was committed by the most likely suspect: Bernhard Netzer, posing as Peter Netzer, with the assistance of Bruno Stossky. Stossky left the reception with the Colonel's cane, carefully guarding against touching it or obliterating Miss O'Hara's fingerprints by wrapping it in his raincoat. After Miss O'Hara had telephoned to say she could not produce the ring, Bernhard and Stossky paid a visit to Colonel Gimbel. He let them in, having no reason to mistrust them. They clubbed him to death with his cane—no witness could be left behind—and stole the raven. Then they extracted the ring and left the feathers in Miss O'Hara's back alley.

"One last crime remained to be committed—the apparent murder of Peter Netzer. It had to be done quickly, for Bernhard learned on Tuesday afternoon that Inspector Egli had arrived in New York and wanted to meet with him on Wednesday morning. But this crime had been planned from the beginning. Stossky was a shady art and antiquities dealer with underworld connections, whose expertise included making and using bombs. Bernhard recruited him, I believe, before leaving Zurich, for assistance in disposing of the false identity he intended to assume as Peter Netzer. After the murder of Bernhard and the discovery of Mr. Kellerman's note, they plotted the apparent death of Peter Netzer as an act of retribution by the Jewish Defense League, which has been implicated in a number of bombings. Since Peter Netzer was already dead—this being the second time he was to be murdered—the plan required a corpse, which would be readily available at the morgue. All that remained was to create a trail of evidence leading to the JDL, and failing that, to Miss O'Hara.

"Mr. Kellerman unwittingly laid the groundwork for the conspiracy theory when he left his note at the hotel desk, but it was the fake death threats to Peter Netzer—embellished with further Hebrew letters following Mr. Kellerman's lead—that sealed the police case against the JDL. Bernhard went one step farther and planted Hebrew letters in Colonel

Gimbel's house and in the morgue. One might ask: What possible motive could the JDL have had to kill Colonel Gimbel? And since when do terrorist bombers wait around until the bomb has exploded to add their signature to the crime? None of that makes any sense, but in fact the Hebrew letters left in those places had exactly the effect Bernhard Netzer intended: they suggested that all the crimes were related and led the police even farther afield as they blamed them on Miss O'Hara or Mr. Kellerman. A little thought shows how absurd this is. But Bernhard Netzer didn't need an impenetrable defense that would survive close examination. All he needed was a smokescreen to confuse the police for a few days while he made good his escape.

"And where is he now? Hiding out with Boris Stossky? Somehow I doubt it. Stossky provided the bomb, which was supposed to blow up a cadaver; but I suspect that the ingenious Bernhard found a way to place Stossky in front of that bomb when it exploded. Pieces of him can probably be scraped off the ceiling in the morgue; the rest has been identified as Peter Netzer. Surely Bernhard didn't intend to share his treasure with Boris Stossky.

"Which brings us back to Helga. She could tell us about all this, and more, I'm sure, if she'd start talking. She might even tell us how she planned to foil her former husband's plan to sell the ring so she could keep it for herself. But she's keeping her own counsel, because she knows how the story ends. Remember what Poe said: You write the ending first, and then you start at the beginning and build up to that. Helga plans to walk out of here, fly back to Europe—or better, someplace in South America or the Middle East—and meet up with Bernhard Netzer, who is very much alive. Of course the police can supply a different ending if they choose. But maybe they've been so drawn into the story that they want to see it through to the end. Whether they'll take advantage of what I've given them remains to be seen."

The moment Borges mentioned Helga, she stood up, her face as cold and white as a block of ice, and headed for the exit, not hurrying, but picking her way patiently through the crowd as if the seminar had been a colossal bore. I kept my eyes on Detective Foley. The last thing she wanted was to acknowledge that Borges might be right. But when Helga had gone about half the distance to the door—she walked more quickly now, as if she'd remembered something she needed to do—Foley nodded to the uniformed cops and they jogged after her. They grabbed her just as she started to run.

She tried to fight them off, squirming in their grip, then whirled around to face Borges as they handcuffed her and dragged her into the lobby. "He doesn't have the ring, you old fool!" she shouted. "He doesn't have it!"

Borges smiled but made no reply. "Perhaps, when the police are done questioning her," he said, "they might engage in a little hard bargaining. Surely she doesn't want to spend the rest of her life behind bars. She's betrayed Bernhard once, and planned to do it again. Maybe she'd be amenable to police persuasion if the price was right. We know she'd do anything for the Ring of Solomon."

Detective Foley stood up and made her way across the auditorium, pretending not to hurry. She was an impressive creature, even in defeat. She strode past me with an expression that dared me to look at her. I watched her out of the corner of my eye. In the corridor Helga could be heard cursing in German like some raving Valkyrie calling down the end of the world. The two cops tried to quiet her but that only inflamed her fury. When Foley added her voice to the uproar, I thought the end was near. The audience, suddenly aroused from their curiosity, raced for the exits.

Bernadette Foley and Helga Netzer weren't the only divas demanding their due. Mary Ann Chalmers loomed over Borges, puffing herself up for the final reckoning. "It had to be the woman, didn't it?" she screamed. "Sooner or later you had to blame it on the woman!" Borges didn't flinch as she hurled her placards down on the table and bellowed out of the room.

Her denunciation was so loud that it roused Professor Selbourne from his slumber. For a moment he sat blinking as if he thought the world might be an illusion. "Who is that young woman?" he asked Borges.

"They told me she was one of your graduate students," Borges said.

The professor blinked again and shook his head. "I've never seen her before in my life."

34. The Imp of the Perverse

Before we knew it, everyone in the auditorium had vanished. The forces of law and order—Detective Foley, Agent Harkins, even Inspector Egli—raced after Helga Netzer and the uniforms to finish what Borges had started, with Rachel Price trotting behind them. The former suspects, including Murray, melted into the fleeing crowd and disappeared. We said our good-byes to Professor Selbourne and I helped Borges down off the dais. We inched our way through the lobby and out to the sidewalk, where I hailed a taxi to take us to his building; there we performed a similarly laborious exercise to get inside the apartment. The whole process must have taken over an hour. And through all this, I wondered, where was our friend Murray—the man Borges had just saved from the electric chair?

Señora Sanchez was out, so I boiled some water and brewed Borges a gourdful of maté and served it to him in his wing chair. For myself I made a cup of instant coffee.

"Thank God," I sighed, collapsing on the couch. "It's finally over."

"Not quite yet," Borges said, sipping his maté through the silver straw. "We still haven't reached the *dénouement.*"

"We haven't?"

"I use the word in its original French sense of unraveling a knot or tangle. The last knot must be unraveled before the detective—or the narrator—can finally escape from the labyrinth."

"I thought we had come to the end."

He laughed. "Remember what you told me about the string quartet? You play all the way to the end—and then it turns out that was only the first ending. You have to go back to the beginning and start over again to get to the second ending. The real ending."

I braced myself for what I hoped was just another Borgesian paradox. "What are you trying to tell me?"

"Let's go back to the beginning," he said with a grin. "Here are the facts as we learned them: Murray Kellerman, the only child of Gisela Kellerman née Mannheimer and the only grandchild of Klaus Mannheimer, was born in New York in 1940 and raised by his father, Rudy Kellerman, a classics professor at Hunter College, after his mother's death in an accident in 1944.

"Here are the facts we didn't hear: Murray Kellerman graduated from City College in 1965, joined the U.S. Marines, and was killed in Vietnam in 1967."

"What?"

"His father, Rudy Kellerman, was devastated by the death of his only child. He retired from teaching in 1968 and sold his book collection to a fellow Austrian émigré and secondhand book dealer named August Schneider; then he retired to Florida, where he died the following year. Schneider discovered the Mannheimer letter about the ring of Solomon stuck in a book he'd acquired from Rudy Kellerman. He knew a younger man, an unemployed mathematician, sometime actor and full-time con artist named Leslie Galton. He and Galton worked out a scam whereunder Galton would claim to be Murray Kellerman, pose as the Mannheimer heir, and inherit the ring of Solomon."

"Wait a minute!" This was going way too fast for me. "How do you know all this?"

"This morning before the seminar I persuaded Rachel Price, the reporter, to escort me to the morgue at the *New York Post* offices. Discovering the truth about Murray Kellerman—the fact that he has been dead since 1967—was not difficult in that news archive. It was something I had long expected. A telephone call to Agent Harkins supplied most of the remaining details. The man we know as Murray Kellerman, whose real name is Leslie Galton, has been under FBI surveillance for many months."

Was Borges just playing one of his tricks?

"I know Murray's been working with the FBI," I said, "trying to set up O'Hara and all..."

"Yes, the sting operation. That began more as a sting on Murray and Schneider than on Miss O'Hara. It seems that our friend Murray—I have to keep calling him that—has been involved in a number of shady transactions with August Schneider. The FBI arranged for him to be offered a sublet in this building, across the hall from Professor Zaragoza—"

Professor Zaragoza!—finally something Borges didn't just dream up. "Isn't that the Professor who usually lives in this apartment?"

"Yes, of course. He's on sabbatical, along with the neighbor across the hall. The important thing about Professor Zaragoza—the crucial link that brought us all together—is that he has a live-in housekeeper."

"Señora Sanchez," I muttered, again reassured: I knew who Señora Sanchez was.

"Actually not," Borges said. "The professor's housekeeper is another lady, whose name I've never known. Señora

Sanchez, without my knowledge, was supplied by the FBI. In fact she is an undercover agent, sent to spy on Murray. Her refreshment cart is equipped with a recording device."

"She's been spying on all of us."

He shook his head. "Not intentionally. I was lodged here to bait the trap. The university assigned this apartment to me, ostensibly because I require a live-in housekeeper. In reality it was because Agent Harkins knew that Murray, subletting the apartment across the hall, would be unable to resist befriending me." A note of vanity had crept into his voice. "Through a wiretap, the FBI had learned that he read and admired my works."

My mind boggled as I tried to make sense of these revelations. Murray a con artist? Señora Sanchez an undercover FBI agent? What next?

From the doorway came the sound of a man clearing his throat. The man was Murray (or, I should say, the man I'd known as Murray and still couldn't help thinking of as Murray). He stood there looking every bit like a con man, with an embarrassed grin scrawled across his face like a signed confession.

"Everyone thought the chess players had met by accident," Borges said.

"Apparently everyone was wrong," Murray laughed. "Including the chess players."

"Checkmate," Borges said.

"Checkmate," Murray replied.

Borges beamed his otherworldly gaze in my direction. "Which of us is the winner?"

I felt like I'd stumbled onto the set of a Samuel Beckett play. "Would somebody mind telling me what's going on?"

"As I just explained," Borges said, "and as I mentioned at our first meeting in this room, the man standing before you is an impostor." He sent his kindliest smile toward Murray. "Tell us your real name."

"Leslie Galton."

"If you don't mind, I'll keep calling you Murray. I've never been able to trust a man named Leslie."

"I don't blame you," Murray said. "I think it was that name that drove me to a life of crime."

He hesitated in the doorway, glancing around warily.

"You needn't worry," Borges said. "I sent Señora Sanchez on a fool's errand that will keep her busy until dinner time."

Relieved, Murray sauntered in and made himself comfortable in his usual chair. "No other FBI agents on the premises?" he asked. "Nobody wearing a wire?"

"Of course not," Borges smiled.

In the Señora's absence, I played the host, bringing Borges another gourdful of maté and a bowl of mixed nuts. For Murray and me there were paper cups of ginger ale, a plate of Ritz crackers and our own bowl of nuts. I was ravenously hungry, and it was all I could do not to scoop up all the nuts and bolt them down. When the nuts were gone, I ducked back into the kitchen for refills and held Borges's bowl so he could feel it with his fingertips.

"I suppose you heard what I told Nick about your background and the nature of your activities," Borges said, picking out a pecan and biting it in half. "It was substantially accurate, I presume?"

"Substantially," Murray agreed, helping himself to a handful of nuts. "I didn't know about Señora Sanchez, but I suspected the FBI had put a spy on me." He gave me a sheepish look. "To be honest, I thought it was Nick."

"And yet," Borges said, "you couldn't help confiding in me, drawing me into your confidence game. Why?"

"I hate to say it, but Agent Harkins was right. I knew who you were and I couldn't help but make friends with you. And I couldn't resist getting you involved in my con. At first it was just for amusement, or vanity, more likely. It was a challenge, like our chess games. Matching wits with a famous writer."

"And detective," Borges added.

Murray grinned. "And detective."

"You knew the FBI was using you as bait, but that only added to the challenge, didn't it? If you could lure Peter Netzer to offer the ring for sale through O'Hara, it would be returned to Switzerland for you to inherit. A much safer method than outright theft."

Murray tossed the handful of nuts into his mouth. "I prefer to operate within the law."

"You needed to show O'Hara that you moved in the right circles and had the right kind of experts at your disposal, such as the Director of the National Library of Argentina. And then when you found out about the curse—you didn't know about it before we read the letter to you, did you?"

"No. My friend Schneider left that detail out of his translation."

"When you found out about the curse, you needed me as a source of arcane information. And when 'Bernhard' was murdered—really Peter, of course—you needed me to find the real killer so you wouldn't be blamed."

"All that is very true."

"But then, what are we to make of the complications you yourself added to the case? It was you who sent the questions to Nick at the *Anglo-American Cyclopedia,* wasn't it?"

"Yes. Professor Alfano left a set in his study—"

"Professor G. Alfano?" I asked.

"Yes, George Alfano, that's who I'm subletting from. He has the encyclopedia in his study, but he's never sent in any of his coupons. And Nick seemed to be so bored with his job, I thought I could spice it up a little."

Borges finished his maté and held out his gourd for a refill. "You heard me mention the curse on the house of Atreus—"

"That's in the encyclopedia,' Murray said, "but I wanted to see if Nick could come up with more, so I sent in a coupon. And then the whole Crébillon thing—"

"You heard us talking about that too?"

"Right. And luckily Professor Alfano also has a collection of Poe's stories, so it wasn't hard to find the Crébillon quote at the end of 'The Purloined Letter.'"

"The police didn't really show you those lines and ask you to translate them, did they?"

"No, I made that up."

"And you planted the *aleph* and the JDL slogan in the note you left for Peter Netzer."

Murray seemed particularly proud of that little stroke. "And it was a damn good thing, too," he grinned. "You said yourself, it threw a monkey wrench into the murderers' schemes."

Borges nodded, admitting that Murray deserved credit for introducing the *aleph* and the JDL. "And you fed information to Rachel Price. She told me so this morning."

"I'll confess to that too," Murray said. "She's an attractive woman. I gave her a few other tidbits you haven't thought of yet."

"The article written by Peter Netzer?" I asked.

"Yeah. I dug that up and leaked it to Rachel. No harm done."

He eyed Borges, then me, and downed the rest of his ginger ale. Then he stood up, spreading his hands in front of him, like a lawyer pleading his case. "You've got to understand, I was fighting for my life. I needed to keep both of you interested in the case."

"And above all there was the challenge," Borges added with a disapproving frown. "The challenge of outwitting me."

"That too. I couldn't beat you at chess—at least I had to make it seem like I couldn't. So I wanted to show that I could outwit you."

"You didn't succeed."

"Maybe not." Murray squinted around the room until his eyes lighted on the large package that had been delivered a few days before, which I'd seen the Señora stash in the corner behind the TV. "I always had the sense—I still have it—that you knew what I was up to. Why did you play along?"

"It was the curse," Borges said darkly.

I could hardly believe my ears. Did Borges just invoke the curse?

Murray cleared his throat. "But do you even believe in the curse?"

"How could I not believe in it?" Borges raised his fist and brought it up and down as if he were wielding the hammer of doom. "I don't like Nazis, and I don't like those who profit from their atrocities, or those who share in their profits"—his voice took on a Biblical cadence as he hammered on—"or their heirs or descendants down through the generations to the end of time."

Murray glanced at me anxiously as he tried to get his mind around what Borges had said. "Then... *you* were the curse?"

"I believe in curses when I am the one putting them into effect," Borges said, stifling a cough. "I did everything I could to bring the Netzers down. So in that sense, yes, I was the curse."

Our throats were so parched from the crackers and nuts that the conversation was literally grinding to a halt. I ducked back into the kitchen for more ginger ale. When I came out Murray was sliding out the package Señora Sanchez had stashed behind the TV, which was wrapped up in brown paper, tape and heavy twine. He bent over to lift it onto a table and started unraveling the twine.

"I have to say," he told Borges, "the analysis you presented at the seminar was masterful. The way you marshalled the evidence and showed where the case against me fell apart. You saved my life, and I'll always be indebted to you for it."

"Yes, you will," Borges agreed.

"Not that the truth wouldn't have come out anyway. Helga Netzer was doomed as soon as the police inspector from Switzerland showed up with those photographs."

"At my invitation."

Murray pulled out a pocket knife and sliced through the twine, pulling it off in long strands. "But there was one glaring flaw in your presentation," he went on. "More than a flaw—I'd have to call it a deception. You allowed everyone to believe that Bernhard Netzer walked off with the ring of

Solomon after he killed Colonel Gimbel. That wasn't true, was it?"

"Of course not."

"Netzer didn't take Grip either, did he?"

"I'm quite sure he didn't," Borges nodded.

"He took a different raven—the one I saw in Colonel Gimbel's living room."

Borges nodded again.

A broad smile spread across Murray's face as he stripped the brown paper off the package, opened the top and peeked inside. "The one he left there after he shipped you the real one with the ring in it. The one that's right here in this package."

"Unfortunately," Borges said, "Colonel Gimbel followed my advice on that point but neglected to do so when I urged him to leave his house and stay with his daughter. I'll never forgive myself for letting him make that mistake."

"How did you know he had an extra raven?"

"He had quite a number of them—that was part of his collecting mania. He told me all about it at the reception, when the two of you were upstairs meeting with O'Hara and the Netzers. So when we agreed that he would send me the real Grip for safekeeping—he was convinced Constance Volpe would try to steal it if he kept it at his house—I advised him to keep one of the fake ones in plain view. On the coffee table, for example."

"So Netzer and Stossky killed him for the wrong raven," Murray said, shaking his head.

"Very sad," Borges said. "But imagine their surprise—and Helga's fury—when they took the raven apart to extract the ring, and found nothing but sawdust. Sad indeed."

Murray didn't look sad. He closed the box, taped some of the brown paper over the top, and hefted it into his arms so he could carry it off. I had no idea a stuffed raven would be so big or so heavy. He shot me a glance that suggested I shouldn't try to stop him. "You figured it all out," he told Borges, "but you know what? So did I, long before you did. So as I said when I walked in: Checkmate."

"May I remind you," Borges said, his color rising, "that chess is a game played by two gentlemen? The winner doesn't actually capture the king. He wins because the king falls under his control. I am the winner because that raven is in my control."

"Not after I walk out with it," Murray laughed. "What are you going to do—call the police?"

"Of course not."

"That makes you my collaborator. If I can get Schneider to agree, I'll give you ten percent. You earned it."

To my amazement, Borges hesitated as he seemed to consider this offer. "I won't take your money," he said. "But there is something you can do for me. Your partner Schneider has a book of mine—my first book, *Inquisiciones*—which he refuses to sell. I want it so I can burn it."

"It's yours."

Murray turned and lugged the raven toward the door. *"Adiós, amigos."*

As always, Borges had the last word. "I must warn you," he said—and Murray paused in the doorway to hear him out. "The curse didn't stop when the Netzers were brought down. It will follow you as long as you keep the ring or profit from it—down through the generations to the end of time. You are not the rightful heir. You have no more right to the ring than the Netzers had. If you keep it, you are no better than they are and you will suffer the same fate."

We sipped our drinks as Murray disappeared out the door. We heard him shuffle down the hallway with his trophy. We heard the elevator door open and then close, and he was gone. He never came back to his apartment.

"I'm disappointed in Murray," I said, shaking my head.

"Don't be," Borges said. "He'll never be able to sell that ring—it's far too valuable. I'm sure he'll do the right thing in the end."

"Whatever that is."

Borges turned his gaze on me. "And what about you?" he asked. "I've tried to give you a few lessons in how to see things with a blind man's eyes. Has it done you any good at all?"

35. The Last Ordeal

I fled from Borges's apartment feeling desperate and disoriented. Everything I believed in, or thought I believed in, had been debunked and overthrown. Everyone I trusted had deceived me. It was late, almost closing time at Sloan House, and raining heavily, but I avoided the subway and walked home. I told myself that things couldn't get any worse, but in that too I was deceived.

The Peruvians met me on the sidewalk holding their suitcases over their heads to fend off the rain. They wore grim expressions: we had been thrown out of our room and banned for life from Sloan House and all related facilities. The news hit me hard. I'd been expelled from graduate school, booted out of the Army, sent packing by Katie, but this was a new low to which I never thought I would sink— to be banned for life from the YMCA! The starving Chileans, it turned out, had been working undercover, ratting out room-overcrowders in exchange for a place to sleep. The Peruvians complained bitterly of a 19th-century war between Chile and Peru. I walked them to the Port Authority Bus Terminal to catch a bus to Paterson, New Jersey, where they had relatives. We traded goodbyes in our best Business English and I was on my own.

I spent two quarters to stash everything I owned in a foot-square locker and walked east along 42nd Street toward Times Square, where I had my pick of porno shops, peep shows, liquor stores and dive bars, all with music blaring through loudspeakers out to the sidewalk. Drug dealers lurked in parked cars, addicts slumped in doorways, hookers paraded in mini skirts offering dates and other delicacies. All I could do was keep walking. I tried not to think, but that—not thinking—is the one thing the human mind is incapable of. What did I try not to think about? Borges and Murray and their fateful battle of wits, and the human debris it left behind. The Netzers and the curse they had brought on themselves, and poor Colonel Gimbel, who'd blundered into its path. But mostly what I tried not to think about was my own life. Somewhere in the maze of forking paths that make up our world, I had lost my way. Back in Cambridge I'd begun as Borges's chauffeur and graduated to his guide, even fancied myself playing Virgil to his Dante; in New York I'd been reduced to a clueless Watson, a narrator so unreliable that I couldn't even trust myself to get the story right. The one bright spot was Lucinda—my mentor, friend, and so much more. Like the woman in the Arabian tale, she'd taken my hand and led me toward the light—she was the eternal feminine, teasing me forward with mystery, incompleteness, misdirection. Why did she seem so sad? Did she suspect that I could only follow her so far? And what about Katie, who'd sent me on this quest? How would she react if I came back empty-handed?

It all seemed so hopeless and confusing.

The rain bore down harder and I kept walking. I walked up the West Side to 96th Street and down again, across to the East Side, downtown as far as the East Village, then wove my way back uptown through the web of shadowy, faceless cross streets. It was midnight, then two in the morning, then three and four and five. I walked with the collar of my raincoat turned up against the wind.

The streets were deserted, as lifeless as the moon. My only companions were the cats and dogs it was raining. If tears streamed down my face, they were the only ones who would have noticed.

It was the dark night of my soul.

At dawn, as the sky brightened, I knew I could walk no farther, that wherever I was—it happened to be the corner of First Avenue and 61st Street—I had reached the end of my journey. Nothing special about that place or time, it was just where existence had taken me, which is special enough. I saw the sun rising in the east and felt a kind of renewal, almost a rebirth—the rebirth of the person I once had been, and now was, and always would be.

At the office, I found Lucinda waiting for me in her cubicle, enjoying her morning coffee. She looked a little sadder than usual, as if she too had spent the night roaming the dark streets. "I have a confession to make," she said before I could open my mouth.

I waited.

"That Arabian tale—'The Tale of the Unlucky Mirror.'"

I slipped into the chair opposite her desk.

"I made the whole thing up, based on what Borges told you. I think he was making it up too."

"But—"

"The Propp footnote I supposedly translated from Russian was actually about some other story. The research notes I read from were fake."

I hesitated. "Then the hero..."

A wan smile flickered across her face. "Who trusted a magician and a trickster, battled with demons, and was finally rescued by a beautiful woman..."

"That was about me?"

"Don't tell me you didn't figure it out."

"I did, just this morning," I admitted, returning her smile. "But I need to ask you something. The beautiful woman must be you. Why is she so sad?"

"Because the hero's going to leave her."

"Lucinda—"

"It's all right. She's known that all along."

I've never felt smaller than I felt at that moment. I wished I could escape without saying another word, but that wasn't an option. "I've made a decision," I said.

"I knew you would."

"The woman I left behind in Boston..."

"Katie."

"You remember her name. Yes, Katie."

"Do you love her?"

"Yes."

"Does she love you?"

"She did once, and she will again."

"You should go back to her. Don't waste a minute. Go back to her today."

We sat together in silence for a long time, comfortable with each other and comfortable with our silence. We both knew it couldn't be any other way. Lucinda was the idea, Katie the reality. But the prospect of having to account for myself frightened me.

"I don't know what I'm going to tell Katie about all this," I said.

Lucinda smiled. "You don't have to tell the truth about what happens on a quest," she said. "Not the literal truth, anyway."

"What other kind is there?"

"The imagined truth. The truth that *has* to be. That's what stories are made of. It's your story, don't forget."

I had to face one more ordeal: breaking the news to Miss Kunkel that this would be my last day at the *Cyclopedia*. I tapped on her door, pushed it open, and found her hunched over a large, open volume on her desk. She covered it with her arms to keep me from seeing what it was. Behind her, the big wooden cabinet stood open; inside was a set of the 11th edition of the *Encyclopaedia Britannica,* with one volume removed.

"So this is the Authoritative Source!" I cried.

She glared at me defiantly. "What of it? The truth is the truth, no matter where you find it."

I couldn't disagree. But I wondered whether that inconclusive account of the Arabian tale had come from the *Britannica,* or whether Lucinda had planted it with Miss Kunkel.

"This is my last day," I informed her.

She chuckled with obvious pleasure. "I knew you wouldn't last. None of them do. How far did you get? Coupon No. 3?"

"Four. But the questions from that subscriber were fake."

She chuckled again, only this time it came out more like a cackle. "No one will ever send in more than four coupons."

"But isn't that because we reject every question as being beyond the scope of our service?"

"Of course it is. But what do you think the scope of our service should be? To grasp the entire universe and break it into coupon-sized tidbits? We will never see more than a tiny part of it, and when our subscribers understand that, they will have acquired the wisdom they were looking for when they bought the encyclopedia."

36. The Truth About Sancho Panza

A month later, back in Boston, Katie showed me an article in the *Globe* that went a long way toward restoring my faith in humanity, or at least in the friend I still called Murray Kellerman. While Borges was in Israel to receive the Jerusalem Prize, an anonymous gift was made in his name to the Hebrew University Museum: a gem-encrusted signet ring, ancient in origin, in the center of which was a brass hexagram representing the seal of Solomon. Although the museum's curators doubted that the ring had actually belonged to King Solomon, there was no question as to its antiquity and fabulous value. Experts identified it as the item sold at auction in Vienna in 1934. And in Philadelphia, a wooden crate containing the remains of Grip—the raven who once belonged to Charles Dickens—was left on the steps of the Free Library, thus resolving the mystery of the raven's disappearance after the death of Colonel Richard Gimbel, who had left it to the library in his will.

Freeing myself from Borges was part of the same decision as parting from Lucinda. The last time I saw him was at O. Henry's that same afternoon. We sat on the sidewalk at the same tiny table as the week before. Borges tied up a few loose ends from the Netzer case—the identification of the corpse in the morgue as Bruno Stossky, the arrest of Bernhard Netzer in Rio de Janeiro, the fate of Mary Ann Chalmers—

and zeroed in on the subject he wanted to discuss. "We need to talk about how you intend to write the story," he said as we scanned our menus.

"What story?" I asked, pretending not to know.

"The detective story we've been living for the past two weeks. You needn't worry—readers will make allowances for your limitations as a narrator. But I want to make sure they understand how I solved the case."

A waitress had appeared to take our orders. It was perky Pat, who had contributed so much to our conversation the week before. "If you don't mind my putting my two cents in," she said, "I think detective stories are overrated. How much brains does it take to find the clues you've planted for the sole purpose of finding them?"

"I don't proceed by collecting clues," Borges said. "As a blind man, I can't comprehend a world consisting of bits and pieces—I must, so to speak, see the whole picture. My method is to visualize the possible universe in which a particular crime could have been committed: there is only one. Once that vision is complete, the solution is obvious."

Pat peered at us over the top of her order pad. "What can I bring you today?" She recorded our orders—which were the same as the week before—and flitted away.

"Twenty-five centuries ago," Borges said, "Zeno of Elea demonstrated the same point in his paradoxes: you cannot grasp the One by adding up the Many. You must grasp the One in its entirety, as you would try to grasp the *aleph,* which contains the entire universe."

"Which of you gentlemen ordered the Waldorf salad?" Pat asked, suddenly looming beside us. Borges grunted and she set his plate in front of him. "I can't say I agree with

Zeno on that point," she added. "Isn't a Waldorf salad just a bunch of apples, celery and walnuts with mayonnaise on them? There isn't any 'salad' there."

"If I had wanted apples, celery and walnuts with mayonnaise," Borges declared, thumping his fork on the table, "that's what I would have ordered. Now if you don't mind, I would like to enjoy my Waldorf salad."

She darted away, undaunted by his rudeness, and he went on: "Do you remember—that first day we met here in New York—when I said we were all impostors?"

"Yes, and look how it turned out!" I laughed. Murray was a scam artist, Señora Sanchez an undercover FBI agent; and Mary Ann Chalmers, I had just learned, was a mental patient who'd escaped from Bellevue. But what about Borges himself? Was he an impostor?

"Of course I am," he declared. "When I said 'impostors,' I wasn't talking about disguises or swindles, but about the conviction, which resides in each of us, that we have—no, that we *are*—an individual self that exists continuously through our lifetimes, and possibly beyond. That makes us all impostors, doesn't it?"

"I guess you could say that."

"Berkeley denied the material world but affirmed personal identity; Hume went farther and denied the self. We are nothing, he said, but a bundle of perceptions which succeed each other with an inconceivable rapidity."

Swooping in from behind me, Pat snatched our empty plates away at a similarly inconceivable speed. "'Succession' implies *time,* doesn't it?" she asked. "As a necessary condition for even that disjointed kind of consciousness?"

"Indeed," Borges said. "Time—though it may be an illusion—is the single thread that gives shape to our intelligence, like the golden thread that guided Theseus out of the labyrinth."

"It's the mayonnaise that sticks the other ingredients together," Pat agreed, skittering off with our plates.

"Like Theseus," Borges went on, "we cling to that thread as we stumble through the labyrinth of shifting appearances, specious doctrines and endlessly forking paths. It is only by grasping it that we can hope to find our way to the light. Ariadne's gift is what enables us to experience ourselves as conscious beings."

I leaned toward Borges as if by boring my own eyes into his I could make him see me. "But what if time *is* an illusion?"

"Ariadne's gift, if you'll recall, was not a thread stretched in a straight line. It was the *ball* of thread, rolled together like Hume's bundle of perceptions. Theseus himself had to unravel it as he ventured into the labyrinth."

"Then is life just the unraveling of an illusion?"

"Ah!" he exclaimed, clapping his hands in delight. "I can't answer that for you. That's something every man has to figure out for himself."

"It's not of the mind, but of the heart," Pat added, refilling our coffee cups. "If you don't mind the woman's touch."

"But if you ever figure it out," Borges said, "don't tell anyone."

"Why not?"

"They'll think you're mad."

I couldn't help wondering if the Borges I'd known really was an impostor in the literal sense. After I got back to Boston, Katie showed me a newspaper article that described him as lecturing at Columbia—and even receiving an honorary degree there—while I spent every day with him on the other end of Manhattan. One of those men must have been an impostor, but which one? The real Borges, I suspected, would have been the one who claimed to be an impostor.

That afternoon at O. Henry's, after Borges made that claim, I asked him: "Have you ever met the real Borges?"

"I saw him in a mirror once," he said. "Or was it in a dream?"

The End

Acknowledgements

I commend the reader to the real Jorge Luis Borges (1899-1986), who was of course the original of the impostor featured in this book, and his marvelous works of fiction, non-fiction and poetry (many of which have been published in English translation by Penguin Books). Without those works, this book and its predecessor, *The Philosophical Detective*, could not have been written. The same acknowledgment must be made to the works of Edgar Allan Poe.

I am also indebted to the many critics and commentators who have written about the real Borges over the years, especially John T. Irwin (the "professor in Baltimore" referenced in Chapter 3), whose *The Mystery to a Solution* (Johns Hopkins University Press, 1994), I discovered after *The Philosophical Detective* was published. This extraordinary work of literary history, analysis and speculation inspired many of the themes and ideas elaborated in this book.

About the Author

Bruce Hartman is the author of nine previous novels, including *The Philosophical Detective,* published in 2014, to which *The Philosophical Detective Returns* is a sequel.

His first book, *Perfectly Healthy Man Drops Dead,* won the Salvo Press Mystery Novel Award and was published by Salvo Press in 2008. In 2018 it was republished in a slightly revised form by Swallow Tail Press. Bruce Hartman's books have ranged from mysteries *(The Rules of Dreaming, The Muse of Violence, The Philosophical Detective)* to comedies *(A Butterfly in Philadelphia, Potlatch: A Comedy)*, techno/political satire *(Big Data Is Watching You!)*, a legal thriller *(The Devil's Chaplain),* and an action adventure *(Parole)*. A graduate of Wesleyan University and Harvard Law School, he lives with his wife in Philadelphia.